BAD BOYS NEVER FALL

SJ SYLVIS

AUTHOR'S NOTE

Bad Boys Never Fall is the second and *final* book in the St. Mary's Duet. The St. Mary's Duet is a **DARK** boarding school romance intended for **MATURE** (18+) readers. This duet is labeled as dark due to the dark themes (strong language, sexual scenes, and situations) throughout. Be aware that it contains **TRIGGERS** that some readers may find bothersome. **Reader Discretion is advised.**

Bad Boys Never Fall is the second and final book in the St. Mary's Duet and it will end with an **HEA**. There will be more books in the St. Mary's Series but they will feature secondary characters.

WHERE

BAD BOYS NEVER FALL

S.J. SYLVIS

CHAPTER ONE

I'D LEARNED from a very young age that emotions were fleeting. They were transient. Interchangeable within the blink of an eye. And the range of emotions I'd seen on Gemma's face in the last few seconds were just that. I watched as they shifted behind her jade eyes. Fear turned to relief. Confusion turned to hurt. Heartbreak turned to betrayal.

As I glanced down at the watery mixture of anger and shock, both masking the pain I'd just caused, I knew that I had made a grave fucking mistake seeking her out that first day at St. Mary's Boarding School. And this? This look she was giving as she crouched down below my feet with my two best friends beside me, her knees scraping against the damp asphalt, likely cutting into her perfect soft skin? This was my fucking punishment.

I knew I was playing with fire.

I knew I was inevitably going to hurt her in the end.

I knew that she and I would crash and burn.

Good girls like her weren't made for guys like me. And bad boys never fell for girls like her.

"I hate you," she whispered through clenched teeth, wet tears still glistening over the curve of her cheeks.

It was that exact moment that I hated myself the most. For letting her in. For allowing myself to kiss her and touch her. I had been an empty shell before she walked into my world, and the only thing inside that shell was anger. That was how I wanted it to be because I knew anger was the only thing that would keep me breathing with my future on the horizon. But again, emotions were interchangeable. One brush of her lips against mine, and it was like the floodgate had been unlocked. Possessive, protective, crazed, lust-driven, fearful. I felt everything at once.

I became unhinged when I'd learned that she wasn't in her room earlier.

When the bus came to a complete stop in front of St. Mary's after we'd crushed Temple on the lacrosse field, I got an alert on my phone. My gaze sliced to Cade and Brantley, and we all popped up out of our seats with Shiner following closely behind. In fact, I was pretty sure our lacrosse gear was still on the bus, but at that moment, it didn't matter. What mattered was how Bain, the guy who stirred the very pot of my life, had managed to leave St. Mary's without the keys to his G-wagon.

When we'd met Mica, Bain's roommate, in the hall, he confirmed that Bain was asleep in his bed.

Confusion sat on top of my shoulders as I watched the little red dot move across the screen of my phone, showing that Bain's car was moving to a location that I didn't even want to think about. That was when Sloane came flying down the hallway, well after curfew.

Gemma. What the fuck was she thinking?

"So, who's going to go at it first?" my father asked with

the same amount of distaste as excitement evident in his tone. My eyes burned to see red, to let my guard down and kill him right here. I wanted to wrap my hands around his throat and watch as he fought for life like he'd done to so many other men before him. But I couldn't. I needed to be rational. There were too many things at play. Too many things in the way.

I wasn't him.

I wasn't a replica of Carlisle Underwood even if, at this moment, he thought I was. My father was beaming with pride. He thought I was on his side. He thought that I was going to pass Gemma around like a goddamn whore and let him touch her. He was so blinded by his own misogynistic traits and thirst for power that he couldn't see the way my hands shook with blinding anger. I was fucking trembling. My fists clenched by my sides, my nails digging into the flesh along my bloody palms.

He would never fucking touch her again.

And neither would I.

Not now. Not after this. I didn't deserve her, and she didn't deserve this.

"Cade? Brantley? I always went first and gave your old men the next go around," my father laughed. "I mean, sorry to tell you, Cade, but your father isn't as faithful as your mother thinks."

Gravel crunched beneath Cade's shoe, but I didn't look over at him. This was a good test for our friendship. This moment right here would determine if Cade and Brantley, my two best friends, who knew just how fucked our futures were, trusted me as much as they said they did, just like it would determine if I let them stay by my side in the long run.

Cade's wide shoulder brushed mine as he looked down at Gemma. Her chest was rising and falling, but she kept her teeth bared and her eyes full of lethal determination. My lips ticked upward, and it wasn't for the reason my father thought. I was proud. I was so fucking proud—even knowing that she was full of hatred for me right now—that she wasn't cowering away. Gemma was brave. I'd always known she was. Whatever she'd lived through in the past had hardened her, and that was good.

"I've already had her," I said, swooping down and gripping her arms tightly. Her delicate chin jutted upward, and a flash of fear crossed over her features only to be replaced with a burning fire. I shoved her toward Brantley who was standing a few yards away. She stumbled over her shoes, the loose rocks and gravel kicking up in her wake, landing in a nearby puddle. "Maybe Brantley would like a go?"

He pulled her against his chest and wrapped his forearm around her upper body. Her little hands came up as she clawed at his skin, and the pink scars around her wrists peeked out as her jacket sleeves fell back.

"No!" The tiny word echoed around us, as did my father's maniacal laughter.

He cupped his hands around his mouth. "Do you hear that, Bain? We have your little plaything! Come out, come out, wherever you are!"

Cade managed to chuckle, but I couldn't force it out. I was too focused on the fear seeping into Gemma's eyes as her resolve fell. She caught my gaze from across the space, and her brows crowded as her mouth drew a straight line. *"Fuck you."*

There it was. That burn of rage. I was glad she was angry, because that meant she had adrenaline, and she was going to need that rush in a second.

"You already have, little one." I winked, and Brantley flung her forward again, as if we were playing hot potato with her. She landed in Cade's arms, and I looked to my father who was watching her with bated breath. *If I killed him, I'd be just like him*. I was smarter than he was. And I wasn't a murderer.

Stepping forward, I tipped my chin. "So, what's the plan? We all fuck her, beat her up real good, and send her back to Bain? He'll know it was me who touched his little whore. It might cause some issues for the future. He'll be even more guarded."

My father took his lingering gaze off Gemma and placed it on me. "There's already an issue, son. Bain knows who you are. They're slowly trying to take each and every last one of my clients." He gestured to the building behind him. *The Covens*. "This one is our biggest consumer. I need Bain to run back to his father and let him know that he can't fucking have it. The Covens buys guns from me and no one else. Bain and his fuck-up of a father touch my shit, then I touch his. Bain's mother is next on my list if they keep it up."

Gemma was struggling in Cade's arms, the muscles along his arm twisting back and forth as he kept her still as my father glared. "Did you hear that, you little whore?" Gemma's mouth clamped shut as she stared at him. The ground behind my feet began to shake. *I was going to strangle him*. "When we're done with you..." He crooked a smile. "*If* you survive, you tell Bain *exactly* what I just said. You got it? You can be a warning."

Her lip lifted, and her white teeth bared again as her head came down. Her eyebrows were crowded above her eyes as she seethed, "I am *fucking* done with men like you demanding things." Then, her head flung back with all her might, and she blasted Cade right in the nose before taking off running into the forest, just like I'd hoped.

Before my father had a chance to grab a hold of the situation and start demanding shit, I stepped forward, taking charge and likely filling him with even more pride. "Time for a game, boys. Go fetch."

Brantley spun around quickly with a devilish smirk on his face, jogging down the hill, and once Cade recovered, he descended too.

My father stood back and lazily placed his hands in his pockets, smiling at me.

"Don't worry, Dad. You've taught me well." I began walking toward the hill that Gemma had disappeared over. "But now that you can see I'm doing what you asked and keeping up with the job you've given me...I expect you to do the same. Leave Jack out of this." I gazed out into the tall trees and foggy air, feeling the bitter taste of deceit in my mouth. "It's not like you'll create a better version of you anyway."

He gave me a curt nod with a glimmer of hope in his eye and started to walk off toward the parking lot. Before he made it to his car, he shot over his shoulder, "Make me proud, Isaiah. Get the point across to Bain...and have some fun. She's a beauty."

Yeah. Fuck you, Dad.

CHAPTER TWO

GEMMA

I'D BEEN PUSHED AROUND ALL my life. I'd been forced to get on my knees and beg. I'd kept my lips sealed and my tongue clipped, letting threats and insults hinder me. I'd been broken, and torn apart, and had somehow morphed into someone who was vulnerable and weak.

But that wasn't me any longer.

It wasn't my brother disappearing and leaving me false hope that made me snap.

It wasn't Richard and his looming threats.

It wasn't the cool floor of that dirty basement or the abuse that followed.

No.

It was him.

Isaiah.

Isaiah was the one to do it.

There was nothing worse than giving someone pieces of yourself and allowing them the power to destroy every last one. I gave Isaiah the few parts of my heart that were the most jagged, the most tarnished, the ones that held both fear and hope, and he broke them in half.

And in turn, it broke me. But it broke me in the best way. Hope had diminished. Guilt was no longer a notion that I felt. Everything that had been holding me back from taking a hold of my life and fighting back was fleeting.

I wasn't going to sit back and let them have me. I wasn't a piece of trash or a little toy for them to touch for their own sick games. I was done being an object. I was done with people using me. *I was fucking done.*

So, when Cade's breath fell over my ear with his grip hard against my body, I was ready for a fight. "Save yourself, Gemma. Fucking run."

And that was exactly what I did.

As soon as my head had collided with Cade's, his arm loosened, and I ran like hell. The moisture in the air coated my sticky skin, the fog hardly giving way to the forest below. My shoes slid on the wet asphalt, and I tripped a time or two, but I just kept running. Sticks snapped, and slippery leaves stuck to the bottoms of my soles. My hair slashed across my face, and my jacket had fallen down over my shoulder, letting the cool night wash over my skin.

I knew they were coming for me.

Just like I had known Richard would the first time I'd run from him, too.

Hurt seeped in as I jumped over a log, falling to my hands for a second. Mud coated my fingers, but I popped back up and kept on running. *How could he do this to me?* Did Cade tell me to run because he wanted me to survive? Or did he tell me to run because they liked the chase? I could hear them behind me. I could hear the rustle of leaves and breakage of branches.

My feet dug into the ground as a familiar tremor ran through my body.

No.

I wouldn't allow the past to revisit me in a time like this—not when I needed to focus and figure out a plan. My legs picked up pace again, the air in my lungs coming out in choppy spurts as blood rushed through my veins. My legs burned from the fast pace, and I felt another slice of pain against my knees. *Just like last time.*

"No!" I whisper-shouted to myself, causing a nearby cricket to stop chirping. Richard wasn't here. He wasn't the one chasing me. My head snapped up as a thought came through. *But...* My gaze roamed all around the forest as I turned in circles. I was surrounded by large tree trunks and thick branches of pine that seemed to never end. If Isaiah had betrayed me once, he'd do it again. He was using me. Was he using me to lure in Bain? My head began to spin as I tried to make sense of it all. It didn't make sense. The way he touched me. *Kissed me. Looked at me.* It didn't make sense!

Nothing made sense!

My feet pulled me backward as my chest constricted.

I couldn't breathe.

I clawed at my jacket and unzipped it, throwing it off to the side. My feet moved backward again, and I fell to my butt, dirt digging underneath my nails, before quickly climbing to stand again.

Was he even planning on giving me the money?

I needed the money. Where would I go without it?

The fake ID?

Richard would find me if I didn't have one. I'd never be able to work. I'd never be able to survive if I couldn't hide behind the identity of someone else. I would have to find a job eventually. Find a place to live. I couldn't do that as Gemma Richardson.

He would find me.

I'd be his.

The chains would go back around my wrists until I submitted.

He'd make me beg for food. He'd make me beg for him.

"Call me daddy, baby girl. I'm all you have now."

His finger would trail down my spine and curve over parts that weren't his to touch. He'd fulfill his threats. He'd spread me wide and make me think twice about running. He wouldn't stop until I told him I liked it. That I loved him. That I was his. That I wouldn't break the rules like my mother did.

"Gemma! Fucking snap out of it."

His hands were running down my arms, and I shook from fear. Not again. No. "Did you break the rules? I thought you were my good girl? Do you want to end up like your mother?"

I gasped and felt for my wrists. I wasn't chained yet. There was still time.

"Gemma. Come on, don't go to that fucking place."

"I'm sorry. Please don't chain me. I won't do it again." His laugh made me double over. The nausea came in crashing waves.

"Cade, she's trembling. She's not with us."

"No. You won't run again. I won't fucking let you." I felt the tears on my face as he shook me. I felt something hard behind me, but it wasn't Richard. It was scratchy and grounding.

"Shaking her isn't working. We need to open her eyes and—"

"Take her mind back...bring her back to the present."

The scratchiness was gone, but the basement was still in sight. There were hands on me. But...goosebumps covered my skin. There were four hands on me. Four. Not two. And they weren't his.

"That's it. Relax."

Where did the scratchiness behind my back go? It was gone. I was no longer being scraped or cut. The sharp pieces weren't rubbing me raw anymore. Instead, it was firm and warm. There were hands on my hips and soft touches running over my chest, dipping down low enough to make me tighten.

"Just let it go. Open your eyes," a deep, raspy whisper wisped around the inside of my ear. Something wet flicked my skin just below the whisper, and I felt my head sag.

The hands were moving. My hips pushed back as fingers splayed over the waist of my jeans. There was a hiss behind me, but it wasn't angry-sounding. It was hot. I liked that sound. I wanted it to happen again. My eyes were shut, and the basement was gone. There was the hooting of an owl overhead, and when warm lips touched mine, I was suddenly hungry. And eager. And angry. I didn't know why, but I kissed back. My back arched as another set of lips touched my neck, and the ones on my mouth were suddenly gone and on my belly.

I gasped, my eyes opening as I shot my head down.

Two big brown eyes peered up at me. Cade's hands were around my hips, wrapping around me like he was steadying me before my knees buckled. I watched as his tongue slipped out from behind his lips and wet the soft skin of my belly, causing things to throb that shouldn't have been throbbing. My heart thumped viciously as confusion crowded me. Cade waited. He stared up at me, looking as hungry as I felt on the inside but wouldn't dare recognize on the outside. There was heavy breathing along my neck, and I knew it wasn't Isaiah. I knew what he smelled like. I knew what his breath felt like on my skin. I slowly moved my head and peeked behind me. Brantley's eyes were hooded as my back pressed into his firm front, but the second he blinked, I snapped out of it.

"Get your fucking hands off me. Both of you."

There was the smallest twitch of a smile on his mouth before his grip loosened. The ground crunched as Cade slowly stood up, wiping a hand over his mouth, but he still kept his other hand on my waist. Brantley stayed behind me too, trapping me between them.

I was still shaken from my lapse in reality, but I remembered exactly why I was in the middle of a dark wooded area, sandwiched between two boys who were sent here to find me. My only question was why? Why were they touching me? Were they fulfilling what Isaiah's father wanted? It didn't make sense. I wasn't Bain's anything. But they made it seem like I was. Was I something more to Bain than he and Isaiah had let on? Regardless of the reasoning, I nearly growled as I locked onto Cade's face, but before I could say anything, something caught our attention from behind.

Cade peered over his shoulder, and it gave me a direct line to Isaiah. I kept my face steady, but hurt flashed within. His words echoed, and it was the only thing I could hear inside my head. *"I've already had her."* As if having sex with me was nothing more than a goal to be met. Another game.

"Why the fuck are your hands on her?" he gritted, creeping in closer and looking more lethal than I'd ever seen him. His brows were hooded over his black-rimmed eyes, and his jaw looked as sharp as a butcher's knife.

It made me irrationally angry to see him, but there was something that sparked to life, too.

My hands pushed at Cade's chest. He hardly moved but ended up stepping aside to let me through. "Don't you dare act like you care now!" Isaiah's resolve fell quickly when he caught my eyes, but I kept going. I kept charging toward him like I was the strong one here. There were too many emotions flinging at me to make me stop, and the only emotion I wanted to grasp onto was anger. I was so angry. The betrayal wiped away any common sense that I had in me to run. "What do you mean why the fuck are his hands on me, Isaiah? You *asked* Brantley if he wanted a go at me!" His mouth opened, but I kept going. "I'm assuming that invitation extended to Cade as well, right? So don't stand there all pissed off because your two best friends wanted to touch me like you did!" The fear and pain were beginning to surface, but I locked it down, steadying my feet, and the next thing I knew, my hand was raising, and I was flinging it toward the side of his face.

I waited for the burn against my palm. I knew he'd feel the sting across his cheek that I'd felt so many times before, but just as I went to make contact, his hand shot up quickly, and he grabbed my wrist, right around my ugly little scars. "Gemma," he snapped. "Stop it."

"Stop it?" I yelled, trying to whip my wrist back. "You... you..." My eyes bounced back and forth between his, trying to keep up with my courage. "You betrayed me! Have you been using me this whole time? You've been warning me that Bain was using me as a toy, but it's you! You acted like I was nothing more than a simple lay. A conquest. You didn't tell your father that I wasn't Bain's girlfriend. I stood there, with your father's hands on me, waiting for you to tell him that I was innocent in all of this. That Bain wouldn't care what happened to me. That I was nothing to him. Yet, you guys stood there and passed me around, threatening to touch me!"

My voice broke, and I felt my wall slowly slipping down. *No. I would not stand here and look weak.* I glowered up at him as his jaw flexed back and forth. He let go of my wrist, and I snatched it away at the same time, crossing my arms over my chest as my body wracked with a chill.

I was done. I was done playing games. I was done with Bain's threats and Isaiah's need to protect me by keeping things from me. *Things like this.* There were obviously much bigger things going on between the Rebels, Bain, and Isaiah's father. And I knew Isaiah's father wasn't a good person, but what I didn't expect was for Isaiah to take my trust and stomp on it. I didn't expect to hear those things come out of his mouth. I didn't expect to feel the heartbreak just yet and for those reasons. *Did he mean what he'd said?*

"I hate you," I whispered, taking a step back. "And I don't

know if you're using me in this sick game with Bain and your father, but I'm done playing." It wasn't fair when you didn't know the rules. Or the objective. I watched as the wall shot up behind Isaiah's eyes. His nostrils flared. His fists clenched. He crowded my space before I even had a chance to step back, and when he glared down at me, he said, "Good."

CHAPTER THREE

ISAIAH

I SLOWLY TOOK a step away from Gemma, fighting every last feeling that was trying to escape out of my chest. I was empty before she came into my life, and now, I was flooded with shit I didn't want to deal with.

I hate you.

Hearing those words cut me deeper than I thought possible. But they were needed. They were needed in the most tortuous way. I hated that Brantley was right. I was stupid to think that it wouldn't end up this way. That she wouldn't be standing here, confused and hurt, and that I wouldn't be standing here, holding my bloody heart in my hands as she threw it back at me. She didn't even know I'd given her my heart. I didn't even know. I didn't even know I had much of one to begin with, and here I was, bleeding out with her standing just a few feet away.

"Why were your hands on her when I came up?" I asked again, looking directly at my two best friends. Anger simmered as I shoved my hands in my pockets, putting more space between Gemma and me. So fucking badly did I want to pull her in close and kiss her to erase everything that had just happened. But at the same time, I wanted to express how angry I was that she went behind my back and snuck out of St. Mary's. If she would have stayed in her fucking room like I'd told her to, then we wouldn't be in this position. I wouldn't be standing here, glaring at my two best friends like I wanted to rip their fucking heads off for touching her.

When I'd walked up, after jogging through the forest for what seemed like hours, I stopped dead in my tracks. Heat had spread to my groin as I zeroed in on Gemma's face. Her head was tilted to the side as pleasure coated her features, but then that heat turned to an inferno when I'd realized that not only were Brantley's lips on her neck, but Cade's were on her stomach. Deep down, I knew there was an explanation—or I'd at least hoped—but right now, I was in the mood to break shit. And their faces would work.

"Calm the fuck down, Isaiah." Cade rolled his eyes as he crossed his arms over his chest. "You should know better than to think that we were out here seducing Gemma after your father came close to fucking raping her."

I cracked my neck and growled. *Not the thing to say to me at a time like this.* "Care to explain, then?" I barked, walking closer.

Brantley sighed as he stepped beside Cade, appearing bored. "She was losing her shit. Freaking out. Saying shit that didn't make sense, like she was revisiting the past...and we couldn't get her to snap out of it, so..."

I saw Gemma move out of the corner of my eye. "So they started touching me, and guess what, Isaiah?"

All three of us looked over at Gemma with her sly little smirk.

Jesus Christ. What did I do to her? The sweet, good-girl version of Gemma was long fucking gone, and in her place was this confident, fiery, hot-as-sin girl taking control of the situation. If I thought she was hot before, when she'd spout off those snarky remarks, now, I was certain that she was the only girl on earth that would make my dick hard. *Stop thinking about her like that.*

My tongue ran over my lips slowly. "What?"

Her cheek rose. "I *liked* it. I liked having their hands on me, and you know what else?"

My blood ran hot as I trailed a heated look down her body. She was filthy from being shoved to her knees and running through the forest, but still, I wanted to pull her into my arms and show her that she was mine. *Even though she wasn't. Not anymore.* "What else?" I asked, my voice thick.

"It worked like a charm." She strode over to me, and I heard a snicker come from Brantley. I stood eerily still, unable to move away even if I'd wanted to. "Your two best friends snapped me out of the panic that *you*"—her finger poked into my chest, and my dick jumped—"put there."

"I think this is our cue to go," Cade mumbled.

I stayed locked on Gemma as I dug into my pockets and threw the keys at him. I waited until their footsteps disappeared before I gripped Gemma around the waist and quickly flung her up against the same tree that my friends had her pinned to just moments ago. Her chin tipped upward, and I saw the way her fear flared, but she didn't back down. Her eyes didn't dart away. She kept a hold of me just as firmly as I kept a hold of her, and for some reason, I really hoped that meant she still trusted me—if even a fraction.

"Don't you mean the panic that *you* put there," I hissed through my teeth, knowing I needed to take my hands off her body and take a step back...but fuck, I couldn't. I was selfish.

It was the entire reason we were even standing here in the first place. "You were the one that left your warm bed, climbed into Bain's G-wagon, and came here when I specifically told you not to." Her lips clamped as her breathing picked up. I moved my hands up slightly so I could fold them around her rapidly rising ribcage, realizing how easy it would be to pick her up and wrap her legs around my waist. "I said those things about you so that my father didn't fucking know that I cared about you. If he even saw an ounce of concern on my face when he had a hold of you, he'd know."

Her shaky fingers came up, and she grabbed my wrists tightly. "He'd know what?"

"That you meant something to me! And do you think he'd let you go unscathed if he knew that I cared for you? He'd find a way to use you as leverage to make me do what he wants. He's already using Jack. He'd use you too." My father was manipulative. I knew him better than most.

Her gulp sounded out around us as I stared down at the shadows along her face. Her features were tight, and the anger was still there, but her voice was level as her nails dug into my skin. "You could have told him I wasn't Bain's girl-friend. That Bain wouldn't care if something happened to me."

I laughed sarcastically, tipping my head up to the stars. "And you think that would have saved you from the compromising situation I found you in? He'd still try to fuck you, Gemma." My shoulders tightened as her breaths rushed out in hot spurts. I was certain she was remembering just how terri-fied she was with him standing over her like he owned her. *God, I hated him.* "And how would you explain knowing that Bain had a car? Or where he parked it? Or how you got his keys? Better yet, how the fuck you knew about the Covens?" I barked the last question out, not knowing exactly how much she knew of the psych hospital, but her mouth slammed shut. "It was either make you seem like you were Bain's little slut and play along, or allow him to see that you meant something to me. One is easily reconciled. The other is not."

Silence fell between us, and it was heavy. Both of our chests were heaving. The air that surrounded us was full of anger and confusion. I gripped her tighter, the cotton of her tank top bundling in my fingers, and her hands around my wrists grew firmer. "And do you, Isaiah? Do you care for me? Because the things you said..."

She trailed off, and I felt my stomach pull. *Say no. Make her hate you. Do it.* "Yes." *Fuck.* Gemma's mouth parted with my admission, and those sweet lips called out to me as heat warmed my veins. "But this..." I pushed my knee in between her jean-clad legs, small pieces of dried mud flying off and hitting the ground below us. "...is over."

There it was. That flash of hurt and confusion all over again. But then the little etch in between her eyebrows smoothed out. "Why? Do you suddenly feel bad for making me a player in your game with Bain and your father? Who's actually using me, Isaiah? Is it Bain? Or is it *you*?"

"I wanna know something," I snapped, ignoring her question solely because I didn't want to answer it. There were too many things that went into my answer, and soon she'd be leaving St. Mary's, and it wouldn't matter. "Why didn't you just wait for me? I thought you trusted me, Gemma. If you wanted to come back here, for whatever reason, I would have brought you myself."

I knew the reason. I knew she had recognized this place, and she was curious. But why didn't she just ask me? Why do this on her own? What was she fucking thinking? If she would have just waited, this wouldn't have happened. My father wouldn't have this perfect visual inside his sick head of her pretty little face, and I wouldn't have stood there, feeling complete fucking terror.

A laugh flew from her mouth and hit me square in the face. Her hair fell behind her back as she looked up to the dark sky in frustration. "It's clear you don't know me at all. Why would I risk you getting caught?" She suddenly brought back those glossy eyes to me, and I stilled. "Did you forget that I know what's at stake if you get caught sneaking out? What happens if you and I both get caught off school grounds, Isaiah? Together? I wouldn't be able to cover for you and lie to the SMC and say we were studying all night! We'd be caught red-handed in our little ploy, and you'd be expelled, and then what would happen to Jack?" Another laugh came from her, and it dripped with sarcasm. "And after meeting your father? I can say I made the right choice. A child shouldn't be left alone with a man like that." Her next words were a whisper. "I should know."

My eyes shut as something in my chest pulled and tugged. I repeated her words in my head, replaying them a few times because I was a glutton for torture. I growled, gripping her torso harder. *Of course I hadn't forgotten that she knew.* Aside from the Rebels, Gemma knew more about me than anyone else. And although I *needed* to stay angry with her over the fact that she put herself in that dangerous situation, I suddenly wasn't any longer. I was more angry with myself, and my father, but not her. *She didn't tell me she was coming back here to protect me and my fucking little brother. Jesus.*

I opened my eyes up again. Gemma was staring at me, and a part of me cracked wide open. "You are too good, Gemma. And that's exactly why this is done." I couldn't stand the thought of her being any more mixed into this than she was. I should have kept my distance once I saw she'd caught Bain's interest. I should have just watched her from afar. It would have been harder, but it was doable. I'd already been keeping hefty tabs on Bain. I could have put even more pressure on him. Get more eyes on her without interfering. Without kissing her. Without making everyone think she was mine and that she was untouchable. I had fucked up by giving her extra attention, by asking for her help with tutoring. I had subjected her to *this*.

Gemma kept a hold of my stare, and I kept going, my grip on her getting tighter and tighter, as if my body knew that this was the last time I'd have her in my hands. "We will continue tutoring. You'll keep meeting me in the library after lacrosse and acting as if you're helping me improve my grades. If anyone asks, you'll say I was there with you, even if I leave. Just like we'd talked about in the beginning. And when it's all said and done, when I'm off probation with the SMC, you'll have everything you asked for, and then you'll fucking leave, and you will never come back." *Then she'd be safe.*

My words were harsh. They implied that I didn't want her to come back. That I didn't want to see her again. And the trembling of her lip told me that she was thinking exactly that. "Fine," her voice cracked as her head turned away.

My jaw ticked, my teeth grinding together as I watched the side of her face nearly crumble. "So, you agree? You and I are done."

Her hands slowly dropped from my wrists, and she brought her gaze back to mine. She put up a good front, but I felt the way her chest caved. She sucked in air as she blinked away the tears. "Yes."

Let her go. Let her fucking go.

The air stilled around us. Everything was frozen. The wind didn't rustle the leaves. The stars didn't glimmer above our heads. Gemma and I locked eyes. My fingers ached to dip underneath her tank top. My mouth begged to be on her warm skin. The perfect bow shape that her lips made opened as a soft breath floated around me. My head dipped down, sweat coating my back even though the night was chilly. My veins flooded with need and pumped blood to every secret spot in my body that only she seemed to bring to life. Our breath mingled as she pressed into my chest. But *no*.

She meant too much.

I'd already hurt her.

My father's hands had been on her. He'd pushed her to her knees and gripped her hair like she was nothing more than a little rag-doll.

I let out a sigh and removed my hands. Her tank top went back down and covered her warm, soft skin. I took one step back, then another, and I felt the cold distance shifting into place. The line was drawn once again.

Gemma pushed off the tree angrily and walked over to her bundled up jacket that was thrown off to the side. I blinked, keeping my face unmoving, wondering if my best friends had taken that piece of clothing off her so they could touch her more.

Although I didn't want to admit it, jealousy was eating me alive. I trusted them, and I believed their excuse as to why things were heated when I had walked up. Gemma confirmed as much.

But she wasn't theirs to touch.

She wasn't my father's to touch either.

Or mine.

When Gemma began to push past me, I grabbed onto her arm and stopped her.

Dark strands of her hair whipped around her face as her stare grew fiery. *Good. She was still angry.* I needed her to keep that wall up so neither one of us was tempted to cross the line again, but there was something on the tip of my tongue that I couldn't swallow. "I'm sorry you had to see that side of my father. I'm sorry he pushed you to your knees and threatened you."

That bright, forest-destroying fire grew wilder in her eye. "It's not the first time I've been shoved to my knees, Isaiah." Then, she peeled my fingers off her arm and kept walking toward the Covens as I stood there with my fists clenched by my side, ready to plow down any mother-fucker who even came close to pushing her down again.

CHAPTER FOUR

THE WALK back to Bain's car gave me enough time to shove away the hurt and pull in the anger. My limbs were shaky, and I had a hard time calming my racing heart. I wasn't sure if I was in shock or if I was truly just that angry about everything that had happened in the last hour, but whatever it was, I was ready to lash out.

The Covens. Isaiah had said, *The Covens.* He gave this place a name that I'd never heard before. I stood with my back pressed against Bain's G-wagon as Isaiah thrust his hands out for the keys, but instead, I stared at the building behind him. The sign was still flickering, but the building itself looked to be quiet. I wanted to ask questions, but there was too much tension between us, and I didn't trust myself to be back on level ground with him.

He wanted to push me away.

I'd do the same.

I came to St. Mary's with no intention of forming relationships that were built on trust with people, and that was how I was going to leave. Although a bit bruised, at least I'd have my dignity back intact.

I reached into my back pocket and pulled out Bain's spare keys, shoving them into Isaiah's hand—the same hand that had just been on my hips a few minutes ago, causing things to twist inside of me that shouldn't have been twisting.

I was still confused. Confused about a lot of things. Was Isaiah using me to get to Bain? To lure him in? Or was it the other way around? I understood Isaiah's reasoning as to why he'd acted like that in front of his father. But I didn't agree with it, and the sting was still there. It stung even more when he'd completely glossed over my question about who was actually using me in their little game, which probably answered the question in itself.

"So, tell me..." Isaiah turned the key, and the G-wagon came to life. If there weren't so many other things to be concerned about, I'd wonder if Bain knew I'd taken his car. "How did you get the spare set from Bain? We searched his room high and low before leaving for Temple. Where were they?"

I crossed my arms over my chest and glared out the window as the psychiatric hospital grew distant. "You expect me to answer your questions, but you won't answer mine?" Something evil stirred in my blood, and I fought the bratty smile that was sliding onto my face. I suddenly felt like we were back on day one when he'd called me a good girl and I snarked a response back. "Maybe I let him touch me like I did your friends."

The car suddenly increased in speed, and I held back a smile. I knew I was being immature, but if I didn't keep up with this whole facade that I wasn't hurt and feeling the shocks of panic still surface, I was afraid I'd break down, and that was something I'd have to save for when I was alone.

Because I *was* hurt, and with that came shame. I was

ashamed that I had given someone the power to hurt me again.

When Isaiah looked down at me, just moments ago, as he pressed me up against the tree with his darkened blue eyes and furrowed brow, and allowed the words, *"We're done,"* to hit my ears, it felt like a slap across the face. It was stupid because I knew we hadn't even really started, and I knew we could never be anything anyway, but it hurt to hear him say it. Especially on top of everything he'd said to his father about me, true or not.

"And did you like it?" Isaiah glanced at me once, and I could see that he didn't believe that I'd actually let Bain touch me, but I could also see that my words had gotten to him, and for a fleeting second, I was glad that I saw the hurt on his face.

I shrugged. "Why do you care? I'm just another piece of fresh ass, right?"

The prickles of betrayal were still there. The question of whether taking my virginity meant anything to him ate at me. What if he'd been kissing and touching me all just for show? Even the times that were in secret? Was it all just to prove to Bain that he couldn't have me? Was this some sick way of showing how formidable he was? Did he fool me into thinking that I meant something to him? Did he fool others? He'd all but said it the first time he'd kissed me in front of everyone. *"I need people to know you're mine."*

"Knock it off, Gemma." His grip on the steering wheel grew tighter as the lines on the road blurred even more. "I told you why I said that, and of all people, I thought you'd understand."

I knew we were getting closer to St. Mary's and that I'd be able to go into my room to sort everything out soon, but instead of keeping my mouth shut, I kept going. In a way, it put me back in control, and I needed that. "Haven't you heard the saying: '*Every lie has a bit of truth to it*?'" I clicked my tongue. "Just food for thought."

His fingers flexed as we rounded the bend. The dilapidated warehouse in its run-down glory sat in the distance, and I suddenly couldn't wait to be back at the school. I needed my sketchbook, and my pencil, and a quiet room where I could digest everything that had happened.

I waited as Isaiah's mouth opened. "Oh, I've heard that saying. I believe it to be true in most aspects." There was a hiccup in my chest, and I almost put my hand over my heart to ease the sting I'd felt. "I wasn't lying when I said fucking you was like fucking an angel. Or that it was nice and pure."

I bit the inside of my cheek. I sliced my attention back out my window so he couldn't read my facial expression, because I was certain there was something on my face that I didn't want him to see. I started to breathe heavily, and irritation was poking at my skin like a thousand little needles.

The car came to a stop, and I threw the door open, stepping out and turning on my heel to begin my walk back to the school. I didn't even care if he put Bain's keys back where they were supposed to go. I just needed to get away.

I heard his strides coming up behind me, the gravel being crushed by his shoe. His hands went into his pockets as his arm brushed mine, and I suddenly felt flushed. "Every time I fucking touched you, it was like touching an angel, Gemma. Perfect and captivating. I felt unworthy every single time."

My brow creased as I felt my wall sliding down. *No.* I wasn't going to let his words demolish the shield I'd thrown up the second he played into his father's hand. If I did that, then a whole round of emotions would come through. I gulped back anything trying to come out of my throat, picked up my pace, and didn't stop until St. Mary's came into view.

Isaiah and I stopped right outside the gate before he reached out with a steady hand and pulled it open, allowing me to walk through. We kept our thoughts to ourselves as we passed by his uncle's little cottage, and I shoved the memories away of the last time we'd walked past it together. My arms came up and crossed over my chest as I lifted my chin.

The hallway was as quiet as it usually was, the black-and-white floor shiny and sleek. I didn't dare look at the dining hall because it looked different in the night. It brought back a secret that only he and I shared, and it was something that no longer mattered, even if my lips began tingling at the mere thought.

Isaiah looked back behind us before turning to face me. I saw the way he looked at me, and it sent little shivers everywhere. His blue eyes were swimming with things I couldn't decipher. His jaw wiggled back and forth. His hand came up, and he rushed it through the dark ends of his hair, and he brushed past me, knowing I'd follow.

I just needed to get back to my room.

"I can get to my room from here. You don't have to walk me." My voice was wobbly, and I knew that I would break soon. The ache in my head was pounding. The feelings of anger and betrayal were slowly slipping away. The need to lash out was gone because a part of me understood. Deep down, I knew what it was like to play a part. I knew what it was like to be someone you weren't to save yourself and others. But my heart hurt. My chest cracked, knowing that I wouldn't feel Isaiah's lips on mine again. I was cut right down the middle in the realization that I didn't necessarily feel safe with him any longer. My secrets didn't threaten to spill off the end of my lips, and that was because I wasn't sure if I trusted him anymore, and that hurt worse than anything.

"I'm walking you to your room," he said, voice lacking any emotion at all.

"I don't want you to. I'm fine doing it on my own."

"Just like you were fine sneaking out of St. Mary's alone?"

His response was like a bite to my skin, because he was right. I wasn't sure I would have gotten out of the situation I had been in if he, Cade, and Brantley hadn't chased me off into the woods.

Everything was so messed up, and it was all I could think about as we both silently walked down the hall to my room, both on edge, wondering if the duty teacher would be making her rounds anytime soon.

My hand rested on the iron-clad knob, and I felt the heat from Isaiah's body lingering behind mine. I shut my eyes, breathing heavily as everything came to a sudden stop. The hurt. The fear. The betrayal. The confusion. The realization that he was trying to do the right thing. Maybe this was him trying to be selfless. Or maybe he really had been using me this whole time to get to Bain.

I wasn't really sure. I wasn't sure of anything anymore.

"Gemma?" he whispered, voice soft, likely wondering why I hadn't moved. *Was he hurting too?*

I kept my head down, voice hardly audible. "There's another reason why I didn't ask you to go with me tonight. It wasn't only because I was afraid that you'd get caught and it'd be all my fault. It wasn't only because I was worried for your little brother." I swallowed as one single tear fell over the side of my cheek. "I knew that I was stepping into something that I wasn't quite ready to share with you yet. It wasn't that I didn't trust you, Isaiah. I just wasn't ready to give you something else from my past." My lip trembled as I thought back to the green awning over my head, feeling the memory peek over my walls right before his father had grabbed me. "I've been to the place you call The Covens. That's why I went back alone."

I felt him come even closer, and I clenched my lips together. His hand rested beside my head against the door as my palm shook along the doorknob. My heart raced so quickly I could hear it in my ears.

"I know."

He knew?

All of a sudden, his hand wrapped around my waist, and he spun me around, backing me up against the door. His arms caged me in, and his chest was moving so fast I felt a small amount of fear seep in. "Don't you *ever* go back there. Do you hear me?"

I didn't answer. Instead, I just kept a hold of his steely gaze, seeing the shadows flicker against the wall behind him. He looked like a villain at that moment. And maybe he was.

He dropped his gaze down to my lips, and I froze. We were both breathing erratically, but there was a sound down at the end of the hallway, and his head dropped before he shoved off the door and growled like a terrorized wolf.

A voice carried through the empty space. "Who's down there?"

"It's Isaiah," he answered, keeping me pinned to my spot. "I was walking Gemma back to her room after tutoring."

"Tutoring?" The voice grew closer, and it sounded like Mrs. Fitz, but I wasn't positive. My heart was beating too loudly to hear anything else. "Didn't you have an away game? Surely you two weren't studying this late into the night."

"Get in your room, Gemma. You're filthy."

I didn't miss a beat. The door was opened, and the smell of lavender and chocolate filled my senses immediately. And for the first time all night, I finally felt safe.

I gulped in the air, and Sloane popped up from her bed, holding a Cosmic brownie in her hand as her laptop slid to the side. "Finally! I woke up, and you were gone—"

The second I latched onto her, I cracked. A strangled cry left my lips as the fear and anxiety I'd kept pushing away since the moment I'd taken off toward the forest was back and in full action.

Two warm arms came around me as I sank to the ground and placed my forehead on my knees, letting the tears wash down over my dirty face and clothes. "Shh. You're okay. You're okay, Gemma. You're here. You're going to be fine."

Sloane was right. I was going to be fine because I was leaving soon, and the thought of Richard, Bain, Isaiah, his father, and the sickening memory of the Covenant Psychiatric Hospital was going to be in the past.

CHAPTER FIVE

ISAIAH

"YOU KNOW what you need to do, bro." I sliced my attention to Brantley, who was resting his elbows against the dining table, looking more smug than usual. He picked up his soda and threw it back before wiping his mouth on his hand. "Just make her hate you. It'll be the easiest way to resist her. There'll be no chance to fuck her."

To fuck her. Like that was all I cared about when it came to Gemma.

Cade chuckled from beside him. "Shouldn't be hard."

"Yeah?" I asked, slapping my hand down on the table, gaining a few quick glances from those who weren't aware that I was seconds from flipping it onto its side. "And how'd that work out for you and Journey, Cade?"

I'd been angry and irritated all day. I couldn't stand to look in Bain's direction, knowing he had a part in last night, even if he wasn't actively present. I had put all the energy I had left into saving face with Mrs. Fitz when she caught me dropping Gemma back at her room well after midnight, which meant, at the present moment, I had nothing leftover to give. My calming vibes and rational thinking were hardly in attendance today.

I could tell Mrs. Fitz had been skeptical when we departed, and why wouldn't she have been? But if she had any suspicion that something other than tutoring was going on with Gemma and me, those suspicions were crushed during art today. Gemma wouldn't even look in my direction, and every time I looked in hers, I wanted to hit something. Her eyes were red, and with the way that Sloane was currently glaring at me, it meant that Gemma had likely cracked when she went into her room last night.

She put up a good front until she turned her back to me and let out her little confession that would haunt me for the rest of my life. Noticing the shake in her voice and watching the lone tear fall down her cheek was so much worse than seeing her hatred brew.

The chip in Cade's hand crumbled. "Fuck off, Isaiah."

Brantley sighed. "Let him be. He's just pissed because we were right." He paused before smirking. "And because he saw us touching Gemma."

My glare was murderous, and I could hear the ticking of the massive time bomb seconds from exploding inside my ears. I didn't have time for this. Although Gemma felt like the biggest issue in my life at the moment, I was balancing something else that neither Cade, Brantley, nor Shiner knew about. Not yet, anyway.

"I'm pissed about a lot of things," I said, my voice seemingly calm, although I still had a load of pent-up aggression simmering on the inside—which wasn't necessarily a good thing. When I was angry but appeared calm and in control, that was when I made bad choices. I was tapping into that overbearing feeling of numbness that cooled my veins, and that was when Isaiah Underwood turned ruthless. "And yes"—I cocked my head at my two friends and dropped my voice—"seeing your hands on her body made me want to strangle you almost as much as I wanted to strangle my fucking father last night."

Shiner peeked up when he heard what I'd said. "What the fuck did I miss?"

Brantley rolled his eyes. "Be thankful you weren't there."

I sensed his agitation before he managed to slump in defeat. Shiner wanted in on the shit that Cade, Brantley, and I discussed privately, and although I'd given him *some* insight on our lives and what I was up against outside of this school, he was still out of the game. It wasn't because I didn't trust him. It was more because the less he knew, the better. "Whatever. Callie's pussy was better than whatever you three got into, I'm sure." He shrugged before snagging his attention away. "But...they're right."

I moved my gaze over to Gemma, seeing her nibble on a carrot stick before I looked back at Shiner. "Right about what?"

"If you want to resist her, make her see you in a different light. Make her see the old Isaiah so *she* resists you. Show her who you were before she stepped foot in this school."

I flicked a crumb off my tie, feeling a shift inside my chest. *Who was I before she came here?* I could hardly remember.

Trailing back down the long table to see Gemma, I noticed that she was smiling at something Sloane had said, which caused my stomach to knot. It was the first time I'd seen her smile all day, and it was like we were back to the beginning, when she had first started at St. Mary's. I had been trying to figure her out from the very second I'd laid eyes on her, and I still was. I distinctly remember thinking she seemed so lost, sitting with Sloane on that Tuesday morning just a couple of months ago. But now? She didn't look so lost, even if I knew, deep down, she was still trying to uncover things about her life that had been hidden from her. Maybe she'd discovered something last night before my father appeared.

Gemma had found her footing in the last few weeks.

But I'd lost mine.

In fact, I was pretty certain that I'd lost myself in her, and she'd found herself in me.

My name on Cade's lips snagged my lingering gaze away from Gemma. "Isaiah can't really go back to his usual behavior. He's still on probation, so there are some limitations, but..."

Shiner played his famous grin, tipping his lip just slightly as he nodded along with Cade. "Oh, yes. I see where you're going, and it never fucking fails."

Their secretive conversation was stroking my irritation. "I'm growing impatient," I snapped, pushing my food away. I hadn't been hungry since I'd seen my father standing above Gemma last night.

"Get a new toy."

I shut my eyes briefly, reeling in my temper. "She wasn't a fucking toy."

Shiner snapped his fingers. "But you played with her."

I was seconds from slamming my fist down onto the table, but Brantley cleared his throat and glanced across the table, gazing into the dining hall. Mostly everyone was seated with their lunches by now, but of course, Bain—being the imperious son of a bitch that he was—slowly strolled the empty space with an apple in his hand, staring directly at me.

Red began to dance in front of my vision, but I dug down as deep as I could to stay grounded. *Calculated behavior was better than impulsive behavior.* I breathed in and out of my nose, hearing something crack in my body from the hostility.

Bain's head tilted with a chuckle as he rolled his dark eyes before turning and going to sit with a few of his friends that were blatantly unaware of his life outside of this school. After last night, I knew that there was going to come a time in the near future where I needed Bain on level ground, so now more than ever, I needed to pull myself back in and stay calm. I gained my smarts from my mother, and I was going to make damn good use of them.

Turning back to the rest of the Rebels, I eyed each and every one of them before I spoke smoothly. "If I find someone new, Bain will think Gemma is free game."

Shiner's eyebrow arched. "And if she's smart, she'll turn him down."

This time, Cade's voice shook, and I was pretty sure I knew why. "And you think that'll stop him?"

I swallowed back the distaste hitting the back of my throat. "Me backing off from her might take some of the threat away. But I have a feeling that Bain isn't only watching Gemma because of me." *And that did not sit well with me at all.*

Brantley nodded, lowering his voice even more. "It has something to do with her uncle, yeah? I mean, they obviously know each other if Bain is his newest gunrunner."

I thought back to the photo I'd snapped that first time Gemma and I went to the Covens. She still had no idea that Bain went there to illegally sell guns to *her* uncle—who was apparently my father's biggest client.

"I think so," I answered as the bell echoed through the vast space, signaling that it was time for the second half of the day. I trailed after Gemma with my heart lodged in my throat. Her smooth legs had two scrapes along the knees that I had to pull my gaze from. "I need you guys to hear this, so listen up." Shiner began to stand, but I held up a finger. "You can stay. This doesn't necessarily apply to you, but you can stay."

He slowly dropped back down into his seat as the dining hall started to empty. Once the ears were away and Bain had disappeared through the doors, not even sparing us a glance, I placed my hands onto the cool wood beneath our trays and breathed out an even breath. "There is going to come a time, in the near future, that I will have to work with Bain."

"You mean work *against*." Cade eyed me suspiciously.

"No." Trepidation crept along my shoulders like a whore running her fingers down the base of my neck slowly and seductively, causing my stomach to hollow out.

Each of my friends was quiet. Neither one of them looked away or spoke. "After I get some things settled, you will have a choice to make." I sniffed, pushing away from the table and climbing to my feet. "I just need you to be prepared."

I turned my back and left them alone, hoping like hell that they chose my side and not the one that was the most familiar to them.

After all, familiar meant comfort even if, in this case, it was morally wrong.

"Do you have any whiskey?" I asked, plopping myself down in the same seat I often frequented when I came into my uncle's moody and depressing office. I loosened my tie and propped my foot up against the ledge of his desk, leaning back in the chair.

"What happened last night?" My uncle's glare didn't faze me, and if I were in better spirits, I would have joked with him. But I wasn't in the mood for games this evening, and I had a very important tutoring session to get to in just a few minutes.

"I came to my senses, that's what." And as bitter as the words tasted, they were true. The only thing that kept replaying in my head from last night was the way Gemma looked after I had hurt her and how proud my father was. Two things I never wanted to see again.

My uncle bent down and pulled open a drawer in his desk. He disappeared for a brief moment before popping back up with a bottle of whiskey. *Fuck yeah. Now we were talkin'.*

My eyebrow hitched, and I grinned. "You surprise me sometimes, Uncle Tate."

He scoffed. "This is for me. Not you. Now tell me, what happened? Mrs. Fitz mentioned to me that she saw you dropping Gemma off at her room as she made her rounds last night."

I paused, keeping my face steady. "Did she tell the rest of the SMC?"

The fucking SMC. Always breathing down my neck. They were almost worse than my father. *Almost.*

He shook his head, pouring a single shot that sat in between us. I eyed it carefully, wondering if he would let me have one. Tate Ellison was a man of good word, but he still had Underwood blood running through his veins, which meant that he was a bit rebellious, even if he wanted to hide it.

"So?" he prodded, picking the glass up.

I clenched my teeth, watching the flickering fire. It almost felt like the flames were licking up my arms as anger began to simmer again. "Gemma snuck out last night while we were on our way back from Temple." The shot glass slammed back to the desk, but I kept my eyes on the dancing reds and oranges. "She went back to the Covens. Stole Bain's car. And when I found her..."

"Jesus Christ."

I ignored his muttering. "When I found her, Dad had a hold of her hair, threatening her because he thought Bain was watching from afar or some shit. He thought she was his girl-friend or something." Silence jutted through the room like the crashing of a wave in the middle of a hurricane. It was quick and suffocating, and I had to force the next words out. "I had to interfere in the worst way possible to show him that I was his little fucked-up clone and that Gemma meant nothing to me. That I didn't even know her. I said she was nothing more than a piece of ass and that I would use her to send a message to Bain."

When I glanced back at my uncle, feeling the guilt creep in, his eyes were shut as his nostrils flared. I wasn't sure what he was angrier about, but to be honest, I didn't really care much. He wasn't a part of this life anymore, even if he wanted to act like he was. There was nothing he could have done if he were the one to go after Gemma. Underwood business stayed within those of the same surname, and from the moment Uncle Tate stepped out of the family business, he had to legally change his name and never speak of it again. Same with my older brother, Jacobi.

"And are you, Isaiah?" he finally asked, pouring another shot. Two was his limit. I was half-eager to see if he'd pour a third. I was certain this school would drive him to alcoholism eventually—at least with me in attendance. He cared too much for the students here. He would have never survived working alongside my father. Jacobi would have. But my older brother was even more selfish than I was.

"Am I what?" I put both feet back on the ground and rested my elbows against my knees.

He swallowed, twisting the cap back onto the whiskey bottle. *Huh. Two was still the limit.* "Are you a clone of your father? Are you following in his footsteps? Did seeing him with Gemma change something for you?"

The last we'd spoken of this, I told him I was taking over the business when the time came because of my father's threats against Jack, so I waited for the surprised look on his face when I answered, "No."

"No?"

Last night didn't necessarily change me. It just made me realize what was already there. *I was not Carlisle Underwood.* The anxiety that I wouldn't allow to fester was beginning to cage me, so I quickly changed the subject, knowing I needed to get to the library even if, the entire time, I would be feeling nothing but irritation and regret.

Part of me wanted to be done with the whole tutoring thing so my life could be a little bit easier. But Jack wasn't safe yet, and until he was, I had to keep up with saving face. I had to keep up with my grades. I had to keep up with the tutoring sessions with a girl who made me see nothing *but* her. I had to continue following Bain, even if I was now certain he was just setting me up the entire time anyway. My job wasn't done yet.

"I need to use your phone."

"Isaiah," my uncle's voice grew more intense, and I clicked my tongue back and forth, making the world's most annoying noise, pretending as if I didn't hear the skepticism in the way he'd said my name. "What's going on with you? Now all of a sudden you're not taking over the business?"

"I just need to use your phone. Or maybe one of those phones inside your desk." I snapped my fingers. "That's a better idea. Give me one of those so no one can trace it back to me."

The tiny crease in between his brows was back. "Who are you calling? And is Gemma okay? After last night?"

I ran my tongue over my teeth as my shoulders tensed. "She's fine. And I'm calling the Covens."

He nearly choked on his spit. "Why the hell would you need to call the Covens? Isaiah. Do you know what you're doing?" He let out an exasperated sigh before glaring at me. "The SMC is just about ready to take you off probation.

They've set a date to reconvene. That's why I wanted you to come to my office. What are you up to? Talk to me."

That had something snapping in my neck. *Gemma could leave after I was off probation.* Plus, once Jack was safe, it wouldn't matter anyway. I would be done following Bain, and I wouldn't need a cover *or* a tutor. She would no longer be a player in this game.

I made a mental note to check on her ID and the other various documents I knew she'd need to completely fall off the face of the earth as who we knew to be Gemma Richardson, even if the thought made me sick.

"Isaiah!" my uncle barked, and it snapped me to attention.

"I'm calling the fucking Covens to see if Tobias Richardson is there." My teeth gritted, and I wouldn't have been surprised if dust had coated the inside of my mouth. "She can't go back there again, and I am absolutely certain that the entire reason she went there last night was because she thought he was there."

I hardly got the sentence out before he spoke. "He's not there."

My head tilted with surprise. "What?"

"He's not there—at least not under that name. I've already checked." He paused, placing both hands on the desk and standing up to glare down at me. "I have Gemma Richardson handled, Isaiah."

I rolled my eyes, standing up alongside him. "Do ya now?" *And he thought that would stop me?*

"I have secrets, too. Let me handle her. You handle the plan that I know you have brewing in the back of your head on how to get out from the family business, and let me know if I can help."

I walked over to the door, keeping my back to him. He knew he couldn't help me. I knew it too. He also knew it was useless to ask me anything else about my upcoming plans, because I wouldn't tell them. I kept my secrets close, and there was a reason for that.

"You're too good to be the Huntsman, Isaiah. You are not your father. You're making the right choice."

But was I?

CHAPTER SIX

GEMMA

Don't even look at him. Don't do it.

My eyes casually grazed the edge of the laptop that the headmaster had given me, and I hated myself for not being able to keep a hold of my emotions. I'd done so well all day long. I didn't look for him in the hallway, even though I knew exactly where he was. I didn't find those piercing icy depths during lunch, even though I could tell he was looking at me, because Sloane would tense each time. When we'd gone to sit outside during the boys' lacrosse practice, I kept my back turned to the field, resting along the fence as I sketched the same thing over and over again in my journal, trying to keep the momentum of anger and betrayal at the forefront of my brain.

Not the betrayal of Isaiah. Even though everything from last night made my throat close up at the mere thought, I knew him—at least, a part of him. I knew, deep down, he wasn't lying when he'd given me an explanation for his vile words and why he didn't jump in to take his father's hands off me. Did it still hurt? Yes. But the betrayal that I felt from Richard was tenfold. His actions were like sharp shards of glass, cutting into me deeper and deeper as the memory of that place continued to resurface. I had a nightmare last night, which I'd already expected. It was the memory that I seemed to unlock by going to the psychiatric hospital—*the Covens*—by myself. It was a memory that I'd buried away for years because reopening that wound hurt more than being shoved to my knees and chained up from innocently asking about my mother. The older I got, the more confused I became over the lies Richard had fed me. But I'd known this entire time. It just took that tattered green awning from last night to open my eyes. I was on the brink of learning more about that night in my deep slumber, but Sloane had woken me up before things progressed.

What I'd managed to gather, though, was that Richard Stallard was the sick one. He should have been shoved into that padded room. Not my mother.

"Stop researching the hospital, Gemma. You won't find anything on the website."

My fingers stilled over the keyboard as I tried leveling my breathing. My heart pounded as I listened to the clicking of the clock overhead. There was a massive wall between Isaiah and I now. It was much bigger than it was when we'd first met. But just because it was bigger, that didn't mean it was sturdy. It felt fragile. Like it was thrown up too quickly, and it would fall down with the slightest crack.

I straightened my shoulders, thinking back to the pep talk that Sloane had given me before I left to come to the library. She wanted me to blow off tutoring. To tell Isaiah to fuck off and that I didn't owe him anything, much less to help him with *raising* his grades. And a part of me wanted to tell him that, but there was an even bigger part of me that broke last night and formed me into this girl that was strong-willed and determined to be independent without two strong hands gripping her waist with whispered promises of safety inside her ear. I wasn't going to hide from Isaiah. I wasn't that girl anymore. I'd been put in shittier situations, and I knew I could handle this. Living with someone like Richard had groomed me to act in ways I didn't want to. I could act like being near Isaiah didn't make my stomach pull. I could pretend that catching his eye didn't make my entire body hot. It wasn't *that* hard to stay leveled. *Right?*

"I'm serious. Leave it be."

My eyes caught his again as I peeked up over the computer. I wasn't going to lie; intimidation looked good crowding his dark features. "Why don't you just sit over there and pretend we're tutoring? Isn't that what you wanted? For things to go back to how you originally planned?" I shut my laptop and crossed my arms over my uniform. I didn't bother changing after school today. I didn't want to feel the denim of jeans rubbing over my scrapes caused by his father shoving me down to my knees. "You wanted me to go back to knowing nothing about your life. Nothing about you or Bain or your daddy issues. I don't ask where you go when you need to leave in the middle of a tutoring session. I cover for you if anyone asks. Yeah, that's about it. Right? I mean, if you're caught out in the hall after curfew, you were just walking me back to my room from tutoring? Yeah? That's the plan? That's your cover?"

He sighed, gripping the pencil in his fist so tightly his knuckles turned white. "Gemma."

My name was more of a warning than anything, and it pissed me off. "Isn't that what you wanted? Correct me if I'm wrong."

I heard the crack of the pencil, but I stayed locked on his face. The intimidation lingered for a split second before something else came over his features. His jaw untightened, and his brows lowered. "I hurt you last night."

I scoffed, pretending I didn't care. "I've been hurt worse, trust me. Don't flatter yourself." *Lies. Lies. Lies.* The hurt I was used to was tangible. Richard didn't slice away at my heart like Isaiah did, so I wasn't used to this silent, underlying pain. And I really couldn't figure out what was better, the physical hurt or the emotional. The only good thing was that I could hide my emotions. I couldn't do that with the scars along my wrists.

Isaiah leaned back onto the chair and continued to stare at me. I wanted to move in the worst way. I wanted to fidget as butterflies coated the inside of my belly, or better yet, I wanted to burn them all together. Too much had happened last night, and I was left feeling desperate and confused. I should have felt anger when I looked into those icy pools, not this annoying trickle of anticipation. There was a wicked part of me that wanted him to say *fuck it* and take me in his arms. I ached to feel his hands around my waist again. I craved to feel that solitude I felt when he kissed me and showed me things that made me feel rebellious and free.

No.

"He's not there, Gemma."

My chest stopped rising as I repeated his words. There was no warm breath leaving my mouth or silent arguments over my body continuing to react to him. The ticking in my ear only stopped long enough for me to confirm who and what he was talking about. "Excuse me?"

Isaiah moved forward, placing his bare forearms on the table. The corded muscles beneath the skin danced out of the corner of my eye.

"Your brother is not at the Covens." He blinked once, and I tried my hardest to unblur my vision as he confirmed what I'd already suspected. "That's why you went, right? To see if your uncle had sent him there four years ago when he left you? You wanted to know why you'd recognized it that first night."

I bit the inside of my cheek so hard it bled. The metallic taste coated my tongue and sent chills flying down my arms. The longer Isaiah stared at me, the more I wanted to break. "That's none of your business now, is it? What happened to our no-questions-asked policy? That stands now that we're back to our original plan, right?"

I swallowed past the rising lump, wanting to shove the laptop off the table as buried feelings started to suffocate me. I knew why the psychiatric hospital was familiar to me now, but there was still a small part of me that hoped Tobias was there. If Richard had sent my mother there, he could have sent him there too.

"I don't believe you," I remarked, gripping the edge of the table. "And how could you possibly know that? Wait. Don't tell me. You're somehow affiliated with that place? You weren't *only* following Bain that night, huh? You know something else." I laughed sarcastically and mumbled under my breath, "Your father probably runs it. That would make sense. He's just as screwed up as Richard."

"Richard?" he asked, treading slowly.

I ignored him. I didn't care if he knew that Richard wasn't my biological uncle. There was a more pressing issue coming to mind. "How do you know?" I asked, putting my watery gaze on his. "How do you know he isn't there? I'm assuming you didn't ask your father such a question, but then again, do I really even know you?" I shrugged, feeling the betrayal of everyone in my life come at me at once. "I mean, sure, I let you take my virginity, but that's beside the point."

"Gemma," he warned again, but I raised my voice.

"How do you know, Isaiah? Wait. Is that even your real name?"

He turned again, rubbing a feeble hand down his face, trying to hide a smirk. "Yes, that's my real name."

Was he laughing?

I quickly stood up, feeling the tears spring back to my eyes but not because I was sad. It was because I was frustrated and angry. Everything was piling up, and if it was his goal to make me hate him, he was achieving it. It was as if he were patronizing me. Like he wanted me to lash out.

"How do you know?" I asked again, placing my hands down on the cool wood beneath my fingers. My legs were shaky, and my knees were seconds from buckling. *Tobias had to be there.* Because if he wasn't, I had no freaking idea where he was.

Isaiah peered up at me behind those black-rimmed eyes. "Because I called the Covens and asked."

Oh no. "You did what?" The question was hardly above a whisper as I sunk back down into the chair. The final string was clipped, and there it was. *Disappointment.* But just as soon as I let the blow hit me, I stood back up, and the anger was rushing. "Are you kidding me?!" My voice was high-pitched, and I placed my hands on my head, gripping my chestnut strands just as tightly as his father had the night before. "You called and asked for Tobias Richardson?!" *Richard would know.* After all, how many people would be inquiring about a *Tobias Richardson?* I was sure when Richard had changed our last names to his mother's maiden name after our mother died, he had done his research.

I gasped, feeling the memory surface again. The one that I'd dug into last night. The one that told me that Richard was a part of The Covenant Psychiatric Hospital— or *The Covens,* as Isaiah called it. I turned my back quickly and darted away from Isaiah and his unmoving features. I ran past aisles and aisles of books until I got to the very end of the library, tucked away in the dark, as my eyes shut

and I was taken back to a time when I was the most
vulnerable.

*"YOU WILL NOT GET AWAY with this, Richard." My mother's voice
was hoarse, like she'd been yelling or maybe she had a cold. We didn't
get out much to catch the germs, but occasionally, she'd have the sniffles
at night. I could hear her. I'd wake up sometimes, looking for Tobias'
warm hand. He and I shared a bed, but every once in a while, I
would climb out and go into Mama's. I sometimes felt like she needed
my hand more than he did.*

*"You mistake me for someone who is weak, Emily." Uncle Richard
laughed, and I shut my eyes, pretending that I was asleep in the back-
seat. Tobias wasn't with us. It was just Mama, me, and Uncle
Richard. I peeked up when I felt a shift, and I glanced out the
window, wondering how I'd gotten into the back of Uncle Richard's
car. My blanket was wrapped around me as I pulled it up to cover
most of my face, seeing the blurring stars through the glass.*

*My mom's voice shook, and I heard another sniffle. Maybe she
was sick. I smiled a little as I thought that, maybe in the morning, I
would get her some warm tea from Auntie. That would make her feel
better. Of course, I would have to have Tobias help me. Auntie liked
him better than me.*

*"Richard. You cannot take me from my children and throw me
into a dungeon. My sentence is finished in a few weeks. What will the
courts say when I'm missing? I appreciate that you kept me from going
to prison, but this will not work."*

*He laughed again, and confusion filled me. What was she
talking about? Sentence? Like a sentence with words? "I own the
courts, Emily. You know this, and you'd do good to be by my side.
You have a face for politics. I don't understand why you'd want any
other life than the one I'm giving you." His words cut off, and the
car came to a stop. I almost fell forward onto the floor, but I pushed
myself back into the leather seat, gripping my blankie as my*

stomach rolled. "Don't worry, though, Princess. After you're through here, you'll be just the way I want you. Compliant, submissive, and obedient. You'll spread those legs when I want, hang on my arm at cocktail parties, and we will raise our children to be upstanding citizens. They will follow the rules, just as soon as their mother does."

My eyebrows crowded as his door opened, and I quickly shut my eyes, pretending like I was asleep. I didn't like when Uncle Richard used that tone. It scared me. He did it a lot. It made my stomach wiggly, and sometimes I would run away and hide. Tobias never hid with me, though. He stayed with Mama. He was braver than me.

"Richard, I will tell everyone in there what you've done to me over the years. I'm done being your little doll. You can't groom me into what you want!" My mother's voice shook as it grew louder, and a tear fell down my cheek. I clenched my eyes tighter as I heard the door slam, making the entire car move underneath me.

"Mama?" I whispered.

"Baby, stay asleep."

I shut my eyes again, gripping onto my blankie. My fingers hurt from the grip, but it made me feel safe. The car door opened again, and I peeked one eye open as my mother yelped. My lips smooshed together as I saw Uncle Richard grab her by her pretty hair and drag her out of the car. More confusion filled me as I saw through the crack that her hands were in handcuffs. They looked more real than the ones that Tobias and I would use as we played cops and robbers in the backyard.

Uncle Richard shouted as he pulled her, and I wanted to scream. "If I can't groom you, then I'll just groom her." The door was suddenly shut again, and I counted to five before I sat up taller with my heart feeling like I'd just run through the forest, playing hide and seek. There was a door with a green curtain-like thingy over the top, and I knew it was the door that Uncle Richard and Mama had gone through.

Mama told me to stay asleep, but Tobias wasn't here. He couldn't stay with her when Uncle Richard yelled. He couldn't hold her hand. She needed me to be brave. I was going to be brave.

My hand shook on the door handle, and the cool air hit my wet face as I crawled out of the car. The pebbles below my feet dug in as I tiptoed over to the door that they had gone into. I looked behind me and saw my blanket half hanging out, so I ran back over, pretending that my feet didn't hurt, and I snatched it, taking it with me. I knew it would make me feel better if I got scared. I couldn't be scared. Mama needed me.

The door creaked open, and I slowly walked inside, thankful for the shiny cold floor beneath my sore toes. My feet fell flat as my eyes adjusted to the bright lights that lined the white hallway. It smelled funny, like it had been cleaned over and over again. I stayed still, trying to listen for Mama, and that was when I heard a scream.

Mama!

I surged forward, leaving dirty footprints behind me as I dragged my blanket down the hall. I ran as fast as I could, pretending that Tobias was chasing me. "Mommy!" I shouted. My face felt really wet. "Uncle Richard!"

"Baby!" I heard Mama's raspy scream, and I came to a sudden halt. My heart was thumping so fast, and I was scared. I was scared, and my blankie wasn't making me feel any better. I turned and stopped right inside a door that was half-cracked. At first, I only saw Uncle Richard. His brow was raised, but the rest of his face remained smooth. "Baby!" My face was suddenly turned as Mama grabbed onto my upper arms. "I love you. Tell Tobias I love him too."

My eyes welled up, and my lip shook. "Mommy?" My head was suddenly crushed into her warm chest, and my arms came up around her waist as she cried. "Mommy, it's okay," I mumbled, giving her my best hug. "Why are you sad?"

Her breath tickled my ear after she kissed the top of my head. "Find your daddy, Gemma. He will save you if I don't come back. His name is—" Suddenly, my mother was ripped from my arms, and I jolted forward in panic.

"Mommy!" I screamed. "Mommy! Wait!" Two men came forward wearing black outfits and pulled her backward. She fought them. Her brown hair swished in front of her face, getting stuck on her cheeks.

"No! Let me go! You cannot do this, Richard!" She looked to the men holding her arms. "He's raped me! Over and over again! He's going to take my kids! I'm not sick! I don't need to be here!"

Uncle Richard's arms circled around my waist as he pulled me away. My arms reached out, dropping my blanket in the process. "Mommy! Come back!"

"No!" Her hands were freed now, and I was glad when she hit one of the men in the face. But then his eyes grew smaller. They looked like little lines below his eyebrows. He was angry. "Let me fucking go! Baby, I love you! Find your daddy!"

I didn't know who my daddy was. I didn't know! Before I could say that, Richard threw me into the hallway, and I hit the hard floor with a big thump. My belly dropped, and my back hurt. I cried out even louder, feeling for the bump that I knew would be there. The door was slammed, and I looked up quickly through blurry eyes.

"Where's Mommy going?" I asked through choppy breaths. Tears fell, and they made me feel cold.

Uncle Richard came and stood above me as I sat on the floor. I wanted Mama. She needed me. But Uncle Richard was looking down at me with the same look he'd always given her before yelling. He bent down in front of me as I cried and cried. I couldn't stop. I wanted Tobias. And I wanted my blankie. I stared at the door behind Uncle Richard, remembering that my blankie fell. But it was okay. Mama could use it. Maybe it would make her feel safe.

"You remember this, okay, little one?" Uncle Richard's finger trailed down the side of my face, and I cried harder. "This is what happens when you don't follow the rules. You were supposed to stay in the car. Maybe I'll have to punish you too."

Fear like no other came at me. I ducked my head into my knees and tried to hide. I couldn't run to the closet. I couldn't look for Tobias *and hold his hand. Mama wasn't here either. I didn't feel safe with Uncle Richard.*

"Judge Stallard?" I heard a deep voice say from somewhere close by, but I kept my face hidden. I didn't want to be here.

Uncle Richard left my side. I could feel him walk away and hear his feet on the hard floor. I shivered as I grew even colder.

"Ahh, yes. Sorry to keep you waiting, Mr. Underwood. It seems the little one left the car when she should have stayed put. I have to keep my eye on this one. She's like a curious little kitten."

A deep laugh sounded, and I finally raised my head a little, just to see who it was. Maybe he could get Mama for me. The man eyed me for a second before turning back to look at Uncle Richard. "It's no problem. I just wanted to shake the hand of the man I am now doing business with."

Richard shook the man's hand as I hiccupped. I wanted Tobias.

"It's a pleasure. I'm glad I have someone I can count on. I'm assuming the shipment went smoothly? I haven't spoken to my men yet."

"Shipment is nice and tidy on the lower deck. Serial numbers have been scratched. Untraceable."

I put my face back down as Uncle Richard spun on his shiny shoes. "That's great. That's exactly what we needed." I heard his footsteps again but didn't dare look up. Tears kept falling, and I was shaking. I wanted it to stop. "When it's time for another batch, I will let you know. We've been getting requests more and more lately. But I have your contact information, Mr. Underwood. I'll call when it's time. I'm going to get the little one home."

The man cleared his throat, and I was pretty sure he was looking at me. I didn't want to look at him, though. "She's a cutie. Even with tears."

Richard laughed. "Crying makes them cuter, don't ya think?"

I hurriedly swiped at my face, clearing off my tears. I didn't want to cry anymore.

"I think we're going to be great business partners, Judge Stallard."

I heard more footsteps, and my heart hurt because it was thumping so hard. My hands shook as I wiped at my face again, and when I saw two new shoes pop into my vision, my eyes grew watery again.

"Say goodbye to Mr. Underwood, Gemma."

My chin was wobbly. I could feel it wiggle. I looked up at two sky-blue eyes, but I didn't say a word. I was too scared to cry again because that seemed to make Uncle Richard happy, and he just made my mama sad.

I didn't like him anymore.

Not at all.

WHEN MY EYES popped back open, I gasped for air and immediately looked for him. *Oh my God.*

"Gem?" Isaiah was crouched down, resting the back of his legs on his ankles. "Talk to me."

Another gasp came from my chest as my mouth gaped open. I sucked in air, coating the inside of my lungs, and locked onto those familiar blue eyes.

It couldn't be.

"H...he..." *No.*

"Gemma!" My name was urgent as his hands came down and cupped my face, locking onto me.

"He...he was there."

"Who was? Where?"

My lip quaked. "Your father. He was there. He was there the last night I saw my mom."

The blood from Isaiah's face drained, and that was when I felt it. That was when I felt the crack right down the middle of my chest.

CHAPTER SEVEN

ISAIAH

Jesus Christ.

Gemma was shaking in my hands. They were still wrapped around her wet cheeks, and I could feel her entire body tremble as the pain and recollection flowed through her. *Fuck. Fuck. Fuck.* I was right. Gemma was more involved in this than I ever knew. A scary thought flowed through me. *Did my father send her here? Did he know something I didn't?* Every muscle in my body locked up, and I felt an ache settle in my bones. I wanted to punch something, throw every last book off the shelves in this godforsaken library. My fingers begged to squeeze my father's neck because he was part of the reason *she* was fucking terrified at the moment.

I didn't like seeing her like this. My heart screamed, and I needed it to stop. I needed her little snarky remarks to come back. I begged for her rightful anger to rear its head again so she could stop bleeding out in front of me.

"Gemma, baby. I want you to breathe." My forehead came down and rested along hers. It was sweaty, and I shut my eyes, wanting to take everything away from her. I didn't know what I was taking, but I would take it. I would take her hurt and make it my own. I shouldn't have been doing this. I needed to leave her be and get through this last stint of tutoring so she could just...leave. But she was determined to uncover things that needed to stay fucking covered. For her own safety.

"I can't." Her breaths were ragged, and I wanted to breathe for her. I wanted to give her every ounce of oxygen in my lungs.

"You can." I gripped her face harder and pulled back, looking down into her eyes. "Breathe for me."

Her head shook back and forth. "Did you know? Did you know that he was there that night? Did you know that your father knows Richard?"

"No," I answered truthfully, and that was when she took a big gulp of air. The small area we were tucked back in smelled of nothing but dust and old, tattered books. It was dimly lit, and I liked it. It felt like we were shut off from the world, even if just for a second. I wasn't thinking about how I needed to take a step back from her. Or how I shouldn't have been the person that was keeping her steady and calming her down. Or how, just moments ago, before she took off running with fear blanketing her features, I told myself to leave her be. I wasn't even thinking about how my father had her pinned yesterday, ready to hurt her and destroy me in the process. All I was thinking about was *her*.

Gemma continued to shake, tears still wetting her cheeks. Her hands came up and gripped my arms as she tried like hell to pull herself out of the assaulting memory she'd just had. I wanted to know in the worst way. I wanted to dig into her mind and learn every last secret that laid behind those secretive green eyes. "How do I know I can believe you?"

"I didn't know," I said, glancing away. "I suspected, though." I was teetering over the edge of right and wrong.

Pulled in two opposite directions. Gemma deserved to know the truth, but she also deserved to stay safe and untouched by this part of the world that I was all too familiar with.

Her head flicked up, that dainty little chin tipping in my direction. I glanced down to her lips as she said, "Tell me."

My chest screamed with the pounding of my heart. *Shit.* I needed to shove her away. She was better off not being involved in this. But the nagging thought in the back of my head told me that Gemma would probably try to find out more anyway. She had gone to the fucking Covens last night without *me* to uncover things. Maybe if I'd given her some insight, it would've pacified her long enough to get her out. To get her out of this fucking school and the spiderweb of lies, danger, and illicit business that she had no business being a part of.

I slowly pulled my hands from her cheeks, and I saw her hope and fear flicker. Her brown hair came over her face as she glanced to the floor, but she slowly looked over at me as I sat beside her, resting my back against the same bookshelf. "That night I took you to the psych hospital, when we followed Bain... I found out something that I haven't told you about." I kept my attention forward, glancing down the long aisle of endless bookshelves. "Bain met someone at the door —the one I found you shoved against last night with my father hovering over you." I heard her swallow but kept going. "Bain was delivering guns to someone there. Illegally. You've heard me talk about the family business..." I was thankful she never dug too much into it, because I never really wanted her to know in the first place, but now, I was wondering if she already knew.

"Yes," she croaked, hardly above a whisper.

"My father and Bain's are both in the illicit trade of small arms. They're gun traffickers. He's one of the biggest gun runners there is. The whole *family business* that I'm set to take over is illegal gun trade, Gem. That's why my father was so angry when he realized the tracker on Bain's car was going to the Covens last night." I looked over at her and hopefully displayed the disappointment I felt over her taking his car and going alone. "That psych hospital isn't *just* a psych hospital. He went there to catch Bain in his territory, selling guns to..." I paused, bringing my knees up to rest my forearms along them. "Judge Stallard."

I felt the icy whip of her shock even without touching her. Long minutes passed, and I kept my ears perked, listening to hear if anyone decided to pop into the library to check on our studies tonight, and that was when I heard the tremor in her tone.

"That's what they were talking about that night, when my mom was taken from me."

I couldn't even look over at her because I was too afraid to see her expression. *I needed to stop this.* She was confiding in me, and I didn't deserve it, but there wasn't much that would take me away from this very spot, even with my father's face lingering in the outskirts of my brain.

"They talked about a shipment. Scratching serial numbers. Something untraceable. Your father looked me dead in the eye that night and watched as Richard took me away from my mom as she screamed in a padded room that she didn't deserve to be in."

Richard fucking Stallard.

I felt unsettled, and I wanted to ask her more. I wanted to know every last fucking thing about her life, and Richard Stallard, and if she knew what his position was there. But I felt her numbness. The sound of her monotonous voice hit my ears and made them ring. I needed to heed the warning that I sensed. *She wasn't ready.*

Her head turned to me quickly, and I caught the wet stripes across her cheeks. "Make it stop."

I'd do anything she told me to do at this moment. My head was telling me one thing, but my heart was telling me another. My stomach dipped, and my muscles locked. Our eyes collided, and I burned. "Make what stop?"

"Everything. My mom begged..." She sniffled, and I broke. "I don't... I can't..." Her eyes shut, more tears coming out of the corners. "I don't want to feel anything right now."

Leave her be.

Walk away.

Disengage in any interest.

Keep her safe.

Remember what you felt last night.

Make her stay away from you.

"Fuck," I growled, grabbing her by the arm and pulling her into my lap. Her legs wrapped around my waist, her hot warmth heating me from the inside out. Her hair came down and covered us like a shield, as if we were in any need of a disguise. I would regret this later, but if she wanted the world to stop spinning for a little while, then that was what I'd give her.

Our lips touched, and I drank her in like I'd never survive without her taste. My mouth coated hers. It moved languidly, sucking and tasting, coaxing her back to life. Her tongue landed on mine, her shaky hands coming up and grabbing my face. Our breathing was in sync, our bodies pressed together, and just like that, the world stopped. Everything stopped. Everything but her and I.

There was no talk of the past.

No intertwining secrets and lies making either of us tremble.

My father wasn't a thought, and neither was Richard, or the Covens, or gun sales, or Bain. Nothing.

This. This was it.

Fuck regret.

Fuck tomorrow.

This was exactly where I wanted to be. I just needed one last little taste.

My hands moved slowly up her back, untucking her white school blouse from her plaid skirt. Her hot flesh touched the pads of my fingers, and her kiss deepened. Her hands moved to my hair, and she pulled, and I followed. I skimmed up her spine, and goosebumps clung to her skin. Heat shot to my groin as she pressed down, taking her mouth from mine and tipping her chin. My other hand came up, intertwining in her hair as I pushed her back down, taking her mouth. *Mine.*

"You're mine," I whispered against her sweet taste. "Give me everything you have. I'll take it."

I pushed my hips up to her warm center, and it was sinful. She gasped, pushing her chest into my face, and my hands quickly left the skin of her back, and I ripped the front of her shirt open and inhaled. *Jesus.* I wanted her forever. I saw nothing but her. I felt nothing but her. She was my goddamn kryptonite, which was exactly why I needed to let her go.

One last time.

Our eyes caught again, and without even speaking, I knew she was in a different place. A different mindset. The past wasn't creeping up behind her anymore. She was here, with me, in this place, and I'd make her forget everything.

"This feeling won't last," I whispered along her ear, gripping the side of her bare thigh. Her skin was like butter against my palm. "But I'll give it to you, anyway."

My mouth landed on her chest, the fabric of her bra inches from my teeth. I wanted to bite her, suck on her nipple, but I was too concerned with her sweet spot. The part of her that I wanted to devour. I gripped the side of her panties, just underneath her hip bone. My finger crooked into its side, and I rubbed at the skin. She withered above me, breathing hard.

"Isaiah." My name mingled with her breathy moan, and my pupils dilated.

I shoved her legs wider as she hovered over me, my dick so hard it pulsed. I wanted to take her and fuck away all our problems. I wanted to erase the feeling I'd had when I saw my father standing over her. I wanted to erase the surge of jealousy that I'd felt when my friends had their hands on her. *She was fucking mine.* I knew her better than anyone else in this place.

The very second I grazed her groin and pulled her panties to the side, I knew I had to listen to my friends when this moment was over. *Make her hate you. Make her resist you. Make her say no to you.* They were right. I wouldn't be able to deny her a single thing. It was going to have to be up to her.

"Jesus," I groaned before sucking her lip into mine. She whimpered as I sunk a finger into her. Wetness coated me, and I wanted to watch her come undone. I was drunk on her. A high I'd always be chasing.

"*Ah,*" she hummed, throwing her head back, still hovering as I pumped in and out. Her little hips moved to their own rhythm, and I sat back and watched with hooded eyes and a parted mouth. Her neck was there for the taking, and my lips begged to suck on the delicate skin. The hickey I'd left a few days ago was hardly there anymore, and I wanted to mark her again.

"Hello?"

Her head snapped down to me as I lurched my head past her. *Fucking shit.*

I squeezed my eyes shut and wanted to ram my fist into the bookshelf. *Fuck.* I felt the moment break in half. I felt Gemma clam up before she quickly stood, shoving her untidy shirt back into her skirt. Her cheeks were flushed, her hair a mess. I zeroed in on her puffy lips and regretful eyes. Gemma didn't want to cave into me, and I could sense that she felt ashamed. She was so determined earlier. So determined to stay angry with me and push me away. And when she broke, she wanted to pick up the pieces herself, yet she let me do it for her. I gave her the fucking permission. *I just fucked everything up again.*

"We're back here," I shot down the aisle, righting my dick in my pants and glancing away from Gemma's blank face. "Gemma was helping me find a book I needed for my report in World History."

Gemma slowly walked toward me, her light footsteps making no sound at all. My forehead furrowed as my chest seized. *What was she doing?* Her arm shot up, just past my head, as she pulled a book down from the shelf. She shoved the dusty thing into my hand and turned around.

I didn't waste any time following after her to see who'd come to check on things. I knew I'd tipped off Mrs. Fitz last night. I wasn't as elusive as I should have been. Gemma and I were both on a slippery fucking slope that just kept getting slicker.

"Mr. Cunningham. What can we do for you?" My voice was level as I plopped the book down onto our study table, right on top of all our scattered papers and books. I eyed Gemma's open laptop, and an inkling of suspicion came through.

I darted my eyes down both sides of the library, glancing at the darkened sky through the far window, seeing the flags on top of the roof of St. Mary's flicker in the wind in the most ominous of ways.

Mr. Cunningham cleared his throat, looking back and forth between Gemma and me. We couldn't have looked any guiltier than we already did. Her shirt was half-unbuttoned, although tucked back in, and her cheeks were flushed with heat. If Mr. Cunningham did indeed have a dick tucked away in those khaki pants he wore, he would know without a doubt that I'd just had my finger inside her wet, little pussy.

My teeth clamped and ground as I stood and waited for his reply. Gemma was eerily still, face emotionless. I placed my hands on my hips, glancing to the left and right again, looking for a faceless shadow. I hadn't heard Mr. Cunningham as he came through the door. I'd heard the creak of the floor, and then his voice soon followed. Gemma's laptop was shut when she'd taken off down the aisle a little while ago. *Someone else was here.* Someone was always fucking watching. It was Bain, or someone he'd sent, but someone had been here, and that was the nice little reminder I needed to push her away.

Gemma broke through my panicky thoughts, my teeth unclenching at the sound of her sweet voice. "Mr. Cunningham? Did you need something?" Her pink and swollen lips tilted upward, and Mr. Cunningham's mouth flattened. He sighed, looking back and forth between us once more before landing on her yet again.

"No, dear. I just came to check on you two, to make sure Isaiah was still staying on the straight and narrow."

I almost choked. I couldn't have been further away from straight and narrow than this very second. I was still up to my usual bullshit. I was just better at hiding it. Add fucking around with the girl I swore I wouldn't touch again, and yeah, I was just as bad as before.

"All is well." Gemma smiled again, but it fell as soon as Mr. Cunningham looked away. The punch to my chest hurt. Before he left through the library door, he turned and glared at me.

"I think it's time you wrap this up, don't you think? It's getting late." *He knew.* I kept a hold of his stare, hoping he'd keep his mouth shut. Not that he could really prove anything. Gemma and I were right where we needed to be, and I was damn thankful that I hadn't gotten an alert that Bain's car was on the move.

I pulled out my phone when the door slammed, immediately texting Mica and asking if Bain was still in their room. He texted back within seconds, and I was thankful for the distraction. I swore I could feel Gemma's emotions all the way across the table.

MICA: He's here. You know I always send a text when he dips out. He's asleep.

ME: Are you sure?

GEMMA WAS PACKING up her things, pushing papers into a binder and forcefully shoving her journal down into her bag as I stood there, completely stationary. Who the fuck was in here messing with her computer? Better yet, are they still here? *Probably one of Bain's friends, just to fuck with me.*

As soon as Gemma snatched her laptop, I was thankful she didn't seem to notice. When she'd slammed it shut earlier, she was moving in a blur of anger. I wasn't sure she even remembered doing so. But I remembered. I remembered because when she closed it, and my eyes landed on her face, the breath was taken right out of my lungs.

MICA: I'm four feet away from his obnoxious fucking snoring. I'm sure.

· · ·

"I NEED you to walk back to your room without me." I couldn't even look her in the eye. "I'll have Cade meet you in a second." The sound of papers rustling stopped. Her quick hands froze along the zipper of her bag. "I need to check on something."

The zipper was quick, and the sound jutted out into the air like a fucking sword. "No, thanks. I'll walk by myself."

My head fell, and a heavy breath climbed out of my mouth. I knew what I needed to do. I let things get out of hand a few minutes ago. I didn't regret it, but it was wrong. This entire situation was wrong. "Gemma, just wait for Cade."

Her tongue clicked as she whipped her backpack off the table, likely not even sparing me a glance. I wouldn't know, though. I still couldn't look at her. If I looked at her, I'd see the regret and confusion on her face again. Or worse, the hurt. "I'm tired of doing things for other people. I will make my own decisions from now on, Isaiah."

I growled, feeling frustrated by everything that was weighing down on me. "You can't really be trusted to make your own decisions, now, can you? You went straight into danger last night! You're being irrational and reckless! Just wait for Cade."

Gemma stormed past me, and I grabbed a hold of her arm. Her hot glare was filled with moisture, and I immediately wanted to retreat. I wanted to apologize, and that was not something I did often. This wasn't fair to her, and I was pretty sure nothing had ever been fair or easy in her life. "Please, just wait."

Gemma whipped her arm out of my grasp, and a part of me wanted to smile at her bravery. She was valiant when she wanted to be. She just needed to dig down to that feeling like I needed to dig down into mine. *Make her hate you.* "I don't owe you anything, Isaiah." Her eyes clenched tightly, and her mouth pursed. "And you know what sucks?" She didn't let me answer as she walked over to the doors that Mr. Cunningham had just gone through. "A big part of me wants to wait here, just because you said so." She scoffed. "I guess old habits die hard. Always trying to follow the fucking rules." Her brown hair swayed as she tipped her chin over her shoulder. "But I'm done doing what everyone else wants. No one tells me the whole truth anyway."

"Gemma!" I yelled, ready to stalk after her, feeling torn between wanting two things. I didn't like the idea of her walking down the dark hallway alone, but I also wanted to stay here and sneak through every last aisle to find out which one of Bain's friends had been in here, messing with Gemma's computer. My head told me to stay, and everything else told me to go after her. My bones were breaking with each stride she took.

I slammed my fist down on the wooden table, the book she'd grabbed from the shelf seconds ago flipping off and falling to the floor beneath a cloud of dust, and I followed after her.

Fucking hell.

CHAPTER EIGHT

GEMMA

"DON'T EVEN SPARE him a single glance, and you know what...forget tutoring tonight. Text him that you're busy with someone else."

Mercedes pulled out the chair beside Sloane. "Yeah, like with another guy. Serves him right."

I tucked a piece of fallen hair behind my ear, almost wishing that I'd worn it down today so I could hide. I had no intention of stooping to Isaiah's level and playing yet another game. It felt like we had been playing a game for weeks. So, to be honest, I didn't have the energy.

I hadn't slept much since Friday, after I completely crumbled in front of him only to flee with anger seconds later as my heart continued to thump from our *moment*. I'd holed up in my room all weekend, thinking about what I'd learned, and each tutoring session that came after felt like an elephant crushing my chest. The only time I left my bed, other than for school and *tutoring*, was in the very early morning to slap my frustrations onto a canvas before breakfast. I was disappointed and confused about what had happened between us in the library, but I also didn't regret it. When he touched me, everything stopped, but I thought it was what I had truly needed at the moment, even as shameful as it made me feel. I was beginning to learn that Isaiah was a sort of isolation for me. Not even sketching was taking away the gnawing thoughts and memories that were distorted and broken. In the past, sketching brought them out, but I'd always been in a trance, unable to sort through them or feel them in the moment. That wasn't how it was anymore. Sketching was replaced with two blue eyes that could see right through me. Everything was just...*gone* with Isaiah. And it was so dangerous. That was why I couldn't even look at him as of late. Not even as we sat a few feet away from one another with a study table in between us. He stayed in the library until eleven each night, never once leaving. He didn't go follow Bain or cut our tutoring time short. I had no idea why, other than maybe he was on edge about Mr. Cunningham checking on us Friday. I couldn't ask, and he didn't give up his reasoning. There wasn't a single word spoken from either of us. Things were left unsaid and lingering.

I shoved my food away, starting to feel weighed down from the week. I'd been feeling the remnants of anger but also anguish from the second I let that memory slip in on Friday. I was sad. I was so incredibly sad for my mom who'd been through something much worse than I thought. I was sad for the five-year-old girl who festered inside me as she watched her mother claw for freedom. I was sad for Tobias because, wherever he was, it probably wasn't a good place. I left both phones in my room this morning, too untrusting of myself if Isaiah decided to text me on the phone he had given me, and too irrational to care if Richard called me on the other.

Something inside me burned to listen to Sloane and

Mercedes and knock Isaiah down a few notches. Everything was so messy between us, and confusion filled every gap that had formed since he found me kneeling below his father at the psych hospital—*The Covens*. I was angry and felt betrayed in a way, but there was the teeniest, tiniest slip in my chest at the mere thought of him that told me just how fleeting those emotions were.

My gaze followed Bain through the dining hall as a whisper of uncertainty graced my ears. According to Isaiah, Bain had met Richard that night at the psych hospital when we'd followed him, and that did *nothing* but stir up anxiety. And although I sensed extreme danger regarding Bain, I also wanted to corner him and demand answers. *Bain knew Richard*. That was something to hold on to.

"Everything is so fucked up," I muttered under my breath, annoyance flashing through because I swore I could feel Isaiah's eyes on me from across the long table. *Was he looking at me?*

Sloane coughed and choked on something, and I whipped my head over to her. "Are you okay?"

Her face was red as she clutched onto her white blouse. She quickly untied the maroon bow around her neck as Mercedes patted her back. Claire, from a few seats down, raised her eyebrows at us and then rolled her eyes, going back to her friends. I didn't pay any mind to her, though. She didn't seem to like much of anyone at St. Mary's unless they had a penis. I couldn't even count how many times I'd seen her sneaking around with a guy following after her. Although, could I really talk much? Isaiah and I had done things on this very table.

My face flamed at the thought, but I wouldn't dare look at him.

"I'm fine." Sloane sipped on her water before putting it

down and looking over at me. "Gemma. I don't think I've ever heard you say fuck."

My lips pursed. "When did I say that?"

Mercedes laughed. "Like, five seconds ago. You said that everything was fucked up."

"Oh." A breathy laugh came from me. "I didn't mean to say that out loud."

Sloane plopped a grape in her mouth before grinning over at me. "You know what you need?"

I half-rolled my eyes, knowing what she was going to say. "To blow off tutoring tonight? I can't." I wanted to. I'd wanted to all week because I wasn't sure how much more I could take, sitting in that quiet library with nothing but the sound of Isaiah's breathing and my rapid heartbeat in my ears. *I couldn't, though.* We had a deal.

"No." She paused. "I mean, yes. But no. You need to let loose this weekend."

"This weekend?" I asked.

"Tomorrow night. Claiming party after the lacrosse game." We met eyes, and she smirked. "You're going to let loose, Gemma Richardson. I demand it. Let's have some fun without the Rebels breathing down your neck like a pack of savages. Fuck Isaiah and the bullshit."

Sloane knew the most about me and Isaiah, although not all of it. She didn't ask what had happened when I came back to our room last week all muddy and in tears. I was certain it was because she knew I wouldn't tell. I wasn't that type of girl. Not to mention, Isaiah and I were like a double-edged sword. Danger on both sides.

Mercedes clapped. "Hell yes! We should pull out all the stops, Sloane. Like..." Mercedes' voice was on the brink of regret. She retreated her next words, but Sloane nodded in agreement.

"Like we used to do with Journey."

Mercedes' lip was held between her teeth as she glanced down the table toward where Isaiah and his friends were sitting. I didn't follow her gaze, though. Instead, I was thinking about tomorrow night and how much the thought of being *normal* seemed so inviting. I needed it. I needed to find another way to deal with everything happening lately, and Isaiah was off-limits. I had to find a way to balance it all until I got out of here, and I had too much dignity to act on impulse with him again. I couldn't rely on his touch. I couldn't rely on Isaiah to silence my confusion and unanswered questions as the blind future dangled right in front of me.

"Oh shit." Mercedes quickly snapped her big brown eyes back to me, and I stilled.

My heart began beating quicker, and my stomach fell to the floor. I was too afraid to look. There were too many possibilities that could have caused her to look panicked. "What? What's wrong?"

"*That mother fucker.* I swear to God, these damn Rebels! They care about no one but themselves!"

Sloane's voice was rising, so I placed my hand on her leg to calm her down. I didn't need any unnecessary looks my way. I hadn't been on the stupid, gossiping St. Mary's blog in at least a week, according to Sloane. I suspected that Isaiah was taking care of it anytime he and I were featured.

"Don't even look down there." Mercedes was trying to appear calm, whereas Sloane was fuming. Her skin was burning hot against my hand.

Slowly, I swung my attention past Mercedes and her wild, curly hair. I saw Claire look down at me with pity before shaking her head at whatever was unfolding. *Why was I nervous?* As long as it wasn't Richard, it was fine. My heart thumped harder. *Wait, what if it was Richard?!* My chest heaved, but instead of looking for Isaiah in the sea of students, I looked for Bain. If Richard were here, coming to get me, it would be his fault. I was certain of it. But Bain's face remained smooth. There wasn't a flicker of accomplishment or even fulfillment there. Instead, he was steady. He watched me, his eyebrows dipping slightly as he tilted his head toward the one place I didn't want to look.

My blood rushed with embarrassment because it seemed like almost every single person was looking at me, which only confirmed that it had to do with Isaiah. Our peers didn't know *everything* that had gone on with us, but Isaiah had made it a point to show them that I was *his*. The kiss at the last claiming was enough to raise questions, even if it had started off as another game in his mind.

Their pitiful stares were the final shove I needed to raise my chin and find those cool blue eyes that I'd grown to love and hate. As soon as I allowed myself to look, it was like ice falling down on my shoulders in the middle of an avalanche.

There he was, sitting with his three best friends, with his white dress shirt undone at the top and his maroon-and-gold tie hanging loosely beneath his neck. His dark hair was standing up like it was Friday evening after I'd run my hands through it in that moment of weakness. I didn't recognize the girl that was on his lap. I was too focused on the way his large hand splayed against her ribcage like he was seconds from gripping her and plopping her down on the dining table like he'd done to me the first night he touched me.

I trembled, feeling sick to my stomach. It was like he had cut me. The feeling was brutal even if I had braced myself. I was back to feeling that overbearing emotional pain I wasn't used to, and instead of letting it envelope me and allowing it to take me down in front of the entire student body, I pushed myself harder onto the seat that was holding me up and looked right back over at Bain. His jaw was set, and his arms were crossed against his chest. He looked angry, and I was too. The rules had changed, and suddenly, I wanted back in the game.

Bain had answers, and I was going to get them, and Isaiah wasn't going to stop me. I wouldn't heed his warnings any longer. Not now.

"Letting loose tomorrow sounds like a great idea," I said, smiling at Sloane and Mercedes.

Sloane's eyebrow raised, and there was a glimmer in her eye. "Heartbreak is code for rebellion. We're gonna have some fun."

"Definitely," I confirmed. But first, I needed to talk to Bain.

———

I WRAPPED the flannel that Sloane had lent me around my body as the cool wind whipped around us. The boys were down below, dressed in athletic pants and long sleeve shirts, doing their drills for lacrosse. My back was turned toward the field again, and the only reason I'd come to practice today was because I had other things on my agenda. Things that couldn't be stopped because my heart had a little tear in it from Isaiah and his show during lunch.

The girl, who I learned was named Breanna, stayed on Isaiah's lap the entire time. Her long blonde locks fell to her butt when she would throw her head back and laugh at something the Rebels said, and I wanted to throw my salad in their faces. All of them. I was more confused than anything, but the silent touches of shame and betrayal were back, and I was wearing them like a second skin.

No more than a week ago, Isaiah had his arms around me, picking up my broken pieces as they scattered on the ground like the crisp leaves that currently sat beneath me. I shouldn't have confided in him again. He told me on Thursday, after shoving me up against that tree just below the Covenant Psychiatric Hospital, that he and I were over. He was only staying true to what he'd demanded that night, although in a crappy way. He and I were no longer anything. In fact, we hadn't spoken in days, but it didn't matter the reason. Isaiah and I were impulsive with one another; it had shown in the library, just one day later. It was obvious we were both running from a past that neither of us could hide from and racing toward a future that we couldn't have. We were intertwined. Our families were somehow twisted in one way or another, and if he knew more about that than what he'd already said, it didn't show.

But regardless, I should have listened to him when he pushed me away. If I had, maybe I wouldn't have been sitting here with raging jealousy brewing low in my belly as I stared at Breanna up in the bleachers with my back turned to him.

"Are you sure you want to do this? I'm all for pissing off the Rebel who hurt you, but...this? Bain isn't someone you should be alone with, Gemma."

"Bain won't hurt me, Sloane." I wasn't fully certain of that, given the first night he had made himself known to me, but after what Isaiah had reluctantly told me last week—that Bain knew Richard—I was certain that if he wanted me gone or if he wanted to hurt me in some way, he would have done so by now. Richard wasn't here to drag me back home, despite the social worker's threats toward him, which meant that Bain hadn't told him a single thing about me.

When I'd first started at St. Mary's, Bain had said he recognized me; he just didn't know where from yet. At the time, I had no idea just how truthful that was. Bain was definitely hiding something, and I wasn't waiting around for Isaiah to tell me what it was.

"And how do you know that?"

I sighed softly, realizing that Sloane was worried about

me. "I have been in more threatening situations, Sloane. I know what I'm doing. I promise. He won't hurt me."

She rolled her eyes as she looked up into the misty sky. "Gemma..."

"Sloane." I grabbed onto her hand. "You're one of the only people I trust in this school. I may hold back some information from time to time, but I will not lie to you." I thought back to when I'd shown Sloane the scars around my wrists. She had been the only person so far that I'd confided in who hadn't betrayed my trust. Well, Headmaster Tate hadn't either, but it wasn't like I'd told him much to begin with. I was still leery of him at times, even if I did feel safe near him.

Sloane's warm breath made a cloud in the chilly air. "Fine. I'm giving you ten minutes, and then I'm coming after you. Got it?"

I nodded quickly, squeezing her hand. I could have waited and talked with Bain at the claiming party—as long as he stayed there the whole time, unlike the last one—just to drive Isaiah crazy. But I wasn't even sure he'd feel that same burn of jealousy that I felt, and I wasn't going to play that game. I had another game in mind—one I wouldn't let him interfere with.

"Okay, go. Now. Their backs are turned."

I quickly jumped to my feet, locking eyes with Bain who sat at the top of the bleachers, as usual, with his pack of friends. When he caught my attention, snagging those dark, beady eyes with mine, I flicked my chin once and quickly walked down the sidewalk and behind the bleachers.

Resting my back against one of the cold metal pillars, I tilted my head, feeling the chill race down my spine. I wasn't sure if it was from the autumn temperature or fear. I stared up at the gray clouds, taking even breaths, grabbing a hold of this messed-up little game in my two shaky hands. I was done waiting on the sidelines. I was still running when this was all said and done, because I knew with complete certainty that the documents I'd found months ago were, in fact, real. It was confirmed in my shunned-away memory. It just took me a while to dig into the past and find the heavy threat that had been there since I was a small child. Richard would do to me what he did to my mother. He thought because he had taken everything away from me that I'd fall into his lap, allowing him to turn me into someone I wasn't. He thought that all the punishments he'd given me, the threats, the fear, the longing touches against my skin that he tried to manipulate into love, would kill the girl I truly was deep down. He thought that sending me to a place like St. Mary's was a punishment. Just another way to get me to oblige to his rules and demands. He honestly thought that sending me away from *him* would make me realize how worthy I was to be his. Did he expect me to beg to come home? Or to be truthful about it? Richard couldn't see the truth because he was so twisted in the head, and I knew that because I knew *him*. I was thriving here, broken heart or not. I had plans that he didn't foresee coming, and Bain wasn't going to get in the way of those. I wouldn't let it happen.

"Did you enjoy your midnight drive in my car the other night?"

My head came back down to level ground, and I ripped my gaze over to the dangerous boy slowly striding toward me. His hair was cut close to his scalp, a diamond stud glittering through the light fog. His footsteps were easy, and the closer he got, the harder my heart beat. Not from fear, though. I was too eager and wild with power to feel the tingles of fear now.

I turned slowly and propped my shoulder against the side of the metal pole bracing the bleachers. His friends were up too high to hear us, especially with the wind cutting through the air. My lips tipped into a small grin. "It's no surprise that you knew. I think you know a lot more than you let on."

Bain moved closer to me. He reached into his coat pocket, and my heart came to a halt for a quick second before I saw that he was pulling out a pack of cigarettes. The lighter flame was bright before he lit the end of one, and he puffed on it for a few seconds before blowing out the smoke and edging even closer to me.

We stood there in silence, and when I realized that he had nothing more to say, I leveled my voice and said, "My first week at St. Mary's, you pulled me aside and said you recognized me." Bain kept quiet as he sucked on the cigarette again. "But you know exactly who I am now, right? And you know Richard too."

His brow quipped quickly, and I hated the sound of this deep voice. "Richard who?"

He was playing with me.

"Oh, you know, the man you sell guns to at the Covens." I saw the flicker of shock ripple across Bain's features. It was hardly noticeable, but I saw as it tore through him. I laughed sarcastically, unable to stop myself. "I have to admit, you've upset some people. I mean, someone else has been supplying those guns to Richard since I was five years old."

After Friday, I had put more and more information together, like pieces from a puzzle. From the fragments of my memory and from what Isaiah had admitted, I knew much more than anyone thought.

Bain stayed silent, and it gave me the push to straighten my shoulders and raise my chin. Fear was a distant thought in the back of my head. I wanted him to know that I knew things about him. I wanted to prove to him, and Isaiah too, that I was taking things in my own hands. I was tired of the lies and half-truths. I was tired of being dismissed. "Want to know how I know that?"

Bain stepped closer to me, puffing out his smoke, causing my nostrils to flare and my lungs to burn. "I'm sure you know a lot more than I'd like. Tell me." Bain's other hand ran down the side of my cheek, and goosebumps clung to my skin. I still pushed back on the fear, though. I would not be intimidated by him. "Did Isaiah tell you all this? Or are you just as curious as your uncle says? He said you were smart, so did you figure this all out on your own? Unable to stay in your fucking lane?"

There it was. The confirmation I needed that there was more to their relationship than the gun trafficking. Bain knew that Richard was presumed to be my uncle. I still couldn't figure out why there was a need for unmarked guns at a psychiatric hospital or why Isaiah called it the Covens, but none of that mattered right now.

"The better question is..." I pushed his hand away from my face. "Why haven't you told him what I've been up to? He wants you to spy on me, right? Or is that just for your own sick pleasure?"

We both heard the crunching of gravel, and I assumed it was Sloane coming to check on me like she'd promised, but Bain's sick smile appeared, and I faltered. "*Maybeee.* But, sweetheart? You are right where I want you to be. You aren't my enemy."

What the hell did that mean? And that "*maybe*" sounded an awful lot like a confirmation.

"Incoming!" Sloane's shout came out of nowhere. I looked to my left and right, but I didn't see her. Bain slowly pointed upward with the cigarette in his hand, and I saw Sloane's panicked face looming over me from the top of the bleachers.

And that was when I heard the chuckle from Bain and the angry shout from Isaiah. My throat closed, and my breathing stuttered. My entire body felt as if it were plunged into lava as I stared wide-eyed at Isaiah with his hand around Bain's throat as he pushed him up against the same metal pole I had been resting on a few minutes ago. "What did I fucking say would happen the next time you looked at her?" Isaiah cracked his neck, and I saw the veins bulging with his angry, hot blood.

Bain laughed, although it was hard to hear because Isaiah's fingers were plunged deep into his neck. He let up for a second only for Bain to say, "Hey, man...take it up with her. She asked to talk to me."

Shit.

Isaiah's hand still stayed against Bain's throat as he whipped his head to me and glared with those ice-blue eyes. Bain made no move to get out of his grasp. If anything, he looked like he enjoyed it. "You *asked* to talk to him?"

"Let him go, Isaiah." My heart was flying through my chest as I tried to sort through what Bain had said to me. *You're right where I need you to be.* That sent panic right into my bloodstream. Adrenaline pumped, and I suddenly felt lightheaded. "Let him go! You're on probation! Do you really want to get caught in the middle of a fight *during* lacrosse practice?!" With Bain's half-threat in my head, I knew now, more than ever, that I needed to get the hell away from this school and anything relating to Richard. My eyes locked onto Isaiah, and I hoped he knew me well enough to know that there was something else going on here.

"Better listen to her. Wouldn't want to get expelled now, would you?"

Isaiah kept his stare on me, and even from several feet away, I could see the blue in his eyes turn dark. He was angry, but I wasn't sure what he expected from me. He couldn't push me away and then pull me in again. I wasn't a tug-of-war rope. He didn't know me at all if he thought I was going to stay in line and keep silent after knowing what I did now. I would *not* be the girl Richard tried to mold me into. Isaiah might not have realized it, but he was asking the same of me.

"Let him go," I said through gritted teeth, and Isaiah reluctantly dropped his hand.

Bain winked at me, and I turned away briefly, still repeating his venomous words in my head.

"I swear to God, Bain," Isaiah seethed under his breath as he placed his fisted hands on his hips. "I hope you know that the only reason I'm sparing you is because I need you."

Bain's head tilted in a cynical way, but he said nothing as he flicked his cigarette underneath the bleachers and turned around. Before he got too far, he called over his shoulder, "Don't fucking take my car again, Gemma."

Isaiah didn't look surprised at all by the words that came from Bain's mouth. Instead, he looked at me with blinding disappointment. I felt myself retreat for a moment. *But no.* I wasn't going to apologize for anything. Isaiah had no right. He had no right to interject himself in this any longer. I didn't owe him anything.

"What the fuck was that about?" He stalked over to me quickly, but I didn't take a step back. I wasn't afraid of Isaiah. Was I conflicted with him? Yes. Did I think he was keeping things from me? Yes. But I wasn't afraid of him. "I told you that you shouldn't be anywhere near this, Gemma. That's why I'm fucking staying away from you! To keep you out of this entire thing! You don't know what you're messing with."

I scoffed, crossing my arms over my chest in a bratty way, ignoring how my heart buzzed with him only feet away. "But I am in this, Isaiah! I've been in the middle of this the entire time! Which I'm sure you knew well before you dipped your cock inside me!"

I paused. *Did I really just say that out loud?!* Glancing around, I felt my cheeks warm, hoping that no one heard what I'd just said.

"Oh, for fuck's sake." Isaiah turned away, his rising chest climbing in speed. "You should know me better than that."

"But I don't!" I shouted, taking a step closer to him. He sliced his glare over to me, but I didn't hold back. "I thought I did, but I don't. You only show me what you want. You hide things. I get it." My voice was a little softer, but I was still feeling the rage climb. "I hide things too. It just is what it is."

Isaiah's hands came up, and he ran them through his sweaty hair, and I could sense the frustration, but I was frustrated too.

"I told you that I was done acting the way people expected of me. I had a moment of weakness Friday in the library, which is now evident after your show in the dining hall today. You made me feel weak and ashamed, and I will be damned if I am portrayed as weak again. I've been weak for almost eighteen years now, and I'm done. I don't owe you anything, and I surely don't owe you an explanation." I took a hefty step back from him because I could feel his warmth, and I didn't want to crave it. I didn't want to glance at his lips and feel the indignity that would come with it. I didn't need Isaiah Underwood to pick up my pieces and sort through my life—even if our paths were intertwined at some point or another.

Isaiah stood there, taking in my words one by one, with his features even and unreadable. *Typical.* I had no idea what was going through his mind, but I wasn't sticking around to figure it out.

"I will see you in the library for tutoring—unless you would like to change tutors and have Breanna tutor you now? Just let me know. As long as you get me what I asked for, I don't really care what you do."

The lie tasted like the past, and I hated that I was being that version of myself again. I'd always been myself around him. I couldn't not be myself around him, which was probably why I craved him so much. My walls fell when we were alone, and the truth always seemed to spew from my mouth one way or another. But those walls were up right now, and I was lying through my teeth. His little brother came to mind, and the truth was, I did care what Isaiah did. I didn't want him to change tutors, because there was so much more than tutoring going on, and would anyone else understand or even agree to do what he had asked of me? Despite everything, I would still cover for him. I would lie without any hesitation or thought to repercussions, and that drove me *mad* because it wasn't for my sake—it was for his. A part of my heart was latched onto his whether I liked it or not.

Isaiah let out a guttural sound and clenched his eyes shut. He quickly turned around, gripping the back of his neck, and stomped away, leaving me there feeling anything but satisfied.

CHAPTER NINE

THE PARTY WAS in full swing, but I was ready to snap something in half. The beat of the song overhead was like a blowhorn inside my ears, and not even the shots I'd taken could take me down a notch. I was on edge. My leg bounced up and down aggressively as I leaned back onto the far wall. The plastic shot glass in my hand crumpled up like a wad of paper as Cade and Brantley tried to talk me down from the ledge.

"Isaiah, this was what you wanted."

I growled through my teeth, eyeing the strobe lights, which gave me an instant headache. It was either the lights causing the throb or the stress weighing down on me. I had too much going on, and despite the plan working overtime in the back of my head and the enlightening phone call I'd had earlier, I was still just as concerned with Gemma as I had been from the start. In fact, it was much heavier now.

"This wasn't what I fucking wanted. I didn't want any of this."

Cade's hands clamped onto my shoulders tightly as his

face blocked the multicolored lights. "I got through Journey, and you can get through this. Keep up with the show, make her hate you, and she'll be better off."

I growled, throwing the neon cup to the dirty floor of the school basement where we held all our parties in secret. "No offense," I started, not really meaning it, "but you didn't have to deal with seeing Journey every fucking minute of every day. Imagine it for a minute." I knocked his hands off me. "Imagine seeing Journey every single day and not being able to touch her. Imagine having to pull other girls into your lap to make it clear that you didn't feel anything for her." Having Breanna on my lap yesterday, rubbing her silk panties on my thigh as she straddled my knee, felt like my organs were slowly failing inside my body. I felt hollow. I just sat there, itching for the bell to ring so I could fling her off instead of digging myself into an even deeper grave.

I was one step closer to ending my father but a million steps away from starting with Gemma.

"Yeah, I'm sure it was hard having a hot chick in your lap," Brantley grunted, and I ignored him, knowing he wouldn't understand anyway. He was the one I worried about the most when it came time to choose sides. He was harder to get through to. His walls were thick.

Shiner popped his hand in between us, holding four shots in the middle of his palm. "Let's just get shitty. Bain is right there with a girl pressed up against his dick, chugging even more booze than we are. He isn't going anywhere tonight."

Yeah, but was Gemma?

Cade snatched a green shot glass, tipping it back and swallowing it whole. "You deserve it, Isaiah. Take some heat off your back. Let's go back to how it used to be. Even if it's just for tonight." He slapped my face with excitement clear in his brown eyes as I grabbed onto another shot. *Just for tonight.* I'd heard that before.

Brantley nodded. "We won our game. Let's celebrate that, if nothing else."

I didn't give two fucks about the lacrosse game today, and I wasn't celebrating anything, but I still threw the shot back in hopes that it would help soothe the ache in my chest. I desperately needed something to ground me so I could get through tonight.

Our tutoring session had been intense last night. More intense than the last few. Instead of Gemma and I being indifferent with one another, now we were both angry. She still wouldn't look at me from across the table, which was exactly what I needed, but *fuck* if it didn't sting. I almost pretended that the little alert went off on my phone, telling me that Bain's car was moving, just so I could get away from the suffocating air, but that was too risky with the SMC becoming more watchful since our little run-in with Mrs. Fitz last week. I was lucky that Bain had been staying put lately, but I was sure there was a reason for that. Just like I was sure that Gemma was about to show up tonight with her two best friends by her side to cut me the same way I cut her.

Gemma wasn't going to hold back. That sweet, goody-two-shoes girl she was at the first claiming party had been morphed into someone else over the last few weeks, and it was mostly by my doing. She was no longer hesitant around other people. She seemed so sure of herself, even while talking with Bain yesterday, which sent me straight to the red.

I felt completely out of control, and I wanted to blame it all on everything that was going on with my father, but the truth was, I felt out of touch with Gemma, and that was what made me antsy. The protectiveness I felt for her had intensified since last week, but she didn't want to be protected by me any longer—and for good reason.

I snatched another shot, although I knew I was at my limit. I was seconds from shooting it down my throat with

Shiner's eager nod in my peripheral when the basement door opened, and three sets of bare legs popped through the threshold.

Every single person looked in that direction. I could feel the shift in the room. I wasn't looking at anyone else, though. My attention was solely on the girl in the middle.

Gemma.

My eyes burned with a hot intensity, and I could no longer breathe. My heart halted, and my stomach tightened. She stood there looking *so* unlike herself that I felt the brunt of shame. It wasn't that she didn't look good, because she did. She looked really fucking good. Hot as hell. Her tight black dress hardly reached mid-thigh, and blood shot straight to my groin as I scanned her tanned, toned legs. Her hair was pulled back in a sleek ponytail, showing off every perfect curve of her face, and her red lipstick was like a punch to the gut. But...it wasn't her. It wasn't the Gemma that I knew. This was a girl who was lashing out because she had been hurt—*by me.*

"Hey, Isaiah." Breanna's voice was like a knife being dragged down my back. "Are we still on for tonight?"

Cade pulled me away, and I knew it was because he could sense my hesitation. "Isaiah. Think about how your father treated her the other night." I couldn't seem to snag my attention away from Gemma, even with Cade's face moving in front of mine. *I wanted her.* No one else. I didn't want Breanna. I didn't want any other girl in this school. I wanted her.

"I'll kill my father," I muttered, watching as Sloane and Mercedes dragged Gemma over to the table lined with shots. She inched her head back, and I swore I could feel the burn of Fireball hit the back of my throat too.

"Isaiah, fucking snap out of it. Have you ever thought that maybe Bain was taking those photos of you and Gemma because he's going to give them to your father or, I don't know... maybe use it as blackmail?" *Obviously.* "If you feel for her what I felt for Journey, you will stay away from her."

I finally pulled myself from Gemma and stared at Cade. I needed to stay on track. I needed to keep myself in line, but I wasn't sure I could. This was the hardest thing I'd ever done, and that was concerning, given my upbringing.

Cade tapped my shoulder once and flicked his chin behind me. "Go over there, put your fucking hands on Breanna's hips, and show Gemma and Bain and everyone in this school that she means nothing to you. Because I'm telling you right now, Gemma Richardson will be the death of you, Isaiah. If she gets hurt because of you, you will never fucking forgive yourself."

Cade was speaking from experience, so I took a deep breath, swiveling on my shoe and stomping back over to Breanna. I was sure it was obvious to her that I didn't really want her, but I was hoping that it wasn't obvious to anyone else. There was nothing between Breanna and me. No lust or passion. I wasn't even sure I would be able to get a hard-on unless it was with Gemma.

A future full of celibacy was what I had to look forward to. Great.

When my palms landed on Breanna's waist, I felt like I was fumbling with a grenade. Her head pulled back, and I knew that there was likely something unfolding behind me. My heart was stretching for another girl in this room, and I wanted to pound my fist into the ground to make the music and low chatter stop for just a second so I could breathe. Breanna's hands came up and touched the sides of my face as she whispered, "It's okay, Isaiah. You can pretend I'm her if you want." *Fucking hell.*

I shut my eyes and sucked in even breaths. "Not sure who you're referring to."

It was pretty evident there was something to Gemma and

me, even if some of our classmates assumed it was only a simple fuck during the claiming party. The faculty, however, was clueless because I'd kept the touching to a minimum and didn't spare her many glances when the SMC was around. Mainly because if they knew I was fooling around with my tutor, they'd never believe our story or accept any excuses if we were found wandering the halls after curfew.

In the beginning, before everything had shifted, I didn't hide my interest in her because I needed our classmates to watch her, to envy her, and to speculate on our relationship so Bain would be forced to back away. But that was a mistake.

Seeking her out in the very beginning was a total miscalculation on my part, and deep down, I'd always known it. I'd always known that there was a reason for my need to hover over her and to watch her every move. Gemma dug herself right under my skin, and I couldn't seem to dig her out, not even for a little while.

"We can play that game too." Breanna's hand crept up my neck and into my hair. "We're all trying to just put a pause on things for a while, right? Isn't that the whole reason for the claimings? To shut things out until the morning?"

I swallowed, looking down at her lips. They were nothing like Gemma's, and I hated it. What was Gemma doing right now? Was she watching this? Was she brewing in hatred for me? Would she push me away the next time I came close to her, because I would come close to her again. I would breathe her air again and put my hands on her body. I just hoped she was stronger than I was and would dismiss me like I deserved.

The music grew louder, and Breanna bit her lip with eager excitement. Shiner handed me another shot, and I took it, relishing in the way it burned through my veins. I skimmed my attention to Bain who was opposite of me, making sure I kept my back to Gemma, and I found him watching me suspiciously. We stayed locked on one another, refusing to look away. Bain and I were cut from the same cloth. Dominance was our first language, and neither one of us would submit to the other, which was exactly why we would be forced to work together in the end.

"Fuck yeah," Brantley said, nodding his head at me. "That's the Rebel I know." I gave him a quick look, and I knew he sensed the question on the tip of my tongue. He scanned the crowd at my back before coming back to me. "*She's fine,*" he mouthed, and my throat constricted. Breanna flipped around with my hands still on her hips and began rubbing her ass on my jeans. I hardly noticed, though, because I was too concerned with what was behind my back. Seeing Bain standing off to the side with someone else did nothing to ease my frustrations and concerns. I needed to see her for myself.

I needed to make eye contact with her.

Just once.

But when I tipped my head over, catching a glimpse of her black dress, my stomach plummeted to the floor. I zeroed in on the fucking idiot daring to touch her ass, and the hold on my rational thinking immediately loosened.

Breanna was shoved away, and I was seconds from plowing down any person that stood in my direct path, but just as soon as I turned around, the lights shut off.

I recognized a voice over the speaker that shouldn't have been.

"It's claiming time."

CHAPTER TEN

GEMMA

Fireball was gross.

It tasted like actual fire going down my throat, and it took everything I had not to cough like an idiot after Sloane had handed me the tiny plastic cup. At first, I'd tried sipping on it, but Mercedes and Sloane laughed before demonstrating how to drink it. I was used to Richard drinking his amber-colored liquid in a glass cup, clinking the ice around like a warning before being scolded. But I took the drink anyway, chucking it back and downing it within seconds. I knew why I'd been so bold. I felt Isaiah staring at me, and I wanted to show him that I was fine, that last night's tutoring session didn't bother me in the slightest. Sure, my heart felt a little banged up, and it took every ounce of strength I had to keep my mouth shut as I refused to tell him what Bain had said to me, but *I was fine*.

Except, now that I was being pulled into a dark room with hands that were unfamiliar resting over parts that only *he* had touched, I felt smothered. The fear of being in a damp, cold room without even a sliver of light had my heart flying throughout my chest. I felt almost as scared as the first claiming party, when Bain had whispered things into my ear that made my skin crawl and caused me to panic. Now that I was a little surer of myself, I wasn't *that* scared, but the fear still laid quietly in the back of my head. The past still brimmed the surface, and I had to remember that I saw the face of the guy who came over to me. I didn't know his name, but I'd seen him around the school at times. I'd passed by him in the hallway and maybe even in the dining hall. He wasn't going to hurt me. His genuine gaze drove into mine before the lights shut off, silently asking me if I was up for this, and I nodded in approval.

I wanted to get Sloane's and Mercedes' go-ahead, but if I looked over at them, then I'd see Isaiah and Breanna again, and I couldn't stomach it. I was on my own right now, and I needed to trust myself.

The door latched, and the room was pitch black. My pulse was strumming, and I took a deep breath as the guy slowly backed me up against the wall.

"Wasn't sure you'd agree to this," he whispered along my neck. His breath smelled of the same alcohol that I'd consumed, and I swallowed back the cinnamon taste that still rested on my tongue. "Someone told me that you were no longer Isaiah's. Is that true? Or should I be prepared for him to knock down that door?"

I breathed out a light laugh, trying to force away the excitement that came with that thought. *What was wrong with me?! Isaiah was currently touching someone else!* "Didn't you see that Isaiah found a replacement? He's not coming in here to stop this." I swallowed, tipping my head to the side to allow him access. "He doesn't care."

The truth I felt behind those words made me clam up, but I tried to relax as rough hands skimmed down the sides of my black dress and underneath my butt. "You sure about that?"

"Yeah, I'm sure."

I wasn't sure. I wasn't sure about anything anymore. I wasn't even sure if this was what I wanted, but I was doing it anyway. I slowly turned back to the warm breath I felt against my neck and placed my lips on his. They didn't feel like Isaiah's. They didn't make my knees wobbly or cause a bundle of heat to burrow in my core, but in a sense, it still felt good. When his hands started to move slowly over my hips and up my chest, my breathing picked up a little.

I wasn't panicking, though, and I wasn't trying to push away memories of Richard from my head. I didn't feel that prickle of danger that I'd felt when Bain had shoved me into one of these rooms during the first party. I didn't feel unsafe.

My tongue moved inside his mouth, and I started to feel a little bit hotter. His hands grew more intense, and I began to lose myself in the moment until I realized that the entire reason why I wasn't panicking or forcing thoughts of my past away was because instead of focusing on the way this guy was touching me, I was thinking of Isaiah. I thought about the time his hands had cupped my ass as he placed me on top of the dining hall table. I thought about the way he made my body hum in the library last week. I thought about how good the high felt when he took me in his mouth against a tree. *How enthralling was that?* It was so wrong to do something like that out in the open, but my body responded, just like it was responding now at the thought of it.

I wasn't kissing some random guy in the middle of a claiming party. In my head, I was kissing Isaiah. My nipples hardened, and I whimpered, feeling out of control. *What the hell was wrong with me?! Stop thinking of Isaiah!* I was driving myself mad, and I felt myself getting antsy. I spread my legs, eager for this guy to make me feel him instead of the one who kept reaching inside my chest and twisting my heart.

"No," I said, taking his hands from my pebbled nipples and placing them on my thighs. "I want you here."

"*Fuck,*" he muttered over my lips in a breathy way. "Whatever you want."

My head fell back again as I pushed Isaiah out of my head. *It's not Isaiah.*

But...it was. The door flung open, and a tall shadow appeared in the doorway. The guy's hands stopped moving just on the brink of where my panties touched the inside of my leg, and I froze. The lone light bulb was suddenly clicked on, and the air thickened immediately. Isaiah stood there, staring directly at me with a fire brewing in his eyes, and that only made me burn hotter. His cheeks were flushed, and his knuckles were bleeding. My first reaction was to race over to him to see what had happened, but I stopped myself before I could.

"What are you doing here?" I asked, keeping my hands on a set of broad shoulders. *Shouldn't he be with Breanna?*

The guy clicked his tongue. "Told you."

I saw his amusement and paused. "Did you bring me in here to make him mad?"

He glanced away, slowly taking his hands out from underneath my dress. I sucked in a breath as I looked to Isaiah, who had murder written all over his face. *Why did I feel guilty?*

"Bain asked him to. And it's not the first time he has done something that Bain wanted. Jeremy over here apparently likes getting his teeth knocked in. Otherwise, he wouldn't have agreed." Isaiah took a step closer to us, but I ignored him and glared at the guy who was just kissing me.

"Is that true?" *I couldn't trust a single fucking soul in this school! Games, games, games!*

His lip hitched. "It's not the only reason. I heard your moans the other night in the library with Isaiah." His gaze traveled down my body as he licked his lips. "You're fucking hot, babe. Who would say no to you?" I felt so dense, and I was instantly angry.

My leg swiftly came up, and I kneed him right in the balls, relishing as he dropped to the floor. "You're a bad kisser anyway."

I stood over him as he cupped himself, and I felt the urge to spit, but instead, I straightened my shoulders and pulled down the hem of my dress. I was ready to get out of this basement. Actually, I was ready to get out of this school. I left Jeremy on the ground, begging myself to keep my eyes away from Isaiah, and walked over to the door with my dignity only half intact.

I would slosh through cool water in the dark underground hallway and go back to my room all on my own. I didn't need Sloane or Mercedes to hold my hand as the familiar feeling of panic came at me from the small area. I was fine.

"Yeah *fucking* right," Isaiah muttered, grabbing onto my arm. He pulled me right back into that stuffy room and pushed me up against the wall.

Jeremy slowly got to his feet, still wheezing, and he half-laughed while shutting the door behind him.

The intensity of the air grew even thicker. So thick I could hardly breathe. Isaiah's blue eyes drove into mine, and I gulped, pressing farther away from him. I feigned anger, but deep down, I was faltering. I couldn't pinpoint my emotions, but the longer Isaiah glared at me, the more I teetered over the edge.

"Why are you here right now?" I bit out. "What are you doing?"

Isaiah's hands clamped down on my wrists as he flung my arms up above my head. My heart galloped, and the hotness I was feeling moments ago while thinking about his mouth on mine instead of Bain's accomplice only burned me more. *Ugh*.

"What am I doing, Gemma?" He laughed in my face, and I could see the irritation on his features. The vein in his neck pulsed as fast as my chest rose. "What are *you* doing?" Isaiah's face grew closer to mine, and my throat closed up. My body was still reacting, and it felt so right to be this close to him.

"What do you mean what am I doing?" I asked, tipping my chin up and leveling him with a glare just as potent as his. "You interrupted what I was doing!"

He rolled his eyes, and his hands tightened on my wrists. He was the only one I would let touch my wrists without feeling the need to pull away. He knew what laid beneath this black fabric. "This isn't you," he whispered, scanning over every inch of my face before dropping his gaze down my body. Butterflies rushed to my stomach, and when I tried to turn my head away, one of his hands left my wrists, and he grabbed my chin. His thumb came up and swiped over my swollen lips, surely smearing the red lipstick that Sloane told me to wear. "This lipstick isn't you." My brows crowded, and my mouth set into a firm line. Isaiah let go of my chin and touched my ponytail that cleared my face of any stray hairs. "This hair isn't you." I gasped as his finger hooked underneath the tiny elastic holding my hair in place, snapping it in half. My brown locks fell in one single whoosh around my face. He swallowed, his throat bobbing with a force that I felt in between my legs. His one hand still gripped my wrists tightly, but the other crept down the side of my cheek and over the dip of my neck so slowly I began panting. The pad of his finger skimmed over my cleavage, and my back bowed, and I couldn't even become angry at the betrayal of my body. It acted on its own. It wanted Isaiah despite everything. It wanted his touch. His kiss. His soft whispers. My body knew I needed that solitude again. *Reckless. Irrational.* That was what I was when it came to him, and it was rebellion in the form of a single touch.

His hoarse voice snagged my attention, and I stared directly at his inviting mouth. "And this dress." His tongue darted out, and he grazed his bottom lip, and I clenched my teeth so I wouldn't kiss him. "This dress isn't you."

My breath fanned over his face, and we locked eyes. My heart squeezed. "You don't know me as well as you think, Isaiah."

His thumb slowly rubbed over my pinned wrists, grazing my ugly scars beneath the black fabric. "I don't have to know all of your secrets to truly know you, Gemma."

I jerked on my wrists, but he didn't let me go, and I couldn't look away from him. I craved his eyes on me, and there was no way I was willingly leaving this room with him inside it. "I don't even know who I am, Isaiah. So how can you know?"

"That's a lie." His dark chuckle brought me back to life, and suddenly, my mouth was a breath away from his. "You know exactly who you are. You know exactly what you want, and you won't stop until you get it." His knee nestled in between my thighs, and I gladly opened them. His words were intoxicating, and I could no longer feel the alcohol in my blood. Instead, I felt him. "You are determined." He pushed closer, and I nearly whimpered. "You are strong." His hand gripped my thigh, and his fingers dug into my skin. "You are brave." His nose traced the curve of my cheek as he finally let go of my captured wrists. His palm came up, and he rested it along the concrete wall, right beside my head. "Most importantly, you know when to retreat from danger. That's why you're running from Richard."

Richard. Not uncle. He said Richard.

I swallowed, trembling underneath him. I needed it to stop. The push and pull between us. I wanted the room to just stop spinning for a minute so I could get myself together.

His words cut through the room. "Tell me to fucking go, right now."

I glanced around the dusty, dirty room as his teeth scraped over my ear lobe. "Wh-what?"

Isaiah suddenly pulled back, the look of pure agony on his face hardly hidden by the anger brewing. "I'm fucking dangerous for you. Just like Richard. So tell me to go."

My brows came together, but I was too stunned to say anything. He was nothing like Richard.

"Tell me you hate me!" he yelled, letting go of my body and caging my head in between his strong forearms. There was a bead of sweat forming on his hairline, and I knew the reason his hair was messed up was because Breanna had been running her hands through it as she moved over him, but I didn't care. "Tell me you wanted that guy instead of me. Tell me you'd rather fuck anyone in this school besides me! Tell me *no*. Push me away."

That was when it hit me. Isaiah wasn't pulling me in and pushing me away because he wanted to. He was pulling me in because he *couldn't* push me away. He wanted me to be the one to do it. And I should have. I should have placed my hands on his chest and shoved him clear across the room because he was right. He was dangerous. His father was dangerous. Richard was dangerous. Bain was dangerous too. All in their own ways.

But I wavered. My fingers scraped along the stone wall behind me, and I stared. I stared into his eyes, seeing the trouble brewing within the blue specks, and it matched mine. We were both stuck. We were both torn between right and wrong, trying to get each other to understand something we didn't even comprehend.

Isaiah's head dropped, and he reared his hand back and slapped the wall beside me. "Go!" The word was like a mountain falling, but I stayed still. He was hurting. I felt him shake along my chest, and it didn't matter that he'd hurt me the night his father had found me—unknowingly or not. It didn't matter that I was relishing in this newfound independence I'd felt while talking to Bain by myself yesterday. It didn't matter that my stomach bottomed out when I saw him with Breanna. Nothing mattered except him.

Life wasn't easy for him.

And it wasn't easy for me either.

Slowly, my hands fell to his chest. I felt the raging beat of his heart against my palm, and when he opened his mouth, it only grew faster. "Tell me you hate me. Tell me to fucking leave, Gemma. *Please*." His head snapped up quickly, and he pinned me with a look that I felt all the way to my soul. "When tomorrow comes, I'm going to start all over again. I'm going to make you hate me so you'll stay away. I won't fucking stop, so tell me to go."

The anguish twisted inside, jumbling everything up, and it was the only thing I needed to push me over the edge. My shaky hand grabbed his hard jaw, the sharpness cutting into my skin. I pulled him in close and let myself cave. My mouth covered his in hungry strokes, and I pushed everything else away. His hands cupped my waist, and he picked me up, forcing my legs around his back, pressing himself against my middle. I moaned, sucking in the stuffy air trapped inside this room full of too much emotion, and pushed right back.

"I'm not thinking of tomorrow," I whispered before biting onto his lip.

His eyes flared, and it forced a dose of dopamine to surge through. "Fuck tomorrow." Isaiah sat down in the dingy chair that was in the corner, and my legs fell over both sides of him. "You're mine tonight."

I shut my eyes, enjoying the way his hands trailed over my back and up to the zipper near my neck. My hair was brushed over my shoulder, and my skin was so sensitive that I felt the wisps of my strands even through the thick black fabric. The sound of the zipper drew my attention to Isaiah, and his hooded eyes drank in my bare skin as he pushed the dress down over my arms. My breasts were on full display. Sloane told me not to wear a bra, and I was suddenly thankful I listened, because Isaiah's mouth was on me, and my body was receptive. I was wet in between my legs, and I wasn't shy about it.

I wanted this.

It was like all the anger and betrayal I'd felt since the moment his father had found me underneath that green awning was coming in full action, and I needed to release it all.

A breathy moan left me as I moved above him, wanting to feel more than the scratch of his jeans. He pulled my nipple into his mouth, and I cried out, gripping onto his hair. The slight moment of pain was a rush right between my legs. I stopped moving, and Isaiah pulled back, looking at me deviously. My hands left his shoulders, and I moved to his shirt, pulling it up over his head. One of my shoes touched the dust-covered ground, and I scooted myself off his lap, shoving the rest of my dress down past my hips. I stepped out of it slowly, enjoying the way he looked at me. His lingering eyes scorched me from head to toe, and I loved every single second of it.

His abs flexed as I walked over to him, wearing nothing but the strappy heels that Sloane had lent me and my black panties. "I don't deserve you," he whispered, grabbing onto my hips and staring up at me with the same intense look on his face that he'd had when he walked in here earlier.

"Maybe...or maybe not," I whispered, slowly lowering my knees to the ground. My hands found the button of his jeans, and his brow furrowed. "But *we* deserve this moment right here. We deserve to put a pause on reality." I pulled the zipper down and realized I was acting blindly. But I was following the cues of my body, and I was eager to be in this moment with him, past and future be damned.

His head tilted back, and his hands flexed on top of his legs when I freed him from his boxers. I swallowed back my hesitation. There was no room for second thoughts. The throb between my legs grew more urgent as I gripped him and stroked down the base and back up again. I thought back to that time in the forest when Isaiah and I stumbled upon Shiner and a random girl. I wanted to do what she did. I wanted to know what it felt like to have him in my mouth. I wanted to watch him lose control, because more times than not, he *was* in control.

"Gemma." He breathed heavily as his hips moved, and his perfectly sculpted stomach muscles flexed.

My mouth hovered over his hard length, and I licked my lips. I was completely fascinated by the lure of his lust and how it was getting into every crevice of my body, but before I could do anything, his hands clamped down on my arms, and he pulled me up off the floor and plopped me down onto his lap. "Get off your knees."

I sucked in a ragged breath as I felt him rub against my wetness. It was coming through the thin fabric that separated us, and I knew he could feel it. "No fucking way will I let you suck me off in this disgusting, dirty fucking basement with your knees scraped up because of something my father did." He swallowed, lifting up and reaching into his back pocket before shoving his jeans and boxers all the way down. The condom wrapper was in his mouth next, and he ripped the foil, pushing me back just far enough that he could slip it on. My panties came down, and he threw them across the room before gripping me tightly and bringing me closer. "I don't deserve you," he said again, lining himself up with me. I rubbed against him, knowing how good it would feel, and it did. It felt so good I nearly cried.

"*Fuck,*" he said, breathing into the crook of my neck. My hands wrapped around his head as I started moving above him. He was everywhere. His lips touched over every inch of my skin. His tongue coated mine, and his hands seemed to move just as quickly as his thrusts.

"Mmm," I sighed as his hand came in between our bodies, and he rubbed circles over my clit, causing my hips to move differently. I was chasing the high I knew would come soon. The orgasm was building, and things were moving faster. The scrapes against his knuckles rubbed across my belly, and I looked down at the reddened marks.

His thumb never stopped moving, but his lips paused against mine. "I knocked down the locked doors, looking for you when the lights went out." I sucked in a breath, my lungs on fire as I moved. *God, it felt so good.* The twisting and pulling over my lower belly were sparking, and I wanted to feel myself come undone. I wanted that blissful feeling that lied to me and told me that everything was okay and that there was nothing bad that could ever touch me again.

"The thought of someone else's hands on you makes me fucking crazy." He bit onto my lip, and I yelled out, feeling the curl in between my legs tighten. He started to pump into me faster, both of us running in circles, frantic for each other.

"God," I whimpered, moving one more time before coming down in full, thundering waves around his body. His arms clamped around my hips, and suddenly, my back was on the ground as I rode out my orgasm, and it was the most intense, blinding thing that I had ever felt.

Isaiah stilled over me, filling me up to capacity. I hardly registered his words as he came down beside my ear, collapsing. "I think I might fucking love you, Gemma." My heart stopped as my eyes shut, trying to push away the uncertainty of everything to come. *"But I can't."*

CHAPTER ELEVEN

GEMMA

I KEPT GLANCING at the art room door, wondering when I'd see his face. It had been a few days since everything seemed to come together only to fall apart again in the basement underneath St. Mary's, and things between Isaiah and me were still just as unsteady. He went right back to keeping his distance from me. His eyes stayed to himself; they never wandered in my direction. His hands were almost always clutching a pencil or book during each tutoring session, as if the object itself was grounding him to the chair. He never left to follow Bain or to go back to the psychiatric hospital. Nothing. We just sat there, in that quiet library, festering in our unwanted thoughts, holding back things that neither of us wanted to say.

No one from the SMC had come to check on us again since Mr. Cunningham, and although Bain's stare had locked onto me every time I stepped in the same room as him, he hadn't interfered either. Everything was at a standstill, and it put me on edge because there was always a calm before the storm.

It was often like that with Richard. We'd have weeks of *normalcy* before he would get antsy and say I was disrespectful or he'd make up some scenario in his head that wasn't true, and then he'd punish me.

I was thankful I was able to skip last Monday's phone call with him, though Headmaster Ellison still had me come to his office to chat. My shields were up, preparing to lie through my teeth to Richard as I pushed away the memory of him throwing my mother into that padded room. I needed a level head when it came to him so I could keep things civil. I didn't want to tip him off, especially since my birthday was soon approaching, and things were about to change drastically. I was too stubborn to ask Isaiah when he'd be off probation and when he'd get me the necessary things I needed to run, but I knew it was soon.

If Richard suspected anything before I graduated from St. Mary's, he'd jump the gun and rip me away even with the social worker breathing down his neck, which was what Headmaster Ellison wanted to talk to me about Monday evening. Apparently, Ann, the social worker, had called and wanted to check on me. I had a hunch the headmaster was hiding something, though, because he'd suspiciously brought my birthday up, and I knew that was likely something he and the social worker had discussed. Once I was technically eighteen, I would no longer be an interest to her. Therefore, no one would be watching out for me, or checking on me, or poking holes in Judge Stallard's story full of lies. The social worker would no longer have an obligation, and Richard would make sure she left us alone.

Part of me was half glad that Headmaster Ellison had mentioned that the social worker had called. I was glad to know she was still alive. Though, I was sure there was a reason for that. After learning more about my dearest *uncle*, I had a feeling that I was wrong about a lot of things. I was pretty sure Richard was following her cues and allowing her to insert herself in our life for a reason. Just like there was a reason Bain hadn't told Richard everything I'd done since coming to St. Mary's.

Anxiety was creeping down my arms and into my fingertips as I swiped the last bit of charcoal on the canvas. I quickly took the thick paper down and rushed over to the supply closet, adding it to my hidden collection of drawings. This was one I didn't want anyone to see—especially Isaiah.

Just as I opened the door to the closet, I saw a shadow outside of the art room. My heart skipped, and a tiny smile crept itself onto my face. Isaiah had mostly been ignoring me, which hurt more than I'd like to admit, especially after our minor lapse in judgment Saturday night, but each morning, I'd see him sit outside the art room door, waiting for me to gather my things and head to breakfast.

He was good at ignoring me and even better at acting like I didn't matter, especially when there were eyes on us, but he still showed up and made sure that I was okay in here. It made me feel protected, even if I told him that his protection was unneeded the first day he'd shown up.

It was our new normal.

He watched from afar, hardly ever looking me in the eye, and I pretended that nothing mattered except my future outside of this school. *Which was exactly how it should have been.*

I straightened my skirt on my hips and grabbed my bag before looking up at the small clock above Mrs. Fitz's desk. I halted with my hand on the strap, realizing that it wasn't time to go to breakfast yet. I turned slowly to the door again, and my heart ricocheted off the walls of my chest. I swallowed the trepidation as I turned the knob.

I had a gut feeling.

Something instinctual, that likely came from all the years of fear and terror that someone was about to catch me doing something I shouldn't have, blossomed in my core, but it suddenly wilted when I saw Cade standing against the far wall with his phone in his hand.

"What are you doing here?" I breathed out in relief, stepping into the open hallway and shutting out the smell of acrylic paints and charcoal dust.

Cade kept his phone in his hand and barely spared me a glance. "Are you planning to go to art college, Gemma? I heard Mrs. Fitz ask you yesterday after class."

The disappointment was there with the fleeting thought of college. But it was the last thing on my mind. "That's not in the cards for me. But you already knew that."

Cade pushed off the wall and slipped his phone in the pocket of his school blazer. His blond hair was pushed away from his face, so I could see the wariness on his handsome features. "How would I know that?"

I rolled my eyes, glancing down the dark hall. "Are you really going to stand there and act like Isaiah hasn't told you that I'm leaving before I even graduate?"

Cade paused in front of me, but I didn't look up at him. I wasn't sure what Cade knew about me. Or the rest of Isaiah's friends. Each Rebel was evasive. They didn't wear their emotions on their sleeves, and they excelled at keeping their faces unreadable, replacing any truth or lie with an even glare, which was why I was having such a hard time knowing what Isaiah was thinking each night in that stuffy library as we pretended to study.

"Why don't you play against me anymore?"

I finally peeked up at Cade's warm, brown eyes. He blinked once, waiting for my answer. "You mean the game you downloaded for me a while back?"

He nodded, looking sincere, but who knew if that was what he was really feeling. I shrugged. "I don't carry the phone around with me anymore." It felt wrong to use a phone that Isaiah had given me. I brought it with me to tutoring, in case Isaiah needed to leave randomly and I needed a way to let him know that someone had come to check on us, but that was it. I didn't want to hold the stupid thing in my hand, waiting for him to text me, only to be disappointed in the end.

Cade sighed agitatedly. "And what if it were Bain in this hallway instead of me? What if he cornered you and threatened you, or hell, what if Isaiah's father showed up randomly and dragged you into some filthy corner inside this school to shove his dick inside you? What would you do, Gemma? Who would come save you?"

Anger rushed to my skin, and I felt the burn on my cheeks. "That seems a little over the top, Cade. Do you really think Isaiah's father is going to come here at six in the morning, pull me out of the art room, and have his way with me?" Never mind about Bain. He wouldn't touch me if he was involved with Richard. He had something else up his sleeve.

He laughed sarcastically. "I'm honestly concerned that you don't seem fearful of that thought at all."

I rocked on my heels. "Cade, you don't know half of the things I've been through. Or what I've witnessed. I know men like Isaiah's father. He wouldn't step foot in this school because there are eyes here. Men like Isaiah's father use other men to do his dirty work." I huffed out a laugh. "Like Isaiah. And you and Brantley."

I nearly choked on the sick feeling I had, remembering how Isaiah's father had shoved me to my knees in front of the Rebels, telling them to have a go at me. He allowed them to chase me through the forest to prove something to Bain, and although that wasn't what happened, or what was planned, he didn't know that.

For all I knew, he thought that Isaiah and his two best friends had raped me and dragged me back to St. Mary's to tell Bain. I wondered if Bain knew what had happened that night. He knew I had taken his car, so did he know what went down after?

Cade ran his tongue over his teeth and shut his eyes briefly before opening them back up and snapping his gaze to mine. He no longer looked like the golden boy that I once thought he was. He looked lethal with his angry scowl and the determined set of his jaw. "Isaiah isn't sleeping."

My head slanted, a piece of my hair tickling my arm. "Okay..." I trailed off because I had no idea what to say or why the sudden change in the conversation. "Did he send you here to tell me that? Is he sleeping in this morning? You know, I didn't ask to have a babysitter. It's fine. You can go."

He dismissed the last part of my sentence. "He's at the pool, doing laps. He does that when he's really worked up about something. He sent me here to make sure you were good. He wants eyes on you at all times, especially now that his father knows your face."

My mouth gaped. "The pool? There's a pool here? It's cold out, though." He had to be freezing.

Cade flicked an eyebrow up as his lips twitched. "It's an indoor pool, Gemma. How did you not know there was a pool here?"

"Is there a swim team?" What else did I not know about St. Mary's?

Cade shook his head. "The pool is off limits. There was a swim team, but..." He shrugged. "Someone drowned or something, so the SMC shut it down. It's supposed to be drained at some point."

My mind got held up on the "*someone drowned or something*"

part, as if that was normal. But Cade continued on past that, once again, dismissing it. "I was hoping you could help."

I took a step back, resting against the door. "Help with what?"

I caught the sharp angle of Cade's jaw as he looked away. "With Isaiah. I've never seen him like this, and..." His Adam's apple bobbed up and down with a harsh swallow. "And I'm worried. I can't get through to him. He has a lot going on, more than you know, and he needs to be sharper. If he's planning on doing what I think, he needs to be focused and tenacious."

A little line of worry etched itself onto Cade's forehead, and it seemed to dig into my belly. I wasn't sure what Isaiah had planned, but for the first time in ever, I could see actual concern on Cade's face. He wasn't hiding how desperate he was, and I ran with it.

"Tell me where the pool is."

———

THE SMELL of chlorine crept under my nose, and a feeling of yearning flew through me. The pool was large, and the dark water looked inviting as it moved effortlessly at the surface. It was so vast and deep that it would be easy to lose yourself in there. To just let the water graciously cover your skin and wash away every last worry.

I heard him before I saw him. His strong arms cut through the deep blue. His dark head of hair would pop up every few seconds, and each time I'd get a glance of his straight nose and jaw, my belly would bottom out. He appeared so strong and capable as he winded back and dove down again. The splashing sprinkled through the air and fell down into the warm liquid, and I felt myself moving closer.

I wanted to learn how to swim.

Maybe I would learn once I grew roots somewhere away from Richard.

"Hey," I shouted, dropping my bag by the door and walking closer to the edge. I was already in my school uniform, except this time, I threw on some thigh-high tights that left a thin sliver of skin showing from below my skirt. My fingers itched to take my shoes off and slide the fabric down my legs so I could at least put my feet in the water.

Isaiah suddenly stopped swimming as his wet face pulled up from the pool. Tiny beads of water ran over the curve of his jaw, and I swallowed. *He was so beautiful.* So dark and dangerous with that constant air of authority surrounding him, but I knew, deep down, he had a strong heart that was desperate for anything good. He tried to hide it, but I could see it. He was right the other night; he didn't need to know all my secrets to know who I really was, and I didn't need to know all of his to know who *he* really was.

"What are you doing here? Is everything okay?" Isaiah waded over to me as I stood above the edge of the darkened abyss. He gripped the side, and I glanced at the popped veins covering his hands and arms from the rush of physical exertion.

"Cade said you're not sleeping."

Isaiah huffed, whipping his head to the left as his temples ticked. A silent moment passed between us before he pushed onto the side of the pool and hauled himself up in one single movement. I quickly took a step back, putting distance between us.

It wasn't that I was afraid to be near him. I'd sat in a quiet library with nothing but the sound of his breathing for the last week. But this felt different. My stomach tensed, and my heart tugged. *Why wasn't he sleeping?*

Isaiah quickly shook out his wet hair, small droplets of water hitting the front of my uniform. He adjusted the low-riding black swim trunks on his hips, and I couldn't help the way my eyes traveled over the hard lines of his abdomen. With every dip and curve, my eyes lingered, remembering how tense he felt beneath me Saturday. A work of art was what he was. I should know, I'd secretly sketched him multiple times this week without even meaning to.

"Cade has a big mouth," Isaiah gritted, standing in the same spot, unmoving as water traveled over his skin and to the floor beneath our feet. "He has no business talking to you about me."

My arms crossed over my uniform as I quickly glanced back at the water, taking my eyes from his body. *God, I couldn't stop staring.* It was one thing being in the library with him, but here? He was hardly wearing anything, and every part of my body reacted. "He said he's worried. That's the only reason he said anything."

His short laugh echoed around us. "And what does he expect you to do about that?"

Hesitantly, I took a step closer to him, ignoring how he was brushing past the matter. "Why aren't you sleeping, Isaiah?"

Isaiah said nothing. Instead, he stared at the wall behind my head, not even looking into my eyes. I craved his gaze so badly it hurt. I wanted to feel that sudden jolt that he gave me when we locked on one another. I hadn't felt it since that night at the claiming. I smashed my lips together, still looking at his perfectly steady face. He had darkened bags underneath the thick mass of damp eyelashes, but he still appeared just as steady as ever. "You know," I started, "I don't sleep much either. Never have, really. Not since Tobias left."

There. Right there. I almost jumped when he flicked his gaze to mine. It was like I could feel the room turn to ice. But it wasn't cold. It was hot. Like the icy burn of stepping into snow barefoot. "I have nightmares," I said, ignoring the way my skin pulled tight at the admission.

"I know," he stated, still staying stark still with the water glistening behind him. I felt the twitch of my brows, feeling the concern whip through me so quickly that I wanted to jump into the pool to wash it away. *How did we get to this?* So much had happened between us in just a couple of months.

Isaiah quickly put his back to me, gripping his neck tightly and showcasing every ripple of muscle along his shoulders and spine. "Do you want to know why I can't sleep? Why I'm here, tiring out my body that's already so fucking tired?"

I stepped closer, and I knew he could feel me. We both studied the pool, nearly standing side by side. He didn't peer down at me, and I didn't peer up at him, too afraid to break the connection. It was heavy and tight. An overpowering tenseness filled the large room, and even the humidity in here couldn't break the cool fluidity of his words.

"I can hear her screams in my sleep sometimes. When things start to get out of control or there's something that I can't fix, it's like my mind instantly goes back to the first time I was ever put into a situation that I couldn't control. My vulnerabilities come out in my sleep."

My hands fell by my side, inches away from his, and I was completely taken aback by what he'd just admitted.

"When my mother was assaulted, I changed. I was barely a pre-teen, but I had seen and knew things that I wished I didn't. So, when the French doors opened, I knew that something bad was about to happen. My father was gone, and so was Jacobi, my older brother. He'd left a while back, leaving me and Jack all on our own." Isaiah sucked in a deep breath, and I knew it was hard for him to talk. I could hear the edge in his voice like a dull razor rubbing over my exposed skin. "It was just me, Jack, and my mom, sitting at the table, eating the dinner the chef had just set down. I saw the panicked look in her eye. The way she looked at me and then to Jack set me into blind action. Once the first man stepped through the door, I dashed forward, grabbed my brother, and I ran. I ran so fucking fast. He was so young that he doesn't remember, but I do. I remember it all. I remember the way his tiny little hands dug into my t-shirt. I remember hearing the blistering screams from my mother as I pushed Jack into the small cubby in the wall between our rooms. I remember every last detail."

Our hands brushed as moisture hit the backs of my eyes. I knew something had happened to his mother, but I never asked.

"By the time I got Jack locked away and ran back to the dining room, it was nearly too late. My mom was lying on the floor in a pool of her own blood. Her face was..." Isaiah paused for a few seconds before finishing. "Her face was unrecognizable."

I wanted to place my hand over my mouth so I wouldn't sob for him. There was a harsh pain nestling in the middle of my chest at the sound of his cracked voice, and although I'd craved to see inside Isaiah's mind since the very beginning, it hurt to do so.

"I don't think about that night often. Everything after was such a blur. Cade and Brantley came with their fathers. They all said I was in shock, but I wasn't." I felt Isaiah move, and I was pretty sure he was looking down at me. "I know how trauma can change people, Gemma. That's why you and I are the way that we are. That's why you and I have something no one else does. That's why we share a connection. We're the same."

My hand shook when his finger hooked with mine. It was a relief to feel him against my skin. Isaiah was comfort and warmth and strength all wrapped up into one person, and with just one single touch, I felt at home. I felt whole. And that wasn't something I thought I could ever feel after Tobias disappeared.

"You asked me why I wasn't sleeping."

My voice croaked as a single tear fell over my cheek and landed on the slippery floor that we both stood on. "Yes."

"I can't sleep because I'm afraid the second I shut my eyes, the same thing will happen to you." I quickly glanced up to him, seeing pure torment and insecurity all over his features. "Whether by my father, an enemy that I haven't even fucking met yet, Richard, or Bain." He swallowed, gripping onto my hand harder and pulling me into his chest. His other hand caressed the side of my face gently, and warmth settled deep within. "You scare the hell out of me because *you* are my weakness, Gemma Richardson, and if the wrong people get a hold of that, like my father or Bain's father, they will show no mercy. You will be used as a bargaining chip, just like my mother."

My bottom lip trembled as I stared up at him. Another stray tear slipped down my cheek, and he quickly swiped it away, the dip in between his brows getting deeper.

"I've been used all my life." It was the only thing I could say. I didn't want to say that I didn't want to be used, because then that meant I didn't choose him, but I wanted to. I wanted to choose him, and I wanted him to come with me and get away from everything that had hurt us or had the potential.

"I know," he whispered, pulling my head into his bare chest. My tears mixed with the water that still blanketed over the curves of his muscles. "Don't worry. I won't let anyone use you anymore."

I quickly pulled back, walls falling and crashing into the pool behind us. Isaiah's face grew serious as I let myself spill. "Bain said something to me."

His jaw wiggled as his hands cupped my face, waiting for

me to tell him, and maybe this was what he had wanted all along—for me to tell him what Bain had said. Either way, I still told him.

"He said, '*You're right where I want you to be, Gemma.*'" I swallowed, letting it all come out in one whoosh. "And his relationship with Richard goes deeper than illicit gun selling. He knows who I am."

The sickening feeling of dread and worry was quickly washed away as Isaiah bent his head down and placed our foreheads together. He nodded against me, our warmth mingling, and then his lips touched mine, and I fell into him. I fell hard and swiftly, and it was irreversible. We gripped one another tightly, and I didn't think either of us wanted to let go.

CHAPTER TWELVE

ISAIAH

WHAT HAPPENED when you were in a battle but you were straddling the line between two enemies? Both sides were dangerous and tricky. It was a war where you couldn't walk into it with guns in your hands or without an army to back you up. You had to be precise and gain control, attack them when they least expected it.

And that was the one thing I kept reminding myself as I stood in front of the house that Gemma grew up in, leaning against my uncle's car at one in the morning. No matter what I found inside, I couldn't attack first and ask questions later.

I had two wars brewing: one with my father and the other with Judge Stallard.

"Where are we?" Brantley asked, flicking his cigarette off to the side of the road.

I held back a groan, stealthily walking over to it and crushing it with my black shoe before bending down and swiping it up. Brantley's dark brows lowered as he leaned up against the car, looking as if he wanted to hit me when I shoved my hand onto his chest with the butt crumbling in between my fingers.

Cade chuckled. "Are you suddenly concerned about the planet, Isaiah? Afraid that a lonesome cigarette butt full of nicotine is going to decompose and seep into the ground and hurt the ecosystem?"

Brantley grabbed the butt from in between my fingers, after I told him to shove it in his pocket, and looked over at Cade. "What are you even talking about?"

Cade shrugged nonchalantly. "I learned about it in earth science. Unlike you, I actually pay attention in class."

"That's because you're fucking lame, bro."

I expelled a heavy breath and looked back at the Stallard Manor that stood nearly as tall as the trees out front. There was a chill in the air, and it did nothing but cool me even more to the core. "I told you two a week ago that there was going to come a time when you were going to have to pick a side."

Brantley and Cade both came over and stood beside me, glancing up to the same home that I was staring at, but they stayed silent, likely wondering where we were.

"I asked you to pick up your cigarette because there needs to be absolutely no evidence that we were here. And the person that lives in that house"—I inched my chin to the darkened windows, almost picturing Gemma's face staring out of them as if I were pulled back in time—"thrives on rule-breaking citizens, and he has many ties in this community and can pull strings like you wouldn't fucking believe. A lonesome cigarette butt would only intensify his stance."

Evidence was artillery to men like Richard Stallard.

"Who lives here?" Cade asked, an edge of suspicion to his voice.

I sighed. "Judge Stallard. Gemma's uncle." He wasn't her biological uncle, which Uncle Tate and I had already concluded, but she let it slip one day when she referred to him as Richard instead of Uncle, and it only confirmed what we'd already suspected.

Brantley ran his hands over his head roughly. "Isaiah, what the fuck? I thought you were done messing around with Gemma. Even Bain has taken a step back from her."

I ignored him. "You two have a choice to make. Right here and right now." I quickly looked at both of them before laying it all out in the open. "You're either with me, or you're not." I held my hand up when Cade opened his mouth. "Let me finish."

Both of their faces dropped. I ping-ponged my attention between them both so I could get a feel for how they truly felt when I let it all out. "I am not taking over my father's business." Silence cut through. I was pretty sure that Cade and Brantley had both stopped breathing. "Before I divulge anything else, you need to let me know which side of the war you want to be on. If it's with me, just know that your fathers will likely be going down with mine. Cade," I started, looking over to him, "I want you to remember that you have a mother. It's possible that when it's all said and done, you will no longer have a relationship with her, as little as it is now."

My heart thumped wildly, gaining traction with each word that came from my mouth. I wanted to believe that they wanted out of the fucked-up future our fathers had intended for us and had bred us for since we were young, but I knew that just because I wanted them on my side, it didn't mean that they were. Wants and realities were two very different things.

Surprisingly, Brantley was the first to speak up. "What are you saying, Isaiah? That somehow, you're going to just walk away from everything? That will not fucking fly with the Huntsman. And what about Jack?"

I knew he'd question my father's willingness to let me go,

but I was staying true to my word. I wasn't giving up any more information until I knew for sure they were with me. "You're either with me or you're not. I need to know now."

I counted in my head with each thump of my heart. Blood rushed and flooded my veins with caution. If they weren't with me, that would mean they'd go down too. My muscles were growing tighter with every second that passed.

"I'm with you." Cade stepped forward and stood by my side, causing me to freeze for a second. "I'm a little perturbed that you even had to ask. We've been brothers since we were in diapers." *Loyal. Cade was so fucking loyal.*

"You've been your mother's son for that long, too. You could pack up with her and leave this life if you wanted. Your father won't be able to come after you when it's all said and done." He'd be stupid to.

Cade laughed under his breath. "If you take my father down along with yours, my mother will probably kiss you herself. Last Thanksgiving, she stabbed him at the fucking dinner table. She hates him, but she's too afraid to leave him." I nodded once before we both turned to Brantley.

His jaw wiggled back and forth like a teeter-totter as he pulled his black hood up to his head. His hands went into the pocket on the front of his hoodie. "Are you doing this all for Gemma?"

"No," I answered. "I'm doing it for me and for Jack. But this?" I nodded over to the looming house full of shit I probably didn't want to see. "This is partly for her. Judge Stallard is affiliated with the Covens and has worked with my father in the past and is now working with Bain's, as you both already know. If my assumptions are correct, Bain is planning on using Gemma for something to get closer to him, maybe to secure a deal, I'm not sure. But Gemma is a part of this, and I will not have that. I want to know all there is to know about Judge Stallard and his position in this. Because after I take my father down and hand over the reins, I'm coming for Richard fucking Stallard, and that means I need to know who he is."

What I meant was that I needed to know how much he'd harmed Gemma and what he'd done with Tobias. Because that'd be next on the to-do list: finding Tobias—for her. I couldn't do that if I accidently tripped and happened to choke Richard Stallard in the process.

Brantley observed the house for a few seconds before coming back to me and Cade. "How tight is your plan, Isaiah? Because if your father knows you're planning on taking him down and it doesn't work, he will fuckin' kill us all." He was worried, and that was something I never saw from him. "We've seen him kill men for less."

My plan was mostly solid, as long as Bain agreed to it, which wouldn't be difficult after I revealed my wild card. Jack was already safe as a precaution, because if things went sideways, he'd be the one to suffer the most. And as soon as I got all the necessary documents for Gemma, including the new identity and everything else she'd need to disappear that she didn't even think of, I'd lay it all out in the open for everyone.

"It's tight. But it's a risk. It'll be a war, Brantley. If you want out, then get back in the car. If you want in, just know this is your only warning that things could go wrong."

A swallow worked itself down his throat before a sinister smile broke out over his shadowed face seconds later. "You think I want to be like my father? You think I want to go around taking orders and killing? You think I want to be in an uphill battle against men like Bain for the rest of my life?" He threw his head back and chuckled. "Who the hell do you think I am? Cade is right. We've been brothers since birth. You think we'd actually choose your psycho father, or ours, over *you* and our brotherhood? We may be a little fucked-up, but at least we're loyal to one another." And it was a shame their fathers were loyal to mine.

He walked over and stood beside me, and we all turned toward the house. Relief settled over me, and it was the first time that I hadn't felt weighed down in days—of course, other than when Gemma was in my arms yesterday morning. It was a breaking point I desperately needed, and although I didn't take it any further than a surrendering kiss before the morning bell rang, it was enough to satisfy me until everything else was handled. One taste of her mouth could last me a little longer. The library wasn't as tense last night either, as if we'd come to a mutual understanding. We were walking on broken glass, and one step to either side would cut us in the end.

Brantley grumbled under his breath. "You're a fucking idiot for thinking otherwise."

I pulled my black hood up, and Cade did the same. We slowly began creeping toward Judge Stallard's house. My phone buzzed, and I quickly pulled it out, fearful that either Gemma or Shiner's name would be on the screen, but it was my uncle.

UNCLE TATE: I tell you that the SMC has set a meeting to revoke your probation and you skip off in the middle of the fucking night and test the waters? Did Bain leave this late? Or was it Gemma this time? I swear to God, Isaiah.

ME: Neither. This is purely business. I'll be back soon.

UNCLE TATE: You better not get caught walking the halls this late. They won't believe that you are walking

back from tutoring. Not after Mrs. Fitz caught you at Gemma's door after midnight.

I SHOVED my phone in my pocket and brushed off his warning. I knew what I was doing. In the past, Bain would sneak out during prime time. The time where he knew the duty teacher would be walking. Or better yet, he was probably the one to tip them off. He'd wanted me to follow him from day one. That wasn't his goal anymore. Bain had desperately tried to get me kicked out of St. Mary's for months, but now his plan shifted to Gemma. He had something else brewing, and it no longer included me being expelled.

"So, you mean to tell me that we're about to sneak into a house this big, and we're not going to trip any alarms?"

A deep chuckle rumbled from my throat. "I hate my father, but he taught me well. Alarms and cameras are off. Even the hidden ones."

Richard Stallard was asleep in his bed, unknowing that the three of us were about to uncover every last secret he held between his thick walls.

———

"WHATEVER YOU TWO DO, don't let me fucking kill him." My hand rested on the knob of a door that was on the side of the Stallard Manor. It looked as if it led to a basement as it was below the ground level of the house.

Cade's arm brushed mine as he and Brantley stood close. "What exactly do you think you'll find here?"

Shit that was going to make my blood run cold. I didn't say that, though. Instead, I said, "Hopefully something that will solidify the fact that Judge Stallard runs the Covens and how much he does at that fucked-up place. Uncle Tate and I both think he sends criminals there, deeming them mentally ill, but instead of sending them to the actual psychiatric unit, he's sending them underground."

Brantley gritted his teeth. "He probably sent my father there."

It was possible. Or maybe Richard's father had. I had a hunch that it went back further than we thought.

"What else do you plan to find?" Cade poked, stopping me before I picked the lock. "No more hiding shit, Isaiah. We're on your team. Let us play."

I began picking the lock, my fingers nearly numb from the cool air surrounding us. "I need to know why Gemma is running from him." My teeth snapped as I thought of her terrified face the first time I'd mentioned his name to her. *And the scars.* "He's hurt her, and I want to know to what extent."

"Fucking bastard." That came from Brantley, and I almost smiled. He could put on a good front and act like he was above women, but deep down, he was just as protective as I was. He only pushed girls away after he was through with them because of buried trauma. I had been the same way— until Gemma.

The house was eerily quiet. Not a single sound was heard. No buzzing of the heat as it ran through the walls, no trickling of a leaky drain, not even the soft whirl of the refrigerator, which meant that I was correct. We weren't on the ground level. We were beneath the main floor. I tapped both Brantley and Cade on their left shoulders, and we all turned that way, using a small flashlight to tell us where the steps were. They creaked under my weight, and we all paused, ears on alert. Part of me wished Richard would wake up and come down here. I wanted to look him dead in the eye and ask him some questions. For starters, like why he wanted his *niece* to call him daddy. The thought of overhearing their conversation a while back lurked in the deepest part of my brain.

"Basement." Cade's deep whisper floated around us, and we inched down farther.

The basement wasn't finished. There was no carpet beneath our feet or flat screen TV plastered onto the wall with sports paraphernalia in frames surrounding us. It was dark and bleak, and it sent an icy punch to my chest.

Something splashed beneath our footsteps, and I brought the flashlight up and slowly began scanning the area. My heart was in my gut, and it kept falling as I spun around, pausing on something in the corner.

I walked over to it, the floor damp under my shoes. The smell of mildew and dirt wafted around us, and when I reached the metal chains, I craned my neck, seeing that they were attached to the ceiling. *If he...*

Sickening thoughts were hitting me from every angle, and suddenly, I was alone. Brantley and Cade were no longer there. It was just me, in the dark basement, kneeling in a spot that I had a high suspicion that Gemma had once been. Visuals of her raw wrists, the pink raised skin that she guarded above anything else, made my blood pressure spike. My head fell forward, and my chest heaved.

"Isaiah."

I cautiously raised my head and grabbed onto the hanging chains with small cuffs around the bottom. I pulled myself up, shaking with the overwhelming need to pull them the fuck out of the ceiling. My thoughts were on a rampage, and I couldn't focus. My heartrate was through the roof, thundering behind my ribs.

"What are these?"

More silence passed.

"Isaiah, fucking speak."

I glared over my shoulder at the two shadows behind me, feeling the room shake around us. "They're chains."

"For what?" Cade asked, stepping forward, keeping his voice low. His firm grip peeled my fingers away from the metal digging into my palm, and he hesitantly raised the cuffed bottom closer to his face, inspecting it. His eyes flicked to mine, and Brantley swore under his breath.

"Jesus Christ."

His office.

"We need to go to his office. Somewhere that he would keep his personal documents." I needed to get out of this basement. I was suffocating. *I would kill him.* I glanced back at the chains as they swayed in front of my face, picturing Gemma chained up. For his own pleasure? To harm her? Both?

"Oh, shit. Get over here." My shoe rubbed over gritty dirt as I spun around.

"Wait. Isaiah." Cade's hand clamped onto my shoulder. "Maybe you shouldn't."

I bristled under his grip. "Get the fuck off me. I'm fine."

"Are you?" He met my eye, and I knew I was slipping. Anger was brewing like no other, and it was taking over my conscious ability to control the situation that I would be face to face with in the future.

I nodded once after expelling a deep breath, and we both walked over to where Brantley was standing. His hands were in fists by his sides, rubbing over his black jeans.

Silence followed us like a deadly plague, and I froze, right there in that exact spot, with the chains swaying behind me.

Richard Stallard was a dead man.

My gaze slowly crawled up the wall, and I pointed the flashlight over every last photo of the only girl I'd ever kill for. A hollow numbness flowed through me, and it was a bad fucking thing to feel. Photo after photo of Gemma bound, naked, cold, and starving. His large hands on her body. A finger here or there trailing down her sleeping face while she lay in her bed, surrounded by fluffy blankets, unknowing that he was standing over her.

Scars.

Cuts.

Scrapes.

Bruises.

He had touched her, and she didn't want him to. He hurt what was mine.

Nausea crept up my throat, but I clamped my teeth down. A feeling that I'd never felt so viciously before flew through me, and I was ready to kill. My hands shook as I clutched the flashlight in my hand, and Cade's hand grabbed it out of my grasp before wrapping his palms around my head tightly.

"Calm down, Isaiah."

I couldn't breathe in normal air. I choked on rage and fury. *I was going to rip his hands from his fucking body.*

"Isaiah!" Cade's harsh whisper did nothing to plow through the debris of my humanity falling to the fucking floor like bricks. He slapped my face, and I quickly whipped it back toward the photos. So many. There were so many. He'd touched her while she was naked and chained. His hand on her neck, her back, gripping her hair.

"He needs to get the fuck out of here, now."

"Think of Gemma, Isaiah." Brantley's thick fingers dug into my arms. "You can't be there for her if you're in prison, and if you do anything right now, that's where you'll go."

I had to get out of here.

I was going to blow the house to fucking pieces. I'd pull the pin out of the goddamn grenade without a second thought if given the chance.

"Go to his office. Gather everything about Gemma, the Covens, and someone named Tobias."

Cade nodded. "I'm on it. Go. Now."

Brantley pulled me as Cade stayed behind, and I let him lead me out the side door that we'd come in. I kept my face straight ahead, my body angled away from the house, because if I caught a glimpse of it again, I would turn right back around and kill Richard Stallard with my own two hands.

I said it before, and I'd say it again: Gemma Richardson was the one person I'd give up my humanity for.

CHAPTER THIRTEEN

GEMMA

MY EYES SPRUNG open when the sound of iron against iron rang out. I'd know that sound anywhere, at any time. *Chains.* My throat closed, and my heart skipped a beat. I kept my back turned to Sloane, facing the wall, which meant that I couldn't see who was opening my door. I listened as the chain clamored against the wood, and I held my breath. *Was it Sloane?* The room had a faint glow to it from the fairy lights that Sloane had hung over each of our beds. We usually turned them off when we went to sleep, but after Sloane caught on that I wasn't sleeping, she kept them on, hoping it'd chase away the nightmares.

It didn't. But it was a sweet gesture.

I listened closely to her breathing, realizing that she was, in fact, still in her bed. I felt the cool air of the hallway float into our cozy room, and I shut my eyes. *Shit.* I moved my hand slightly, reaching for the phone under my pillow. It had to have been well into the middle of the night, but hopefully Isaiah had his phone on.

Not that he could do anything for me. By the time he'd answer, it'd be too late.

Whoever was in my room would be done with me by then.

And if it was Richard, we'd be long gone.

I held back a whimper and pushed back on the fear that was too familiar to me. My stomach was tied in knots, and my heart raced. I was hot and tingly from panic, and I didn't know what to do.

It's not Richard. It's not Richard. It's not Richard.

My mouth tasted of blood as I began to feel lightheaded. Terror coursed through me, and when a strong hand landed on my shoulder, I wanted to die right there.

I wouldn't survive if Richard took me.

"Baby."

A shaky gasp left me unable to speak. I quickly turned over and dug my fingers into Isaiah's hand, seeing the worry etched over every perfect curve of his face through the shadows of my room. His dark eyes went directly to my mouth, and his thumb hurriedly brushed over my parted lips.

"Why is your mouth bleeding?"

My eyes shut again as a shudder traveled through my body. I swiped my tongue over my lips, tasting the metallic liquid before swallowing. My whisper was like a broken record playing off in the distance. "You scared me."

Isaiah cursed under his breath, slowly trailing his hand down my arm and clasping our fingers together. I peeked through my heavy lids, willing my heart to calm down as he pulled me up. The covers fell to my lap, and I blinked a few times. "What are you doing here?"

I caught Sloane's staring eyes from across our small room, and she rolled them before turning her back to us. "Fucking knock next time, Isaiah."

He said nothing. He didn't even look in her direction. His

skin felt hot against my palm, and worry nudged me. "Are you okay?"

Again, he said nothing, but his body language said enough. He was tense. All over. He pulled me to my feet, his fingers clenching mine tightly. We padded over the soft rug, and he opened my door, pulling me out into the hallway. "Isaiah, what's going on?"

My mind was reeling. My thoughts were wavering over a fine line of panic and suspicion. I glanced behind me, seeing nothing but the flickering sconces on the wall and the dark-red carpet that lined the hallway. Goosebumps were covering my skin as Isaiah pulled me even faster down the girls' hall and then quickly down the boys' hall until we were outside a door.

"Isa—" I didn't get a chance to finish his name before he opened the door and pushed me inside. It slammed shut, and I realized it was the first time I'd ever been in his room. It was dark, and the bed on the left was messy, whereas the one on the right was made. I wondered where Cade was, since they were roommates, and a part of me wanted to ask, but Isaiah's face was suddenly in front of mine, and he peered down into my eyes with something unreadable passing behind his. He looked unguarded and almost vulnerable.

I raised my hand, my chest rising and falling with concern, as everything else faded away. All of our uncertainties were gone, and I was seconds from feeling his warm cheek pressed to my palm, but he caught my hand in his instead. His stare drove into mine, and with the silvery moonlight streaming through the window behind him, he didn't even look human. He looked too perfect to be real.

My sleeve was slowly pushed up to my elbow with the work of Isaiah's fingers, and I saw that his hands were shaking. *What was wrong with him?* My arm was extended, and I held my breath, briefly glancing down to my scars. He'd seen them already, but he was staring at them with a tight face. I pushed back on the need to secure my wrist to my chest when his lips touched the side of my delicate skin.

"What are you doing?" My voice was breathy as I watched him trail light kisses around the entire diameter of my scarred wrist. Isaiah's mouth stayed on my skin until he slowly dropped that arm and started on the other. The air whooshed over me, and something clicked inside, telling me just how much I enjoyed his lips on my flesh. My wrists didn't get touched often. They didn't even feel the misty air most days. They were sensitive, and Isaiah's mouth overtop of them made heat spread to my stomach.

"Isaiah," I whispered again, my heart bouncing all over the place.

His eyes moved to mine when he dropped my arm. We stayed like that as he fingered the hem of my long sleep shirt and pulled it up over my body. I was too confused and worked up in all the right places to stop him. His touches were soft, but urgent too, like he was cautiously branding every inch of my skin with his.

Isaiah suddenly crowded my space, pushing me up against his door. My back hit the hard wood, and his chest was pushed against my front. I was suddenly frustrated that I'd put on a tight tank top underneath my long sleeve shirt because the fabric felt itchy against my skin. My hands were flat against the solid wood, and my heart climbed with speed as he suddenly gripped my nape and tilted my head up. His mouth grazed the base of my throat, and I was certain he could feel my pulse thumping. The softness of his lips caressed me, and he laid kisses on every part of my neck, dipping just below my collarbone.

"Isaiah, I thought we weren't doing this anymore. After Sat—" To be honest, I wasn't sure what we were doing, but I didn't think it mattered at the moment.

His hands fells to my hips, and he forced me around, covering my back with his heat immediately. My mouth slammed shut, and my eyes widened. My core shrunk as heat pooled in between my legs. The feel of his large hands, so sturdy and protective, gripping my waist had every thought vanishing.

This was just who we were when we were alone.

Too desperate to think of anything but each other.

"I need to touch you," he whispered, his hot breath coating my ear. A shiver raced down my body, and my back bowed, pushing my butt onto his hard front. "Let me touch you, baby. *Please.*"

My cheeks heated, and I smashed my lips together.

His tongue ran a line all the way from my ear to the back of my shoulders, landing over my spine. I wanted to turn around and plant my mouth on his, but something stopped me from doing so. His hands left my hips, and his fingers slipped underneath the thin straps of my tank top. He pulled them down slowly, and a ragged breath left my mouth. The way he was touching me was sensual. He wasn't rushing to strip me naked. He was taking his time. He was slowly running his lips over parts of my body that had only been touched one other time.

My eyes sprung even wider at the thought. *Wait.* My body tensed when his lips touched the skin of my back that I didn't think about often. No one saw my back, not even when he and I had sex. *Could he see it in the dark?*

I stepped one foot back in between his and tried to turn around in a blur of panic, but Isaiah quickly crowded me again so I was unable to move.

"No." His voice was gravelly, and his chest rose quickly against my skin.

"Isaiah," I rasped.

"He doesn't get to touch you anymore." His lips landed on

the faint marks that had since healed and faded. It'd been at least a year or two since Richard had gotten that brutal, probably disgusted with the ugly marks that he had put there. Isaiah pulled the straps the rest of the way down and quickly yanked on my tank top, leaving it to rest along my hips. I was bare in the front, and despite the sudden rush of panic and confusion, my nipples were hard and begged for his touch. His touch did things to me. It quieted me and coaxed me to be in the present.

Isaiah's nose grazed the side of my cheek from behind, his fingers diving low beneath the waistband of my shorts. "Where else has he hurt you, Gemma? I want to remove his fucking touch from your perfect little body."

Tears sprang to my eyes, and my answer was blunt. "Everywhere. He's hurt me everywhere."

Isaiah stiffened from behind me. He wanted to ask me more. I knew he did. But I didn't want to talk anymore. I just wanted this solace I had with him. I wanted to just *be*. With him.

And I think he knew that because he quickly untensed, gripping the waistband of my shorts and pulling them down my legs slowly. My core tightened, and I almost moaned. The fabric ran over my thighs, and it sent tingles up to my middle. My head tipped backward, my hair tickling the bareness of my back.

"He doesn't get to hurt you anymore." His fingers hooked into my panties, and I turned my head, locking onto his eyes. They were wild and untamed, and I wanted to stoke the fire I saw. The passion. There was an unbelievable amount of torture attached to this moment. For us to touch like this, knowing that there wasn't a future. It was almost forbidden from the beginning. With every threat from Richard, Bain, and his father. Yet, here we were, knocking them down one by one for just a little taste.

My mouth was claimed by his, and our kiss was deep. His tongue coaxed mine to life as if he were sucking my soul up my throat and down his. "Put your hands on the door above your head."

Excitement flared, and thoughts of the past were floating away like ashes from a fire. Isaiah's fingers dove further into my panties as he held me in place with his other hand, digging into my hip bone. His finger skimmed over the sensitive bundle of nerves, and my legs grew unsteady. "*Mine,*" he growled, nipping my lips again. "And I will break every one of his fingers for hurting you."

I sucked in air as he circled me, and I felt my wetness coat him. I whimpered, almost begging him to touch me in the way that I wanted, in the way that I deserved. If I could just stay here with Isaiah, in this room, for the rest of forever, I would.

"I'll protect you, Gemma. Even when you're gone."

His finger inched inside of me, and I whimpered, throwing my head back onto his shoulder. Isaiah ground into me, and the tight grip he had on me never wavered, and I loved it. I loved feeling his strong hands. I felt safe with Isaiah, even after I questioned my trust in him.

The dip in my confidence was only a reaction to my past.

I knew all along that Isaiah would never hurt me.

"That's it," Isaiah said, putting another finger inside of me. I moved my hips, basking in the curl deep in my belly. It felt so good. All of it did. His fingers. His lips on my sweaty skin. His hard length rubbing me from behind. "Feel me inside of you. Fuck my fingers and know that you deserve to be worshiped. Do what feels good for you and *only you.*"

I moaned, moving quicker. My hands started to slip from the door as I threw my head back. My legs started to get wobbly. Isaiah's grip on my hip left, and he cupped me around the waist, holding me up. "There it is, baby." His mouth was on mine, and his teeth sunk into my bottom lip. "I fucking love feeling you come apart for me. I fucking love feeling you move against me, chasing that high that you deserve over and over again. It's addicting, and I can't stop myself from wanting every single part of you."

Crashing waves hit me from the core and pulled me to the brim of insanity. I yelled out, and Isaiah's mouth came over mine as he quickly removed his fingers and shoved my panties down to the floor. I was still moving my hips, riding out my orgasm, as he spun me around and propped my leg up around his hip. He gripped my bare ass with his hand. "You are fucking beautiful, and you deserve the world," he said, pulling his pants down and pushing himself into my sensitive middle.

Stars coated my vision when he entered me, and it nearly brought me to the edge again.

"Isaiah," I gasped, wrapping my hands around his neck. His muscles were moving fluidly under my touch as he pulled back and entered me again and again. I matched his pace, basking in the way my body was humming. Blood was rushing to every part of my body, and the room was spinning. We met each other's middles, thrusting and gripping one another as if we were about to slip from the other's grasp.

Isaiah pulled away from my mouth, and his eyes bounced back and forth in between mine. "I fucking love you, Gemma. So much that I would burn the world down for you."

My eyes shut as tears pooled. Hearing those words did something to me. It opened up a gate inside my chest that I couldn't seem to close.

"Do you understand me?" he asked, thrusting into me again. I gasped at the rising ecstasy in my blood. "I love you, and I will not stop trying to make the world a better place for someone like you." I could read between the lines. Isaiah knew something about Richard, something that I didn't even want to touch.

I nodded against his chest, placing small kisses over the sweaty skin. I couldn't say anything back to him because I knew if I opened my mouth and said those three little words, I would break in half. So, instead of saying anything, I brought my lips to his, and I kissed him. I kissed him with everything I had, and he kissed me back just as passionately. We met each other with deep thrusts, and I moaned into his mouth, feeling my high come back. His fingers drove into my skin, and I bit down on his lip, feeling myself let loose around him. He pushed in a few more times as I moved my hips, and his hands suddenly left me, bringing my tingling legs back down to the ground before he pressed his hand against the door and shot something warm down the front of my belly.

He hissed in between his teeth as he gripped himself, sweat falling from his forehead and running down the side of his cheek. I watched in awe as he stroked himself as the white liquid left him. *Wow.*

"Fucking hell," he muttered, glancing up at me sharply with hooded eyes and swollen lips. He was still gripping himself, and I bit my swollen lip, not wanting to leave his room to go back into our uncertain realities. I didn't want to think about anything other than this moment right here.

Isaiah shook his head back and forth slowly as he dropped himself and crowded my space yet again. He bent down, grabbed his shirt, and slowly ran it down the front of my belly to clean me. Then, he threw it to the side, gripped my ass again, and picked me up, wrapping my legs around his body.

"Fuck tomorrow," he whispered before depositing us both on the bed until morning.

CHAPTER FOURTEEN

ISAIAH

I TRAILED HER EVERY MOVE. From the second we parted ways this morning, it felt like there was a gaping hole in my chest that just kept growing wider the longer we were apart. I wanted to follow her every move, walk her to each class as if danger was lurking behind the paintings on the walls, but the biggest danger of all was the man she had grown up with who hid behind his large, mahogany judge's bench, sending criminals away because they broke the law.

But what about him? No one was above the law, even if men like my father thought so. Judge Stallard was an abomination, and he would never fucking touch Gemma again.

"Hi." Gemma's sweet voice lingered in the empty library, and just like that, I came down off the ledge. The second we locked eyes, her cheeks flushed, and her bottom lip was tucked in between her white teeth in an adorable attempt at hiding a smile.

We hadn't talked much since last night when I stole her from her room and claimed every part of her skin, which was the only thing on my mind today. Even in the dining hall, with the chatter and clanking of the kitchen, the only thing that I could focus on was Gemma sitting at the end of the table with Sloane and Mercedes. We would catch each other's gazes, and something would pull in my chest, and I nearly pushed my chair out and sat with her.

But I didn't.

It wasn't because I didn't want to. It was more because I felt the heavy presence of fear on my shoulders. I didn't feel fear often, but it seemed the more I fell for Gemma, the more it surfaced, and it felt like my profound duty to make everything safe and rid the world of people like Judge fucking Stallard.

Everything felt off since seeing those photos of her and feeling between my fingers the iron links that were held tightly to the ceiling in the basement. Those chains had been cuffed around her delicate wrists at one point or another. *Fucking hell.* It was vital, now more than ever, that Gemma left and stayed away until his actions were brought to light and shoved down his throat.

"Hey," I finally said, smiling down at her. Tonight, we wouldn't be stuck in the library, thinking of all the things we wanted to say or do only to end up keeping silent and sharing stares. Tonight, we were going to forget about it all because I wanted normalcy with her. We didn't have much more time, and it was something I needed in order to keep myself in check. I stared at her a little while longer, the air growing heavy with everything that swam around us, but the longer I gazed, the more her cheeks flushed. "I like seeing you like this," I said, placing my hands down on the table that sepa-rated us. Her fingers were fiddling over the woven string of her journal like she was nervous.

"Like what?"

I hummed under my breath. "Flushed." I fought back a

grin when her cheeks grew even more red. "And…" My chest cracked slightly. "And happy. You look happy." Maybe even a little refreshed, too. Like breathing in the air on a spring day. I liked it. I liked her like this.

Gemma's gaze quickly fell to her lap, her fingers stilling on the string of her journal. "About last nig—"

"Nope." I straightened and gripped the edge of the chair I was standing over.

Gemma's head flew up, her bright-green eyes leery. "Isa—"

"No," I said again, this time a little more urgent. "I meant every word I said last night, Gemma." My chin dipped, and my tone grew serious. "You are addicting, and all fucking day, I've had to sit back and watch you from across the room, too afraid to touch you because—" *Shit.*

Gemma's eyes held that same curiosity that I often saw when we were in these heated conversations. "Because what? The SMC? Bain?"

I scoffed. "Fuck the SMC. They're the least of my concerns."

"So you don't care if you get in trouble anymore? You're still on probation, Isaiah. What about Jack? And your father?"

I shook my head, agitated that we were discussing anything regarding them. "The SMC has set a meeting. My uncle tells me they're taking me off probation. Not that it matters. I'm no longer following Bain when he leaves to go on his little business trips. I'm no longer feeding my father viable information." *He just didn't know that yet.*

Gemma's mouth instantly parted. "What? Why?"

"Gemma." My hands left the chair that I was gripping, and I rounded the side of the table. My feet creaked over the old floor, and it echoed throughout the library. "Let's just forget about it all for the night, yeah?"

Her hand landed in mine, and it was warm to the touch.

So warm it melted away the worry that started to creep up at the thought of my father and Bain. Not only was Richard on the forefront of my mind, but so was Bain and our upcoming talk that he had no idea was coming.

"Do you know something?" Gemma's question made me pause for a second. I wanted to squeeze my heart to make it stop beating so fast. "Last night...you—"

I cut her off by pulling her to her feet and grasping her chin tightly with my hand. "You'll be gone soon." My teeth clenched as I felt her body tense in all the wrong places. "I have everything you need. I'm just waiting on one more document."

Her perfectly arched brows crowded, and I zeroed in on her parted lips. "What do you mean? All I asked for was a new ID and some money..." She glanced away, mumbling under her breath. "Part of me doesn't even want it."

"What? Why?" Surely, she wasn't planning on staying. Not after the shit I just saw in that basement.

Her voice broke, and I felt the trembling of her chin. *Fuck*. This was exactly why we were leaving the library. I didn't want this tonight. I didn't want to watch her break and feel the world caving in on us. If anything, we needed to cave in on it. Gemma and I together could put stars in the sky. That was how it felt when we touched. It was...intense and powerful. All-consuming. Like the fucking universe swallowing everything in its path. My ribs felt like they were ready to crack open at any given second with her in my arms.

It was terrifying.

"I... It makes me feel like this thing between us was just part of a shady deal. It all started with you needing someone to cover for you and tutor you, and then I asked for something in return. It feels like I'm being paid to..."

"To what?"

She swallowed and brought her attention back to mine,

bypassing my question. "What other documents are you getting for me?"

I breathed out a loud sigh, conflicted over the fact that she just held something back. I wasn't going to push her, though. She'd been pushed enough, especially last night as I claimed parts of her body that I knew had been touched by Richard. I shifted on my feet when heat shot to my thighs. Last night was more than just hot. The way I brought her body to bliss was fueled by more than attraction and lust. *The things I said to her...*

"Isaiah?"

I cleared my throat, dropping my hand from her chin and pulling her away from the table. "I'm getting you everything you need to disappear, Gem. You'll need more than a fake ID and some money to get away from a man like Richard Stallard." Her fingers clenched down on mine, but I kept moving us toward the door. She stopped for a second and pulled her hand away from mine and went and grabbed her journal from the table. We left everything else, which were just the books that neither one of us planned to open. Once she was by my side again, I intertwined our fingers and walked to shut the lights off. "You'll have a new social security number, a birth certificate, a license—even though you really need some driving lessons..." *Maybe I should teach her how to drive before she leaves.* "A passport..." I trailed off, glancing down the hall before we stepped into it. I didn't want to say any more in case there was someone skulking behind a hidden corner. Bain's plans were still unknown to me, but I knew they had to do with Gemma, and I didn't fucking like that.

Just a few more days.

"Oh." Her whisper was a mix between shock and confusion. "Where did you get all that stuff from?"

Jacobi's face popped into my head at the thought of our phone call. *My older brother.* The person I'd hated for so long yet still held a tiny amount of admiration for. I admired the selfishness he had. If I were as selfish as him, maybe I wouldn't feel the sharp pricks of dread in my back every time I looked at Gemma. "There are people that work for my father who would do anything for money, despite their loyalty to him."

She stayed silent as we continued down the quiet hallway. Most of the faculty members were still awake, but as long as they didn't see Gemma and me actually leaving the school, they would just think we were walking back to our rooms after tutoring. Though, the SMC was hardly a thought in the back of my mind. They could expel me all they wanted. Jack was no longer a loose end for my father to use and taunt me with. In fact, I hadn't heard from my father in days. After the whole thing with Gemma, he'd checked in and wanted to know what Bain's reaction was. After I fed him some bullshit, I told him Bain would likely no longer be messing with the Covens, which was a total fucking lie. He believed it, though, which meant he trusted me, and it was always good to have your enemies' trust in your back pocket. It pushed him to look into his other business relationships that he felt Bain's father was trying to steal. It got him far away from the situation that would soon be in my grasp.

And it was no surprise that he hadn't called to inform me that Jack was no longer at home and in the care of Mary, our nanny. Jack was on vacation as far as anyone knew, and my father didn't even notice.

Fucking piece of shit.

"Not to change the subject," I said, most definitely aware that I *was* changing the subject, "but I have some ground rules for tonight."

Gemma paused, both of us tucked behind the door that led into the side entrance of St. Mary's. "Rules? What exactly are we doing? Isaiah, if the duty teacher sees us..."

I clicked my tongue, stepping back to give her a look. "I thought you liked breaking rules, Good Girl."

She scoffed, rolling her eyes playfully. Even through the shadows, I could see the pink on her cheeks. "Fine. What are we doing, and what are the rules?"

"We're having fun." I winked at her and grabbed her hips, pushing her up against the wall. "Because we deserve it."

———

"FINALLY." Shiner tipped back his flask, swallowing whatever liquor he had in there. "Where have you guys been? You have the only working lighter, and it's fucking cold."

I stepped over the crunchy leaves and pulled Gemma beside me. She was clearly confused as she ran her gaze around the small wooded area, locking onto our friends—Shiner, Brantley, Cade, Sloane, and Mercedes—as they all sat on logs.

"What is this?" she asked, whipping her adorable face over to me. She was excited. Her eyes sparkled underneath the stars, and her mouth split in two. She turned back to everyone else. "Did you all just say screw curfew or...?"

Sloane laughed, popping to her feet and running over to Gemma, taking her from me but not before scowling in my direction. I chuckled, half-annoyed that she didn't like me but half-pleased because I knew the only reason she didn't was because she knew more about me and Gemma than anyone else—or at least I suspected. Sloane was protective over Gemma, and I was okay with that.

"Girl, we used to do this all the time before..."

A twig snapped, and we all glanced at Cade. He was building the fire we were about to light, and his jaw clicked back and forth like a ticking time bomb. "Before I went and fucked everything up," he said dryly before looking over at

Sloane. "Sorry, I just knew that's what you were going to say so I might as well say it myself."

I dug into my pocket and threw the lighter to Cade who caught it with a cat-like reflex and went back to his fire-building. Ready to sit down, I tipped my head to Brantley who remained silent as he watched the girls who sat on the same log together, laughing about something.

"We used to have these small fires on the weekends when there wasn't a claiming party."

Sloane started again, ignoring Cade and his remark. "It used to just be me and Journey and maybe an occasional girl for Shiner over there."

I chuckled when he wiggled his eyebrows.

"Oh." Gemma wrapped her arms around her middle and shivered. I stood up and whipped my black jacket off before handing it to her. She graced me with a thankful smile, and I paused at the sight of it, lingering on her soft beauty.

Sloane was right. These secret bonfires were a norm for us before Journey left. Everything seemed to change after that night, and not just with Cade, but with all of us. It was when reality started to set in, and the Rebels and I saw our futures for what they were.

I knew that things would never go back to normal, and I'd accepted that, but now that I had Gemma, I felt a sense of hope that I didn't know was missing. I was hopeful that things would go my way for once so that we could have more nights like this.

More nights full of normal, harmless shit that teenagers did. Like gathering around a fire with your friends, drinking booze that was stolen from a teacher who was too stupid to lock it up in their desk, eating s'mores, laughing, dancing. All of it. It was all I wanted, and it was all Gemma deserved.

Shiner handed his flask to the girls, and Gemma wrinkled her nose after taking a sip before passing it to Mercedes. The flames came to life a second later. "So, you guys have never been caught doing this? No teachers have ever come out here looking for the fire that was burning?"

Brantley was still staring at Gemma, probably wondering the same thing I was. *How had she survived what she'd gone through at home and still managed to become this decent, kind-hearted girl who held respect for people in power?* She was the kindest student we had at this school, even if, deep down, I knew she had a fiery spirit when provoked.

Brantley eventually tore his eyes away before answering her question. "We're facing the opposite end of the teacher's quarters, and we all know Headmaster Ellison doesn't really care as long as we're being safe."

Gemma nodded, looking away from Brantley to land on me. I flicked my chin, and she slowly stood up, staying locked on me as she walked over. I placed my hands on her hips, feeling a fire zip through, and spun her around fast and plopped her down on my lap. A rush of air left her mouth as she wiggled over me, no doubt feeling my growing hardness beneath her. Nuzzling my nose into her long hair, I sighed, letting every worry melt away right along with the fire.

Time passed by quickly. We all laughed and joked around, each of us buzzed on the alcohol that Shiner had brought with him. Gemma had another sip or two, and I felt her body relax along mine and knew that she was forgetting everything that was soon approaching for us. No one other than Cade and Brantley knew that Gemma was leaving. No one knew that, by this time next week, she would be far gone, and people would be looking for her.

"So..." Shiner started, his words elongated due to the excessive drinking he'd been doing. "Mercedes..."

Everyone paused, and I held back a laugh when I saw Mercedes giving Shiner a weird look because he remained silent, appearing deep in thought. I was interested to see what would come out of his mouth.

"This is getting awkward," Sloane whispered, smashing her lips together, looking at Shiner who was apparently thinking of a sleazy line to lay on Mercedes.

He cleared his throat and leaned forward, placing his forearms on his bent knees. "I haven't really met you."

Mercedes tilted her head as Gemma turned on my lap to look at Shiner. I gripped her hips and whispered into her ear, "Are you doing that on purpose?"

"Doing what?" she whispered back, and I chuckled.

Mercedes crossed her arms over her jacket. "You've met me, Shiner. We have world history together. You literally sit right behind me."

Shiner cocked a coy grin and glanced at Cade and Brantley who were also waiting for his ridiculous line. *One-Liner-Shiner. He was famous for his lines.* "Oh, yes. Trust me, I know. You bent over two days ago to grab your pencil."

Mercedes froze, and her eyes widened a fraction, but Shiner kept chugging along. "I meant that I haven't *really* met you."

"What does that even mean?" Mercedes was becoming impatient, and Sloane was shooting him a look like she was about to throw a burning log at his face.

"I mean, like...meet, as in my dick meeting your pussy."

Mercedes' mouth dropped open, and I placed my forehead on Gemma's back and shook with quiet laughter. There it was. The famous One-Liner-Shiner in full drunken action. *I'd missed nights like these.*

"Surely that line isn't part of your famous one-liners." Mercedes rolled her eyes and scoffed. "I don't understand why girls lift their skirts for you when you say things like that! It's so crude."

Shiner threw his hands up in protest. "Okay, fine. So...you don't like dirty talk. Noted."

I couldn't help it. I let out a laugh and felt Gemma laughing too. Sloane was holding back a smile as Mercedes whipped her curly hair away from her face, fully disturbed at what Shiner had said to her. I saw that her cheeks were a little red, though, and I wondered if she secretly liked it.

"You know what I think we should do," Sloane said, swiping the flask back out of Shiner's hands and taking a gulp. "I think we should play a game."

Cade sighed. "We're not playing truth or dare."

For once, Sloane didn't say a rude remark to him. She shook her head, understanding why he'd said that. "No. Let's play hide and seek. Remember when we did that the first time we came out here?"

"Hide and seek?" Gemma sat up a little taller. "I haven't played hide and seek since I was seven." There was a hint of nostalgia lingering within her wistful words. My arms wrapped around her all on their own, and I pulled her back into my chest. Her skin felt so warm as I ran my thumb in small circles underneath her shirt. "I used to play it with my brother."

Sloane and Mercedes both snapped to attention, but my fingers didn't stop moving, even if I was surprised that she had admitted that. Gemma was so guarded and private with everyone. Even with me.

"You have a brother?" Sloane asked, completely baffled. "What?"

Gemma nodded but kept quiet. I took control of the conversation so it didn't bring us back to the heavy moments that I was destined to stay away from tonight. "Hide and seek sounds like a grand idea. Nothing like chasing you girls in the deep, dark woods to keep the night alive."

Shiner clapped his hands and winked at Mercedes, who rolled her eyes in response. "You can run, but you can't hide."

"Girls against boys?" Sloane stood up excitedly, allowing Gemma's admission to pass.

"Always," I answered, tapping Gemma on the leg. She stood up and turned around and mouthed, "*Thank you,*" at me. But she didn't need to thank me for saving her in moments that made her uncomfortable. I was always on her side.

"You up for this?" I asked, pulling her in closer and tipping her chin back. Her emeralds sparkled with excitement beneath the stars, and the shadows of the fire played across her high cheekbones, begging me to take her back to the school to be alone.

"You think you can catch me?" Her white teeth sunk into her lip, and I hurriedly swiped my thumb over it.

I gazed into her eyes, feeling myself snap in two. "I won't stop until I do."

CHAPTER FIFTEEN

GEMMA

THE FOREST WAS quiet as Sloane, Mercedes, and I descended down the hillside with the fire disappearing behind us. The bushes rustled with the wind, and for the first time, I didn't feel the inkling of panic poking from behind. I was safe. I knew I was safe. I wasn't running for my life from Richard, and I wasn't allowing myself to cave in to the past that I pushed away.

I felt it brimming the surface. I recognized it prickling the sides of my brain, but instead of pushing it away and pretending it didn't exist, I allowed myself to see it, feel it, and dismiss it. All because I knew I was safe. I was with Sloane and Mercedes, two girls that welcomed me into St. Mary's and hadn't judged me once. The two girls that had made me feel better when I was hurt over Isaiah's actions, even if they didn't know all the details. They were my friends, and they cared for me, just like I cared for them.

Isaiah was giving me something tonight, and maybe he

didn't even mean to, but he was gifting me a normalcy I so desperately craved. It was a nice pause on everything else, and I was enjoying it. I was enjoying *him*. *Us*. I was enjoying the laughter and the easy conversation without fear, regret, or dread lingering, and it made me feel strong. It was like he knew I needed this moment to heal what had been broken last week.

"Let's go this way," Sloane whispered, veering us off the worn, dirt path and into an area that was crowded with bushes and trees.

Mercedes and I followed closely behind, and once we were tucked underneath a tall pine tree, we placed our backs against the large stump and watched through the spaced out branches for the guys to finally wander through. *If* they wandered through. How they'd find us in this large forest was beyond me, but I knew eventually they'd show up.

"I cannot believe what Shiner said to me." Mercedes sighed agitatedly and pulled her knees up to her chest. "What a dick."

Sloane laughed. "He just wants in your pants."

"Maybe because there isn't anyone else to feed his ego. He has never even spoken to me in class. It's like I'm invisible to most of the guys in this school."

I peeked forward. "Did you bend down in front of him like he said? To grab your pencil?"

Her lips pursed together as she nodded. "I didn't even think about it."

"Then you're not invisible. He probably hasn't pursued you because he knows you're not like the other girls here."

Her eyes dropped. "What do you mean?"

I smiled. "You're nice, Mercedes. You're kind and pretty." I shrugged, calling it how it was. "He probably feels intimidated by a girl like you. You're not the type to pull your skirt up for a little bit of attention from a guy like him. You have depth. Anyone can see that."

Sloane nodded. "It's true. He knows you're too good for him." She paused before adding, "And you are."

I laughed. "And the same goes to you, Sloane."

She shook her head. "That's not true. I'm not nice. I think most boys are afraid of me because I don't put up with their shit. Not even the Rebels."

We all laughed and discussed how different we all were. It was true. We were all so different, yet we somehow fit together perfectly. They were both really good friends, and I knew my heart would form a tiny gap in it when I left them behind without even a note.

"I'm going to miss you two." I froze the second the words left my mouth. *Wait. Shit.*

"What?" Sloane asked, glancing over at me. Her hair was pushed behind her ear, and she gave me a skeptical look. "You mean, like, when we graduate?"

I nodded quickly, glancing away. *Maybe tonight relaxed me a little too much.* "Yeah, that's what I meant. You and Mercedes are planning on going to an Ivy League, right? Didn't you two already apply?" To be honest, I hadn't really been keeping up with everyone and their college plans. It was never an option for me, so when it was brought up, I usually shut down and detached.

Mercedes blew breath out of her mouth. "Yeah, but that does not mean we will get in."

"Sure you will," I answered. I had faith that they both had exciting new adventures waiting for them after high school. Me on the other hand... I couldn't even see past next week.

"What are your plans?" she asked me as Sloane stayed quiet, seemingly lost in her thoughts. "Art school? Didn't you say that Mrs. Fitz talked to you about putting together a portfolio for one of the schools she was connected with?"

She did, and the entire time we were talking, I felt my heart sinking to the floor.

"Yeah, we're working on it," I lied.

"That would be amazing, Gemma. You'd do so good. It's, like, all she talks about during art class. You're not even in my class, and she pulls out your work as an example nearly every day."

My cheeks heated, and pride went through me. Mrs. Fitz was constantly pushing me to do more and to create things for my portfolio. I was certain she thought that was what I was doing when she'd given me permission to use the art room any time I wanted—within normal curfew times, of course. Except, it wasn't. Not really, anyway. I didn't plan on showing anyone what I'd drawn. Ever.

"Shh," Sloane shushed us, and my thoughts scattered. Excitement bubbled in my belly at the thought of Isaiah's hands wrapping around my waist again. Last night had been on my mind the entire day, and I wanted to ask him more about what went on through his head last night as he ran his mouth and hands over parts of my body that were only ever touched once before, but he had a way of distracting me, and I did exactly as he wanted. I pushed the tough stuff away and focused only on the present moment.

And it felt good to do that. It felt good to be in the moment with him. It always had.

"Listen to them," Sloane whispered above a soft laugh as we listened to the guys arguing about which way to go.

Mercedes bent her head to ours. "We should split up, confuse the hell out of them, and then sneak up when they least expect it."

"Yes! Let's do it. Girl power, baby."

I silently laughed at Sloane, and then the three of us crept out from underneath the tree with the smell of pine flowing through my nose and into my lungs. Sloane went straight, Mercedes went to the left, and I slowly trotted to the right. I had no idea where I was going, and I really didn't want to venture off too far because, now that I was alone, I was afraid things would start surfacing that I didn't want. Although I felt lighter now than I had in weeks, there was still an edge of caution always present.

I tip-toed toward a large tree in the middle of a large opening and paused, looking up to the sky. A tiny smile stretched on my lips when I realized where I was.

I turned slowly, my hands coming down by my sides that were completely swallowed by Isaiah's large jacket. It smelled like him, and I breathed in the clean scent of his body wash and cologne. It reminded me of safety and something wildly tempting.

I knew exactly where I was in the forest.

I was in the same spot he had brought me to the night of the pep rally bonfire, when he'd told me about his little brother, Jack. It was the first time I saw Isaiah as vulnerable, and it was then that I realized he was just as human as I was.

Closing my eyes, I inhaled his scent, tipping my head up to the stars. Leaving him was going to be hard. Necessary. But hard. *So hard.* I didn't want to leave, and that hurt even worse. It wasn't supposed to be like this. I was supposed to be running from Richard and healing myself in the process from everything that I'd seen and been through, but instead of healing myself, I was leaving with an even bigger broken heart.

"You were supposed to stay with Mercedes and Sloane. It's a good thing I found you."

I shrieked, snapping my head back down as my entire body tensed.

I tipped back, glancing into Isaiah's dark eyes before

moving down to his mouth. My heart came to life, and the thoughts of a broken heart left. I knew, without a doubt, that I'd never feel this way again. There was no way something like this ever came twice. The feeling he inflicted in me when our eyes connected wasn't even a word in the dictionary. We were connected, bound by something neither he nor I could ever name. The two of us were thrown together by fate only to be pulled apart in the end by things that were out of our control.

I spun around in Isaiah's grasp and wrapped my hands around his strong neck, pushing my fingers into his hair and bringing our faces closer. He kissed the tip of my nose gently, and I shut my eyes, feeling him everywhere.

"Even when you're far away from here, I'll never stop looking for you." His lips moved over my mouth. "I will find you, Gem."

I didn't wait for him to kiss me. Instead, I kissed him. I kissed him hard, like it was the last time I'd ever kiss him. His grip on my body grew tighter as I slipped my tongue into his mouth, exploring and tasting, trying to memorize everything about this moment. I quickly pulled back and grabbed onto his hand, pulling him farther into the forest with his hooded gaze questioning me from behind.

"What are you doing?

I smirked, feeling bolder than ever. "Do you remember the last time we were in this part of the forest?"

Desire swam inside my veins, and I felt drowned by the need to feel his hands on me. Maybe it was the small amount of vodka that was making me so adventurous, or maybe it was the fact that I knew my time with him was coming to an end. *Don't think, Gemma. Just do.*

Isaiah's tongue darted out as he planted his feet, pulling me into him instead of the other way around. "I remember every moment with you."

A giddiness had me jumping up into his arms, and he quickly caught me, wrapping my legs around his middle. I felt so light in his grip, and with the way his mouth curved into a devious grin, I knew he enjoyed having me there just as much as I did.

He pushed himself into my middle, and my eyes widened. "Tell me what you want, Gemma. What's going on in that pretty little head of yours? I'd love to get in there and see everything you're thinking. You have been a mystery since day one."

His eyes bounced back and forth between mine as he continued moving through the wooded area, surely coming up to the same tree that he had me up against the first time we'd come down here. In fact, I didn't care what tree it was. He could have me anywhere.

"Do you want me to make you come again?" His hoarse whisper was like the tree bark rubbing against my skin. "Is that what you want? To feel what you felt last night?"

I thought for a moment, taking in his blunt question before answering. "Yes," I rushed out, feeling the sturdy tree behind me.

A coy smile worked itself over his face, and I bowed my back, pushing my chest against his. *Why did I get this way with him?* I was an entirely different person when he and I were alone. Like my body did the speaking for me. It craved him. His lips on mine. The way he got lost in me. The way I got lost in him. I loved it. Everything else just disappeared, and that was enticing as hell.

"Say it," he demanded, inches away from my mouth. "Say it so I can hold onto this memory and play it over and over again to get me through everything to come. Let me have this."

I needed it too.

My heart thumped hard as I gazed up at him. Things

suddenly turned dark, and the trees were swaying as my head spun. My lips tipped with a grin, and I'd never felt so bold in my entire life, but seeing Isaiah's reaction to me and knowing that he was seconds from kissing me again, I looked him in the eye and said, "Make me come, Isaiah."

CHAPTER SIXTEEN

GEMMA

THE DOORS to the library opened, and everything seemed brighter. My eyes found him immediately, and my heart fluttered. I'd waited all day for this. The entire day felt like some wicked form of foreplay for us. The fleeting, heated gazes. The subtle touches as I'd pass by in the hallway that hardly anyone would notice unless they were actively looking—like Bain. Isaiah and I decided to be cautious with each other. Even though we both knew what was coming, Isaiah wasn't all for flaunting me around, and I felt the same. Bain still skulked in the shadows, neither one of us really knowing what his plans entailed, and with his threat about Richard, I was all for being careful. Plus, I liked when Isaiah and I were alone. Our guards were down, as if we were in a safety net.

I knew why he'd used Breanna that one day. I knew why he'd tried to push me away and hurt me. He wanted me to hate him. He wanted everyone to believe that there was nothing between us. I understood, and we'd come to a silent agreement over it. Some things just didn't need to be said or explained because there were just too many uncertainties.

There had always been uncertainties in my life. For the longest time, all I saw when I looked to the future was Richard. I didn't know what the future held, but I always knew Richard would be in it, controlling me, giving me just enough to keep me asking for more. He was a heavy presence in my life from such a young age that, up until recently, I couldn't see past him. Richard Stallard, my presumed uncle, was like a thick wall placed right in front of my eyes, and if he was somehow involved with Isaiah's father and Bain, I wanted absolutely no part of it. I didn't want to tip any scales, even if I did feel that things had changed within me.

I felt more myself now than ever. I was stronger, but that didn't mean I was safe. Isaiah was right. I was smart enough to know when to leave. It didn't make me weak to run; it made me smart. And I'd much rather be smart than stay and risk my life. Because that was what I would be doing if I stayed here, even for Isaiah. I'd be risking my life, because Richard had plans for me, and he knew when to cross his T's and dot his I's.

That wasn't to say I didn't want to stay, though, or that I forgot about the original plan between Isaiah and me from time to time—like when he and I were in our own little world. I couldn't ignore the pang in my chest when I thought of leaving him. Before Isaiah became a constant in my life, I was exhilarated by the idea of a fresh new beginning. But now, I was no longer just leaving Richard when I ran away.

I was leaving Isaiah. Sloane. Mercedes. And I was leaving behind a safety that I'd never felt before and a life that I hadn't seen coming. Like last night, when I was gathered around a bonfire with them. It felt so real and normal. St. Mary's was more a home to me than Richard's house ever had been, and it hurt to think of leaving it behind, especially when I was alone and I thought of Isaiah. He made me feel worthy and like I deserved more than I was given.

"Hey, you." Isaiah sauntered up to the table, and I peeked up at him through my thick eyelashes. The second I caught his gaze, I felt the heat rush to my face, thinking about last night. *And just like that, the dread disappeared.*

"Hi," I quickly said before my smile fell as Isaiah dropped a large piece of paper onto the library table and began unrolling it. I watched as his steady hand smoothed it out and realized right away that it was a map. I was pretty sure it was the same map that was hung in the headmaster's office behind his desk. I would know. Each time I went down there for my weekly phone call with Richard, I would stare at the same place on the map so I wouldn't have to see Headmaster Ellison's wary gaze scrutinizing me.

"What's this?" I asked, pushing my journal into my lap. I'd caught Isaiah glancing at it from time to time as if he were curious of its content, but he never asked to see what was inside. *Thank God.*

"After tomorrow's lacrosse game"—he glanced away from me at the last second, and my core instantly cooled—"I will be obtaining the last document you'll need for your runaway package."

My heart sank to the floor right along with my stomach. I swallowed back the bitter taste of disappointment and nodded my head. Thick tears formed in the backs of my eyes, but I sucked them back down, knowing this was coming. "Oh." I cleared my throat as my fingers gripped onto the leather backing of my journal. "Okay, so..."

"So you'll be leaving the following day."

It only took a second for my eyes to fly to his. I opened my mouth to...protest? I wasn't sure what I was going to say, but I did know that it seemed like my entire body seized up and the room tilted. Sweat started to form on my back.

"Right. Leaving." I nodded, grasping onto the determination in his gaze, hoping it would give me the same strength he seemed to yield.

"You *have* to go the next morning, okay? After the game tomorrow, I'll come get you from your room when the halls are clear. I'll give you what you need and..." His voice trailed off, and he glanced away again. He stared behind me and looked down the aisle with his hands pressed firmly onto the table that separated us. "And then you need to leave."

Something about the way he tensed made me question him. "Why the next morning? What's so significant about the next morning?" I had a weekly phone call with Richard tomorrow night because that was when he returned home from his business trip. The headmaster had already informed me of such. I was to go to his office at 6 o'clock sharp, and I'd call Richard to give him an update on my time at St. Mary's and tell him for the millionth time that I was following the rules and being the good girl that he had *raised* me to be, and then I'd sit with Headmaster Ellison for a little while and chat like we'd started to do over the last couple of weeks. There was another small gap forming in my chest at the thought of Headmaster Ellison. I was beginning to like him. The unexplainable bond I'd felt with him from day one only seemed to grow stronger with my time here at St. Mary's. The familiarity of his presence was no longer a slight acknowledgment to me but more of a constant. He felt safe to me, too.

"Gemma." Isaiah walked over to the side of the table and bent down beside me, resting the back of his legs on his heels. His cool-blue eyes peered up at me beneath his dark lashes, and my heart hurt at the conflict I saw. "Last night, before we went to the bonfire, you asked me if I knew something."

I nodded gingerly as Isaiah's head fell down, showing me his dark head of messy hair.

"I do. And I have something planned. Something big is going to happen, and I can't do it until I know you're gone and you're safe." My throat clogged at the cracking in his voice. I didn't like seeing him like this. I didn't like seeing him worried or conflicted or hurt. I didn't like feeling the insecurity within him. My brows folded, and a tremor of fear coursed through me. Sometimes it surprised me when everything heavy was weighing on us again. It was so easy to lose sight of the mess we were in when he was in front of me. When he and I were alone, touching, looking into each other's eyes, I lost sight of the main goal: leaving for safety. I would be free for the first time in my entire life, and that seemed so scary at times, because although I would never fully feel *alone*, I actually would be. I was a twin. It was like having your soul split in two. I could feel Tobias, not physically but emotionally, and I hoped that someday he would find me. But until then, I would be alone, in a world so much bigger than I ever imagined, without anyone. I'd be navigating the world blindly, running for my life with a new name, and I was pretty sure the only thing that I would be thinking about was everything good that I'd left behind.

I felt incredibly attached to Isaiah, and I knew that all the freedom I'd feel with getting away from Richard wouldn't taste nearly as good because there was now something tying me to this school and this life.

I hated that I felt tethered to someone, and I didn't want to admit it when I was alone, but it didn't matter because my thoughts always came out on paper, and the last few times I'd lost myself to sketching, I'd found myself blending the charcoal until I got the perfect almond-shaped eyes that I was aiming for. The memories that I'd pushed away, the violence in my childhood—all of it—always came to me when I sat, mindlessly sketching. But things had shifted recently. I began drawing other things. Like *Isaiah*. And that was when I realized that I was hiding him, too.

My throat began to throb even thinking about it. So much anger and resentment was buried beneath my thick layers, and a big part of me wanted to tell Isaiah everything. He didn't know all of it. He didn't know the real reason I was running, and lately, there was hardly anything holding me back from telling him.

Except fear.

I was still afraid of Richard, and I was afraid of what he was capable of.

"Isaiah. If you're planning something for Richard...don't. The only thing I need is what you're giving me so I can disappear. It's the only way." My heart galloped in my chest, and I heard the thumping within my eardrums.

"You're still going to disappear," he whispered, reaching up and pushing a stray hair away from my face. "But when things are safe, I will come for you, Gemma. So take this"— Isaiah pulled out a black Sharpie and threw it onto the table —"and mark where you'll be, because I will come for you."

I held my breath as my head spun. "Wh-what do you mean?" I glanced back at the map and then to Isaiah again. "If you're planning on doing something to Richard, please don't." I shook my head as anxiety rattled through me. *He knew something.* "I know that Richard is connected to Bain, and the Covens, your father...whatever...but his plans for me have nothing to do with anyone but himself. Do not do anything to Richard on my behalf, Isaiah. Don't screw up your life for me."

I thought back to last night when he said he wasn't following Bain anymore or giving information to his father, and I began to feel dizzy. Richard's plans for me had nothing to do with anyone else but him. He was selfish and wanted me for himself. I had nothing to do with his business with the psychiatric hospital or the illicit gun selling. I was Richard's little angel that he wanted to keep in a box, up in that big house of his, to do with as he pleased.

"Don't put me in this! Don't do something because of me. What about Jack? What are you planning?" I was frantic and could feel myself spiraling.

"You're already in this, Gemma. I'm just the one pushing you out." Isaiah's words did nothing to soothe me. I wasn't afraid for Richard. I wasn't telling him to leave Richard alone because I wanted to protect the sick bastard. I was afraid for Isaiah. And Jack! Richard was a complex man, and he had more friends than enemies, which was a baffling thought given everything I knew about him.

I glanced at Isaiah's pleading eyes and felt like I could see all the way through him. I knew him, and I knew that he was hiding something. "Do you know why I'm running?"

Isaiah's jaw clenched, and the room grew cold. It felt like hives were eating away at my skin with each passing second, and when he looked down to my wrists, I almost pulled them back.

"I know that he has chained you up." Something dark crowded my vision, and my breathing picked up. "I know he's touched you in places that he shouldn't have." Chills coated my arms. My lip trembled, but I fought back the tears because if I broke, I was afraid of what I'd say. "I know he's cut you and has bruised your beautiful, flawless skin." Isaiah's fingers swiped over my cheek, and I shut my eyes, holding tightly onto the invisible wall to shut out everything Richard has ever done to me. "I know that you told someone that Richard abused you, and they allowed him to twist it all so no one believed you. That's how you ended up here."

"Stop," I whispered with blurred eyes.

Isaiah's hands rested on mine that were clutching my journal. "Please just mark where you're going so I can find you when it's all said and done. It's the only way I'll let you go. I won't look until I know it's safe for us both. I'll keep it safe until I can trust that no one will follow me to find you or hurt you to get to me. I'll keep it safe just like I'll keep you safe."

I shook my head. With the thoughts of Richard crowding my vision, the fear came back, and it slithered into every hopeful part of my body and turned it dark. "I can't risk it." I paused, feeling the cut right to my chest. "That's not why I'm running, Isaiah."

His fingers stilled over mine. "What do you mean?"

I took my hands from his and dug the heels of my palms into my eyes, allowing my shaky whisper to fill the empty library. "From the second I got here, my plan has never veered. *Survive*. I needed to follow the rules, keep my head down, and when I got what I needed..."

"You mean the new identity and money?"

I nodded. "The police know my name and who Richard is. He has friends in law enforcement all across the United States. It wouldn't matter if I went halfway across the country. If my name were to go through their database, it would lead to Richard, and then he'd find me again. It wouldn't matter if I told them everything. He'd just pay them off or lie and tell them that I was mentally ill like my mother—which isn't true. There is no outrunning Richard if I stay Gemma Richardson." I paused, sniffing up the emotions. "So my plan has always been the same. Get a new name and run like hell and never look back." Part of me didn't even care about the past anymore. All I wanted was out.

The library was quiet, and I kept going. I kept going because maybe if Isaiah knew everything, then he'd understand why I couldn't tell him where I was going. He'd have to accept the heartache like I was. We'd have to just deal with our fate. "I'm not running because of the pain he's caused me in the past. I'm not running because he's chained me up and hurt me. I'm running because of what he has planned for the future."

"Look at me."

I began to shake in my seat. I heard the chattering of my teeth but was too blinded by the panic crawling up my back to make it stop.

"Gemma, breathe, baby. It doesn't matter what he has planned, because he doesn't get to hurt you anymore."

My words were choppy and cut short. "It's easy for me to think that when I'm with you. I'm not looking danger in the face when you're in front of me."

"That's because I'm shielding you from it." His hands came around my face, and he pulled me onto the floor and into his lap. "Trust me when I say I'll protect you and keep you safe, Gem. *Please*. What does he have planned for the future? If you're not running from what he's already done, then what are you running from?"

Tell him. I wanted to tell him. The way his strong arms folded around me made me feel like I was in a world where Richard didn't even exist. Nothing existed except for the warm breath of Isaiah moving over the crook of my neck.

"Gemma," Isaiah's voice was distant in my head, and I was afraid that meant I was slipping into the past. "Has he raped you?"

Even my voice sounded far away. "I...I don't know. No. I don't think so. One time, after Tobias was gone...I woke up, and he was there, hovering over me, but..." Isaiah's body tensed, and the memory was surfacing. I quickly shut it down and grabbed onto Isaiah's shirt.

"God, you're shaking like a leaf. It's okay. Don't tell me anything else. It's okay." His graceful touches and warm shushes in my ear didn't stop me from plowing through the walls that were coming up in tens.

"He will," I blurted, feeling goosebumps bubble on my

arms. "He will rape me, and that's why I can't tell you where I'm going. I won't risk it, Isaiah." I pulled up and looked right into his eyes. "And he made Tobias disappear. He'll make you disappear, too, if he thinks you're a threat to me. If he thinks you'll take me from him."

The blue in Isaiah's eyes turned dark and angry. Rage was plastered all over his features when he snarled, "I *will* take you from him."

My hands began to sweat, and everything seemed to crash all at once. Tears spilled over my cheeks, and I shook my head. I saw the way that Isaiah's eyes became worried, and I felt his hand press against my heart.

"Hey, calm down. Your heart is flying through your chest. Gem, fucking look at me."

A sob escaped me, and then everything went dark.

Three months prior. September 14th. 3:53 p.m.

My backpack was light on my back as I gripped the straps with my sweaty hands. There wasn't much in there other than a few articles of clothing, my old journal, and the worn photo of me, Tobias, and Mom. Richard's office was unlocked, and I knew it was only because he'd rushed out the door when the school had called him.

I couldn't believe how careless I had been with my drawings, and I wasn't waiting around to see how my uncle would handle the accusations that came with them. I'd heard him telling the principal that I was mentally unstable. That I was making it all up. That everything in that journal was fabricated from my mentally unstable brain.

He was a good liar and an even better manipulator. I knew that now, which was exactly why I was running.

The floorboard beneath my feet creaked as I stepped over the threshold, looking for any indication or clue that caught my eye. I didn't have much time to snoop, but I didn't want to leave until I at least tried to find something that told me where he'd sent Tobias. I knew it had to be on his computer. It was the one thing he guarded above all else, and after the last time he'd caught me in here, it never left his side. He protected it more than anything.

I swallowed past my fear and rising anxiety of the clock ticking quietly in the back of my head. A bead of sweat fell over my temple as I sat on his computer chair and clicked the button, silently thanking anyone who would listen that his computer was unlocked. My heart sped through my chest so hard it was painful as I moved through folders, taking in as much information as I could. There had to be something on here. There had to be.

There were a million folders to sort through, and I wasn't sure I'd be able to get to them all. I knew my time was running out. Each second that I sat here was another second that he could pull his car into the driveway, and I'd be done for. I'd be chained up in the basement for who knew how long. I didn't know where we went from here, and I didn't want to find out. My heart stalled as I clicked through another set of folders. There was one that caught my eye.

The title was a date.

My birthday. Tobias' birthday.

December 6th.

My finger shook over the keyboard as I squeezed my eyes shut, taking a deep breath before clicking on it and reading as quickly as I could.

It could have been another case file of his, but I'd once heard someone say they didn't believe in coincidences, so I didn't either. As soon as the folder popped open, a breath of air got stuck in my throat.

There wasn't a single case file in the folder. Instead, there were tiny thumbnails of pictures.

Hundreds.

And they were all of me.

I blinked a few times as I clicked through them, tasting the bile rise up in the back of my throat.

There were some of me sleeping peacefully in bed, all within the last year or two. It was as if they were in chronological order. My hair got longer, and my breasts got fuller. My cheeks had lost their chubbiness, and the angles grew sharper. I sucked in another breath when I moved from the ones in my bed to the ones in the basement. The rush of cool blood flushed through my veins as I saw my naked form, cowering on the dirty floor with my wrists wrapped in chains. I had no idea when he'd even taken them, but by the look on my face, I wasn't conscious.

A lone tear fell over my cheek and landed on the wooden desk below the laptop, and I had the urge to take the sleek piece of technology and slam it onto the floor. I wanted to stomp on it and destroy every last picture he had of me.

I knew why he had them.

I didn't realize the signs of his obsession until after Auntie left. After Tobias whispered to me in the darkest of nights that what was happening in our home wasn't normal, I started to look at things differently.

Richard didn't care for me like he should.

Our entire upbringing was wrong. So incredibly wrong.

The lies that were fed to me, the punishments, the moral codes and rules that were nothing more than a sheer way to control me. To make me his.

The fear that was buried deep within my chest started to brew, and I was seconds from slamming the laptop shut and leaving, but there was a single file in the bottom left-hand corner of the folder that begged to be opened. The curiosity came from the irrational part of me asking for more fear, and I let it override the rational part, the one that was screaming at me to just leave. To flee.

When the folder popped open, I scanned what appeared to be a spreadsheet of some sort with several dates leading into the new year.

The first date was my and Tobias' birthday with the words: Gemma enters adulthood.

A sickening feeling coiled in my belly as I slowly stood up. The fight-or-flight instinct was going to war inside me as I continued to read the upcoming dates and their purpose.

December 7th: pull from school.

December 9th: meet with Dr. Bink and bring a photo of Emily for reference.

December 15th: first surgery - nose.

My pulse thumped and thumped as I tried to make sense of the spreadsheet. Why would I need surgery on my nose, and why was there was a note to bring a photo of my mother to a surgeon? I didn't understand. But then, small snippets of memories came crashing in, the ones I had pushed away until I no longer could. The things my uncle would whisper to me when I was being punished. The name he would call me as he ran his finger down my bare spine with a thick, raspy voice and a bulge in his pants. "Emily. You'll be my Emily. I won't let you make the decisions your mother made. I won't let you break the rules like she did. You are mine, and you'll do better."

He was turning me into his own messed-up version of my mother. A muffled cry left my lips as I continued to read the rest of his plans. The rest of the surgeries. He had individual notes with each date and appointment. He was even planning to get me colored contacts. Eye doctor: sky-blue contacts. *He wanted to take my vibrant green and change them to the shade my mother and Tobias both had.*

The flight instinct that was fighting to pull me from the computer and force me out the front door won when I'd read the last date on the spreadsheet with the title: Wedding.

That was when I slammed the computer down. That was when it all came back to me. Everything had made sense at that moment.

Richard was planning on keeping me forever.

He was planning on doing more than just touching my spine as he chained me up in the basement.

He wanted me to stop breaking rules and to fear him and his punishments so I would obey him and do what he wanted.

He wanted to turn me into my mother and then marry me.

The videos I'd found a few months ago confirmed that he and my mother were sexual with one another, that they'd had a relationship of some sort, but I remembered when things fell apart. When she wanted to leave with me and Tobias. How she didn't want him to touch her anymore. And then soon after, she was gone.

And he turned into someone else entirely.

I took off through the door and didn't look back. Reading those things was the last thing I needed to take off. Tobias would have to find me, not the other way around. He said he would come back for me, but I couldn't wait any longer.

I just couldn't.

Not if I wanted to survive.

"How long has she been out?" The voice was muffled through my hazy thoughts, and I fought to open my eyes. I wanted to open them so I could stop seeing the dark forest that came after what I'd found on the computer. I could almost feel the sting of the branches whipping at my legs as I ran toward freedom. It was like I was there, but I wasn't at the same time.

Make it stop.

"A few minutes. Off and on. She's been mumbling things. Go get my uncle. See if he can get the nurse."

I could hear footsteps pounding. *Was that real? Was that in my head?*

"Gemma, baby. Open your eyes, please."

I felt the vibration in my throat, and there was a soft touch to my face.

My lashes felt glued together, and although I felt myself coming back, my eyes didn't want to open. The vulnerable, sad, and scared girl that I truly was on the inside didn't want to see the look of pity on the faces that stood above me.

I was afraid.

Embarrassed.

Shameful.

"You're safe with me." Isaiah's whispers soothed the panic that still simmered just beneath the surface. "Tell me what you need."

The tickle on my cheeks told me that my eyes were finally opening and that Isaiah's smooth voice was the one thing that I could hold onto and focus on because I knew I was safe with him. I knew Richard wasn't about to pop out of the corner and beat me for telling someone the things that I knew, and even if he had, Isaiah would take him down. I wasn't in the basement with chains around my wrists. I was in the library with Isaiah's scent wrapped around me like a weighted blanket.

I also knew he wasn't going to tell anyone my secrets if I gave them up. He knew how important secrets were. He had some of his own.

And I trusted him.

I trusted him with my secrets. My body. My mind. Everything.

I trusted Isaiah Underwood, and although my heart felt torn to shreds, I loved him with those tiny, frayed edges.

My eyes chose that moment to spring open. My lip trembled as I locked right onto his face, and all I wanted was for him to make it disappear.

"There you are," he finally said, eyes bouncing back and forth between mine. There was a small divot in between his eyebrows, and his jaw was set to stone. "Don't do that to me, Gemma. I need you to stay with me."

My head was pressed to his chest as soon as he helped me to my feet, and his hand ran down the length of my long hair. His heart was thumping so violently in his chest that I could feel it against my cheek, and I only wrapped my arms around his waist tighter.

"I got a hold of the headmaster. He said he's coming."

Isaiah's grip on me never loosened. "Tell him never mind. I have it handled."

Cade's voice was closer now. "Shiner, you got that?"

"Yeah, I'll let him know."

Silence filled the large library, and although I wanted to know when Cade and Shiner had gotten there, I didn't speak. I didn't want to. All I wanted was to stay in Isaiah's arms and pretend the last ten—or however long it was—minutes never happened. I wanted to go back into my bubble of keeping my secrets silent so I didn't have to face them.

"She shouldn't be alone tonight. I'll stay with Brantley again."

Isaiah's hand ran down my hair once more before his head lifted from the top of mine. He whispered his next set of words, but I heard him clear as day. "I don't want to let her go, Cade. How did you do it with Journey?"

Cade's answer was distant as his footsteps faded. "I had no other choice."

I think Isaiah knew right then that neither did he.

CHAPTER SEVENTEEN

ISAIAH

GEMMA FELT fragile in my arms, but I knew she was anything but. The images that were forever embedded into my memory of her chained and hurt told me just how strong she actually was. She was braver than most people I knew.

I could see now why she always clammed up when Richard was brought up. The thought of him took her away from me. It took her to a place that her mind couldn't even fathom, so she shut down. That was trauma. I'd seen it before, and I had to say, it cut much deeper when it was happening to someone you cared about.

"Here's some water." Cade walked further into our room, holding a bottle of water he must have snagged from the mini-fridge and handed it to Gemma. Her hand shook when she reached out and grabbed it, opening the top and taking a small sip.

"Thank you."

Cade glanced at me, and I could see the troubled look on his face. He knew what she'd been through. He saw the photos, and although he couldn't get into Richard's office the other night, we'd seen enough to know that he would never get close to her again.

Cade was worried about me, too. I could see it. I was spooked when she'd gone limp. Absolute terror flew through my body when her small frame slipped in my grip. I'd called Cade, and he and Shiner rushed to the library in the dead of night with Brantley not far behind.

Looking over at Cade's bed, I saw that the covers were tossed onto the floor. He must have been sleeping when I'd called, and that was likely because of how hard we'd practiced earlier. We had a big game tomorrow, and Coach made us redo our weakest plays over and over again until we got them right—as if lacrosse was really that big of a fucking deal.

I stared as Cade ran a hand through his messy hair before giving me a subtle nod while pushing his phone back in his pocket. "I'm going to sleep in Brantley's room." There was a quick notch in the way he slanted his head to my phone that sat on the table between our beds.

Gemma finally raised her head. "You don't have to do that, Cade. I don't want to kick you out of your room."

"You're staying in here," I said, swiping my phone off the table as I stood up. I quickly read Cade's text as he assured Gemma that he was fine with sleeping in Brantley's room.

CADE: Collins texted. The last document is ready. He'll slip it onto the bus during the game. He was inquiring about payment.

MY STOMACH WAS tense as I put my phone back down onto the table. The question was on the tip of my tongue, and my fingers twitched to let out some pent-up aggression. I knew I had to let her go. I was a strong enough man to push her out the door when I knew danger was soon approaching. But there was something that she was hiding. I was missing a piece of information, and although I wanted nothing more than to just slip under my covers and hold her against me all night long, I couldn't. Not even knowing how desperately she needed my stability instead of the raging monster inside. It was clawing to get out from the dark instinct that was driven into me at such a young age, threatening to make someone bleed—someone being Richard Stallard—but we were running out of time, and I needed to know all there was to know so I could handle it appropriately.

"Isaiah?" Gemma's soft voice brought me back down as I stared at her from across the room. *When did I get over here?*

Cade was almost through the door when he paused and turned back to look at me. Our eyes met, and although his face remained expressionless, I knew he saw the anger stemming from my shaky hands. He knew me better than most, and he would stay if I needed him, but I shook my head, letting him know I was fine. Gemma was my main priority. As soon as the door slammed shut, I glanced over, and she was sitting perfectly still on my bed. Her eyes darted away almost the second I caught her, and a sense of awareness hit me. Her trauma had come back in crashing waves earlier, and those waves were still hitting her.

I knew how that felt.

I slowly crept over to her, and her chin dropped down so low that I couldn't even see her face. I hated that she wouldn't look at me. My knee hit the floor as I bent down in front of her, realizing that I would never bend down for anyone *but* her. My hand came up next and rested on her chin as I felt a single tear drop onto my skin. A stab of pain hit me in the chest, and I didn't even want to speak. I shut my eyes briefly and dropped my hand, resting both of them on the sides of her thighs. My head came down and landed on her knees.

"I know you don't want to tell me," I started, hating how weak and desperate I sounded. Gemma needed me to be strong, but I was slipping, and she was the only one I'd ever slip in front of. She was the only person I'd ever let see through my vulnerabilities, because she recognized my fear. "But I need to know everything." Raising my head, we locked eyes briefly, and I saw the way her mind was moving. "I will tell you what I have planned, if you really want me to, but it won't matter. You will be far away, and I promise you I will not let you come close to this. You don't need anything else fucked-up in that perfect little head of yours."

Her lip trembled as she stared at Cade's bed behind my shoulder. "Perfect little head? It's messed up in my head." A sarcastic laugh huffed from her mouth, and my lip twitched.

"It's messed up in mine, too." I paused. "The only time it's bearable is when I'm with you."

The teeniest, simplest smile formed on her lips, and my entire chest grew warm. *There she was.*

I grabbed onto her chin again, and I swiped my finger over her bottom lip. "Seeing you smile is my favorite thing. You need to do it more often. Promise me you'll smile more when you're gone."

Her head nodded, and the smile vanished along with the warmth I'd felt down to my soul. Silence filled my room, and the only thing I could focus on was the way Gemma's hands were clutching onto my blankets.

"Gem?"

Her glossy, green eyes struck me so quickly it was like a cut to my skin. A faint swallow worked itself down her throat, and my ears began to ring. "He's planning on marrying me."

I blinked once. Then twice. I slowly took my hand from her chin so I didn't accidentally squeeze it tight with the rage engulfing me. *Did I hear her right?* I slowly stood up and placed my hands on my hips, prepared to make her repeat herself, but she pulled her knees up and wrapped her arms around them, continuing.

"He and my mom were in some type of relationship or something. She didn't want him anymore. I remember. She told him no all the time. She cried a lot, and that night..." Gemma glanced up to me as tears brimmed the surface. "That night, when he took her to the psychiatric hospital, the night your dad was there, he acted as if she was mentally ill and unstable, but it was only because she wasn't doing what he wanted of her. She wanted to leave after..." She paused, thinking. "After the court let her go. I'm not sure what that meant. I'm assuming something with the group home Richard's mother ran, but he lied. He lied and said she was sick, but she wasn't, and it was all because she didn't want to be his wife." Gemma sniffled, and my back stiffened at her words. "He plans to make me a replica of her. I saw it all on his computer the first time I ran away. He plans to pull me from school the day after my birthday, and he has surgeries planned." Hands of anger were slowly wrapping around my neck, choking me. "He is going to make me his bride because he thinks, after all the years of abuse and brainwashing, that I'll just comply. That I'll marry him and follow his sick rules and...and..."

"That will not happen." My pulse beat violently against my skin as I pushed Gemma further onto the bed and scooped her up in my arms. She shook as she sobbed, and I felt my heart thud to the fucking ground. It was painful to see her like this, to feel her fear like it was my own. To know all that she'd been hiding and fearing since the moment she set foot in this fucking school. *Jesus Christ.* "Do you trust me, Gem?" Her head nodded quickly as her tiny hands wrapped around my body. I pressed her head hard into my chest, my hand nearly covering her entire face, and whispered, "Trust me when I say he will never *ever* touch you again. I said I would burn the world down for you, and I meant it."

Richard Stallard would be the next to burn, right after Carlisle Underwood.

———

MY PHONE VIBRATED a few times in the early morning hours before the sun had even risen. Cade's bed was empty, his uniform still hanging over the back of his computer chair, so I knew we hadn't overslept.

Gemma's right leg was hooked over mine as her head rested on my chest. The golden-brown strands of her hair covered half her face as I stared down at her partially hidden cheek. Lungfuls of air escaped me as I slowly turned away, grabbing my phone to see who had texted.

UNCLE TATE: Meeting with SMC is in twenty minutes. Tell me you're awake and you're coming. Let's not give them a reason to not revoke your probation.

ME: I'm up.

UNCLE TATE: Good. Tell Gemma that I wrote her a note to take classes off today. Is she feeling better? Did she have any more fainting spells?

ME: She's okay. She's asleep right now. I'll explain later.

. . .

I SLOWLY SLID out of bed and couldn't even fathom looking down at her angelic state all tangled up in my covers, but I did anyway. I stared at her the entire time I got dressed. I watched as she mumbled in her sleep, pulling the blankets up to her chin and snuggling into my pillow. I traced the red rings around her wrists and almost bent down to kiss the raised skin, but I kissed her forehead instead.

It was a sweet action. Something I'd never expected of myself, let alone falling in love with someone. But here we were. I was twisted and hooked and willing to change my entire future for her. I was nearly ready to give in to losing a small piece of my humanity.

All for her.

And it was worth it.

"Isaiah?" Gemma's sleepy voice had me pausing at the door with my back to her.

I quietly turned around and began knotting my tie so that the SMC wouldn't roll their eyes when I sat down for the meeting—as if I cared at this point. "Yeah, it's just me. I'm going to my meeting with the SMC."

Her eyes fluttered open, and she pulled down the covers just a little, showing off the tops of her breasts. I tore my eyes away, wanting to savor her body once again. "Oh. I better get up and get ready for classes. I hope Sloane isn't worried about me. I meant to have you text her before we...slept."

I hid a smile at the pink on her cheeks. "Cade let her know that you were staying with me, and my uncle wrote a note for you to skip classes today." I walked over the short distance to her and sat on the edge of my bed, knowing that I was basically eating up borrowed time.

"Oh." Gemma's cheeks burned a bright red as she looked away.

"Stay here for the rest of the day. There's food and water in the mini-fridge. I'll come back before we leave for the game."

Or maybe I'll just come during lunch. A grin started to creep onto my face, but Gemma's question wiped it right off.

"Does he know?"

My head slanted. "Does he know what?"

She gulped, fiddling with the blanket with her dainty fingers. "Does Headmaster Ellison know I'm...leaving?"

"No." I clenched my jaw tightly. I'd fill him in after it was all said and done. He would interfere, and I couldn't have that.

I watched the relief settle onto her face. I smiled at her and ran my thumb down the side of her cheek. She peered up at me shyly, and I couldn't help but bend down to kiss her again.

Our lips connected, and a rushed noise left her as my hands caged her head on my bed. *How will I survive without her?*

I hastily pulled away and stood up. The small indent in between her eyebrows had me considering not even going to the meeting, but instead of staying, I gave her my best smirk and lowered my voice. "I changed my mind. I'll be back during lunch."

"Lunch?" she asked.

"Yeah," I said, walking backward to the door. "I'll come back here to eat."

She smiled innocently, which quickly fell when I said, "*You.* I'll come back here to eat...you." Then, I winked and walked out the door and down the hall with denial stabbing me in the back.

We had only hours left—if that. And denial was the only way I was going to get through it.

CHAPTER EIGHTEEN

GEMMA

I WAS LEAVING in less than twenty-four hours, yet all I could do was pace my room from the second Isaiah went back to his classes after lunch. I was filled with nerves, and dread, and a whole bunch of other things that I couldn't pinpoint.

Should I pack?

Should I only pack the necessities?

Should I make it seem like I went missing instead of running away?

I made a mental note to go to the art room in a little bit, maybe right before I went down to the headmaster's office for my weekly phone call with Richard, to grab some of the drawings that I'd stuffed in the supply closet. If anyone found those, they'd know for sure that I ran away, and they might not stop looking.

The phone that Isaiah had given me had pinged on my bedside table, and I rushed over to it, seeing that Sloane had texted me.

I asked her to have a full-on girls' night with Mercedes

before Isaiah got back from his away game later, and she gladly accepted, wanting full details on what was *truly* going on with Isaiah and me—especially after I had stayed in his room last night. She, along with Mercedes and the Rebels, knew that Isaiah and I were *more*, but she still wanted the dirty details, and I was fine giving some of those details up.

SLOANE: I'm going to the dining hall and bribing the staff to make us something special for girls' night. I passed Isaiah in the hall. He said he was coming to say bye to you in a few when they got the bus all loaded up.

I SMILED, relishing in the tiny moment of happiness before reality came rushing back in.

I was leaving.

I was really leaving. Tomorrow. My throat began to close at the thought, and I realized just how badly I didn't want to go.

"Why couldn't my life be different?" I said aloud, plopping onto my bed. I tried to look into the future, knowing that, no matter what, I would be safe because I would be far away from Richard, but the fear was still there. There were questions without answers being thrown around my head. Like, what if Tobias came back? What if Richard learned of my relationship with Isaiah? What did Bain really have planned? What if Richard hurt Isaiah? Isaiah never did tell me what he had planned, but I knew not to ask again. The only thing it would do was make me stay so I could somehow try to protect him, and I was smarter than that. I had to trust Isaiah, and I did. I really did.

I swiped at my cheeks and nodded sternly to myself. *I trusted him...and I loved him.* Something warm crept down my limbs at the thought of those three little words, and I knew, tonight, I would tell him. I had to tell him because I wasn't sure when I'd get my chance again, and he needed to hear me say it. I'd shown him. I'd given him my everything, so he had to know. But Isaiah Underwood deserved to hear me say it.

I loved him.

And he deserved my love.

Every bit of it.

The knock on my door startled me. My hand flew to my chest, and I glanced in the mirror to make sure my face was clear of tears. We had one day left before things became very, very real, and I was going to make every moment count.

A smile brushed against my lips as my hand landed on the iron knob. The door opened, and I smiled wide only to crash and burn a second later.

Fear sliced at my throat. My tongue was too heavy to move. The blood drained from my entire body and landed right on top of a set of shiny black shoes.

No.

No, no, no.

My lips parted as a strangled gasp left my mouth. Richard stepped into the room as quickly as his strong grip pinched the front of my throat. My natural reaction was to become submissive and cower, but something inside of me had switched the second I came face to face with him. Strength. Determination. Rage.

The sturdy walls of St. Mary's Boarding School that felt so protective were like an invisible shield coming down over my body. I wouldn't submit to him. *Absolutely not*. Submitting to him again was about as dismissive as allowing him to marry me. *Wasn't happening.*

I was angry and so damn close to freedom that I wasn't going to start over now.

This ended here, and it ended now.

"Let me go," I choked through a half-closed throat, trying to jerk out of his grip. Richard pushed me up against my desk, the wood cutting into my back as my journal fell and plopped to the tile floor. The leather binding unraveled just enough to pop open to the last drawing that I'd sketched.

Isaiah.

My breath seized as I tried whirling around in his threatening grip, trying to run as far away as I could because I wouldn't give in this time. I wouldn't go back to that dark basement to play make-believe with him. I knew there would be no more chances for me. He would never let me out of his sight now. I could no longer fool him. He gave me a second chance because he was forced to, and I ran with it.

I turned eighteen in just a few weeks, and I knew that was the end goal.

Legally, I would be an adult, and he would make me his. There was no way around it. He'd already had the marriage certificate drawn up and tucked away so nicely into its own section of the *Gemma* file on his computer. The signatures would be there. Judge Stallard had too many connections with too many important people. No matter what shade of crazy he was.

The deep-brown color of his eyes looked black as he glared down into my face, squeezing my neck so tightly I had no other choice but to claw at his skin.

"I hear you've been a bad, bad girl, Gemma." His hand constricted tighter, and black started to creep into my vision. *No!* I wanted to sob.

How did he get into the school and into the girls' hallway? Did the headmaster lead him to my room? Did I misjudge Headmaster Ellison's good character? How stupid could I have been? To trust him? To trust anyone?

Isaiah. He was coming.

His face flashed before my vision, and a deep instinctual

moment came over me where I thought, for just one fleeting second, that I could get out of Richard's grip by raising my leg and kicking him. But he was too fast. He saw what I was about to do before I even had a chance. His other hand grabbed onto my thigh, and it felt like he'd broken it in half when he slammed my leg back down to the floor. The grip around my neck lessened just a smidge, and I struggled to get away, but instead of letting me get far, he pulled me back and into the bathroom where I fell to the floor, hitting my head off the sink on my way down.

The throbbing came instantly, and something warm ran down the side of my cheek. *Shit*.

"You're just like your fucking whore of a mother," he snarled, pulling me up by the back of my hair. I screamed out in pain, feeling like every last strand had been pulled out. "I thought I could trust you. I thought I had broken you after all these years, molded you into the woman I wanted." His nose ran down the curve of my jaw, and I almost threw up from the recognition of his Old Spice cologne. "At the very least, I thought I could trust Headmaster Ellison, but I was wrong."

I whimpered, wishing like hell that Isaiah would break down the door and find me. Was he coming? If I knew anything about Richard, it was that he could survey an area well, and he never went anywhere without knowing all the ins and outs. He always covered his bases. That was, until his mother had her unexpected stroke, shutting down the group home, but nine times out of ten, he was prepared.

Judge Stallard was fast on his feet, and he didn't make the same mistake twice.

"I thought I told you that you were mine, Gemma."

My vision was growing blurry, but I fought like hell to stay awake and alert. I dug my toes into the bottoms of my shoes as he pulled my head back even further to run his hot breath over the side of my neck. The same side that held a faint bruise from Isaiah's deep sucking from last night. Just as the thought came in, Richard's teeth sunk into that exact spot, and a guttural scream left me, feeling the sharp sting of a bite.

"I told you I would teach you how a man treats a woman. How your body and mind could escape into pleasure by *my* hands. Not some fucked-up little teen boy who has no business putting his dick inside your little cunt." The hand in my hair pulled tightly again, and I cried out. The other hand went in between my legs, and he grabbed me there, stunning me for a quick second before I heard my name being called from my room.

Sloane.

Panic flew through my veins at the thought of him hurting her. Because he would. Richard was in a bad spot. There was blood on both of us. There was even blood on the floor. There would be no talking himself out of this.

Leave, Sloane. Just leave. Please leave. Run.

"Gemmaaaa!" she sang. "Where are you? I got Betty to make us s'mores for tonight! She said we can come get them here in a few. Oh, and I want full details, by the way. Did Isaiah stop by yet?"

My uncle pulled my hair again as he dragged me to the bathroom door, kicking it wide open and startling Sloane. Her eyes flicked from him to me, and then came the horror. Richard gave her no room to speak or even run. He was over to her within seconds, holding me by his side. I was too stunned to do anything. Too confused by the black gun he had whipped out of his pants at some point, directing it right at her face.

"No!" I yelled, pulling away just enough to be pulled back into him again. "Don't! Don't hurt her!"

Sloane's hands went up slowly as she took a small step

back, leaning onto her desk with the twinkle lights hanging just above her head. Her gaze drifted to mine, and something passed between us just before Richard snarled in her direction. "Did you know that she was fucking the Huntsman's son? Did you encourage it?"

Confusion flashed along her features, and I quickly answered, "She didn't know! She warned me against him." *He knows. He knows who Isaiah is and what we've been doing.* I suddenly didn't want Isaiah to come find me. Richard had a gun, and he was crazy enough to shoot Isaiah on the spot.

Richard didn't give Sloane a chance to answer him. Instead, he raised the gun up high and slammed it onto her forehead, making her crumble at our feet.

A muffled cry left me, and I pushed and scratched to get out of his grip, but he was strong. Even with all the fight I had in me, he was too fucking strong.

What was I going to do? *Think, Gemma! Survive.*

"I'll never be yours!" I screamed, throat raspy from the tears and pain. "Never. I will never be yours, just like my mother was never yours."

Richard laughed, letting go of me quickly. I fell to the floor and scooted all the way back to my bed, scrambling to get to my feet. I wasn't going to pretend that I wasn't intimidated. Fear was bubbling up in my core, threatening me as it climbed up my throat, because I was looking into the eyes of a man who'd hurt me. Who had convinced me that he cared for me and that the way he treated me was normal. That my punishments were just what *parents* had to do to make good citizens. But his punishments were set in place to break me. To make me crave his approval. He tried to manipulate me, and when Tobias caught on to his lewd behavior, Richard had gotten rid of him. Just like he'd gotten rid of my mother.

The back of my hand wiped over my face as I smeared away the blood dribbling down my cheek. My uncle squared his shoulders, still holding the gun in his hand, as a pitifully sad smile curved over his lips as he watched me climb to my feet through the swaying of the room. "Oh, baby girl. You have no idea what I have planned for you. You'll be begging for me by the end."

I shook my head, tears and blood streaking over my cheeks and hands as I mentally pushed back on my fear. "I know what you have planned for me, *Uncle*. And you can't make me a replica of her. I will never be her. I will never be what you want. I won't be your good girl, you sick fucking bastard." My attention shot to the door behind me, and deep down, I knew there was no way out. But I was going to try anyway. As soon as he threw his head back and laughed at my insult, I darted forward, but one smack to the head and I was on my back, drifting in and out of consciousness.

Survive, Gemma. Just survive.

CHAPTER NINETEEN

ISAIAH

MY CHEST FELT TIGHT, like a rubber band was wrapped around my torso, and it just kept getting tighter as the seconds passed. If I didn't have to meet up with Collins in the next town over during my game to get the last document for Gemma, I wouldn't have been going. Lacrosse was only a way to pass the time at this school. A way to blend in and shield myself from prying eyes like Bain. Now, it didn't matter. There were much bigger things going on than beating some lacrosse team full of punks who didn't even know how to hold their own dick.

"Are you good?" Brantley asked, bringing his head down when we both shoved our lacrosse gear into the back of the bus.

My abs flexed with the twisting of my stomach. "Something feels wrong," I admitted, resting my arm along the bus door as other players threw their bags on top of ours.

"That's just tomorrow creeping up on you. Things are about to change. It's heightening your stress."

I shook my head, pushing off from the bus. It wasn't heightening my stress. It was heightening my senses. "I'm going to go say goodbye to Gem. Something feels off. I'll be right ba—"

My words were cut off when I saw Shiner jogging down the sidewalk without his bag. He was lasered onto me, and his face was flush with sweat. Brantley and I both froze, seeing that Shiner's features were pulled a little too tight to be normal.

"What's wrong?" I snapped, meeting him halfway.

He was out of breath but forced the word out anyway. "Bain."

My heart began to slip. "What about him?" I snarled, looking around the school grounds, waiting to see his smug fucking face. All he had to do was wait another day, and he'd have what he wanted.

"I passed him going to my room to get my shit. He was coming out of the girls' hallway. He looked me dead in the eye and said, *Ask Isaiah where Gemma is.*"

My feet hit the sidewalk, and I took off running. My heart, lungs, and soul all seemed to stay behind. I felt nothing but panic and rage slithering through my veins as I hopped over the curb and flew to the side entrance. My peers were a blur of maroon as I ran past them, not stopping once until I got to the girls' hall. I paused, silencing the thumping in my ears as I sliced my eyes down the quiet corridor. *Where was everyone?*

It wasn't a good sign. I knew it wasn't. There wasn't a single girl loitering. Their doors weren't opening or closing.

There was no one in sight.

My pulse danced behind my skin in angry booms. I prowled down the hall and stopped outside of the linen closet. The same linen closet that Gemma and I had been in when we first made our deal. I sucked in a heavy breath, swung the door open, walked over to the shelf tucked away in the very back, and reached underneath, unhooking the Glock 19 and pushing it into the back of my lacrosse shorts.

Maybe I was being impulsive, but there was something intuitive about my mechanical thoughts. Too many years of growing up, walking into situations with my father, unprepared. And maybe I knew, deep down, that something was seriously fucking wrong.

I felt it in my bones.

I had felt it in my bones last night when I had Gemma in my arms.

Something didn't feel right.

I felt eerily calm with her tucked away in my bed, and I should have known that something was about to go wrong.

Shit. Shit. Shit.

Leveling my breathing, I exited the supply closet and continued down the hall. I knew my heart was beating a mile a minute, but the only thing I focused on was the single door that was half opened.

"Gemma?" I shouted, pushing my hand on the tall slab of wood. The chain echoed off the side as the door slowly slid open, revealing nothing but her and Sloane's empty room. Gemma's bed was untouched. The phone I'd given her was on her bed. "Gemma!" I shouted again, knowing she wasn't in here. *Fucking shit.*

"Isaiah?" My uncle's voice sounded far away, but within a second, I saw him rushing into Gemma's room with a red face and rising chest. "What's going on? Shiner ran into my office and said something was going on. What the fuck is going on?" He spun around Gemma's room and looked for anything out of the ordinary, just like I was doing. But there was nothing. Everything was in place. The only thing that caught my eye was that Gemma's desk chair was pushed in a little too far at her desk. I bent down and noticed that the two front legs were sticking up from the floor, and that was when I saw her journal.

Sliding it out from underneath, I quickly closed it and held it tightly within my grasp. Cade showed up next as my uncle was walking around the room. The bathroom door was closed, and he was seconds from knocking when Cade said, "She isn't anywhere. I can't find her or Sloane. Mercedes has no idea where she is, and it seems that all the girls had been sent to various places in the school. Mary's Murmurs had some announcement for the girls to meet in the library about some stupid Sadie Hawkins dance that they were planning."

"She was fucking taken!" I yelled, gripping the top of my hair. "Get Bain. Right fucking now."

Cade gripped me by the shoulders, and I was too busy trying to control my breathing to shove him away. "Do you think she might have left early? Maybe Bain tipped her off. Threatened her for some reason? Maybe he forced her to go. Blackmailed her or something."

"What are you two talking about?" My uncle's shout went through one ear and out the other. I shoved Cade's hands off my shoulders and stomped over to the bathroom, knowing that Gemma wasn't in there because she hadn't answered me. I was still going to check, though.

"She didn't fucking leave. I hadn't even given her the documents. She knew that tonight was our last night. She would have told me if Bain had said something."

"What documents?" Uncle Tate threw his hands up. "And leaving? Isaiah, I told you to leave Gemma up to me!"

I got in his face the second I saw red. "Leave her up to you? You don't even know half of it, Uncle!"

Fuck. Was there oxygen in here? Why couldn't I fucking breathe?

"Goddammit! Someone get Bain!"

I shoved the bathroom door open, ready to walk over to

the mirror to slam my fist in it. I didn't even want to see the horror on my face that I knew was there. Reality was sinking in, and everything that I had meticulously planned had just vanished into thin air, like Gemma.

If he had her...

I stopped immediately the second my foot stepped inside the bathroom. My eyes darted to the sink first, and my stomach shrunk. Bright-red blood lined the side of it, and there were drips on the white tiled floor.

"Isaiah." A small voice caught my attention, and my head snapped to the left as my uncle rushed in behind me. He immediately grabbed onto Sloane who was lying in the bathtub half hidden behind the shower curtain.

"Shit!" I yelled, diving down to my knees to look into her eyes. She blinked several times, and I had the urge to shake her tiny shoulders to get her to speak, but fuck, she was bleeding. It was selfish, but a part of me hoped that it was her blood on the sink and not Gemma's. At least Sloane was alive.

Uncle Tate brushed Sloane's matted hair away from her eyes as he bent down and placed her on the floor in between us. "Sloane. Are you okay? What happened?"

Sloane looked from my uncle and then over to me. Her shaky hands gripped onto my forearms, and she cried, "He took her, Isaiah. He...took her."

"Richard? Her uncle?" I asked, placing my hand over hers. Fuck, she was shaking just as badly as Gemma was last night in the library. Shiner's voice carried from the room, and I heard the faint worried tone from Mrs. Fitz, too. None of that mattered, though. It wasn't Gemma's voice that I'd heard, and it was the only one I cared about.

She was gone.

Sloane nodded slowly before wincing. "I think so..."

"What did he look like?" A hopeful part of me hoped it

wasn't Richard that took her, but that would only mean it was one other person. *My father.*

"He was tall…" She winced again. "It was her uncle. I know it. He was saying stuff… I think he's the one that put the marks on her wrists, Isaiah. It had to be. She was so scared."

My chest caved, and my entire being shook. I wouldn't have been surprised if the walls of St. Mary's trembled along with it.

"What marks?"

I met my uncle's eye, and the same determination that I often saw in the mirror was there, and it was prominent.

Sloane pulled us back with her next words. "He asked if I knew she was fucking the Huntsman's son and if I encouraged it. Gemma said that I didn't know. She was trying to pull him away from me." Another tear slid down Sloane's face, and I sat back on my ass, sick to my stomach. "Then he hit me with a gun, and he must have dragged me in here."

"Jesus fucking Christ." Uncle Tate climbed to his feet and began pacing the small bathroom. He opened up the door, and Shiner, Cade, and Mrs. Fitz were all standing there. I could feel their eyes on us, but all I could do was stare at the sink with blood on it. Everything felt out of control.

Everything.

I couldn't get a grasp on it.

"Isaiah," Sloane started, but both of our heads turned at the sound of my uncle's phone ringing. I briefly glanced at Mrs. Fitz. Her plump, rosy cheeks were ghastly white, and I probably looked the same. I slowly stood up and bent over to pick Sloane up. I bypassed everyone, unable to meet anyone's gaze, and sat her down onto her bed.

"Headmaster Ellison, you have to see these. Something is very, very wrong."

As soon as I left Sloane on her bed, Cade walked over and

stood beside her. Our gazes collided, and we both knew that shit was about to turn bad real fucking fast.

"Just a minute, Mrs. Fitz. It's Beth."

"Speaker," I demanded. Beth was my uncle's assistant who knew a lot about the students at this school. She was quiet and often in the shadows, but it was always the quiet ones who knew the most.

"Beth?" my uncle rushed out. I walked closer as he pulled the phone from his ear and put it on speaker. Shiner shut the door because the girls' hall was becoming busier as they came back from their *meeting*. I was certain it was all a big ploy to begin with.

Staring a hole into my uncle's phone, my pulse had begun racing again, and my fingers twitched. *Where the hell was she?* Back in the basement? *Fuck, this was all my fault.* Bain. It had to have been Bain. He must have told Richard. *The fucking photos.* But why?

My uncle's voice came crashing back in. "You didn't see anyone walk in? No other adults other than faculty? Did you see Gemma leave?"

I could tell Beth was leery. "No...nothing suspicious has caught my eye. I didn't even hear the door open. I was calling to let you know the mail came. The results are back."

My uncle's hand tensed on the phone, and my eyes climbed up to his. He was hesitant but must have thought better of putting the phone back to his ear, because he said, "Read them. Right now."

Beth paused. "Are you sure...? I was just going to leave it on your desk. I haven't opened it."

"Opened what?" I asked, noting the way his chest rose a little faster. "Uncle Tate, does this have something to do with Gemma?"

"Open them, Beth. Read them."

The shuffling of a paper came over the speaker, and my

uncle spoke with authority as he looked at each of us. "Not a word to anyone."

Beth's voice had us all looking down to the phone again, and I tensed, fearing nearly anything that could come out of her mouth. *Results?*

Her breath was loud on the other end, and I walked a little closer to my uncle. "Oh, wow. It's...it's confirmed, Tate. Gemma Richardson is your daughter."

CHAPTER TWENTY

ISAIAH

My mouth clamped shut with horror.

Everything slowed.

The phone fell to the floor, and it felt like hours had passed before I heard the crashing of it hit the ground.

Gemma Richardson is your daughter.

Gemma Richardson is your daughter.

Gemma Richardson is your daughter.

I watched in absolute confusion as my uncle's face morphed from shock into anguish. His clenched fist came up to his mouth.

Gemma Richardson is your daughter.

"No," I said.

Sick. I was going to be sick. I shook my head. "No. No. No. She...she can't be your fucking daughter. The test is wrong." I pointed my finger in his face. "If you suspected she was your daughter..." My hand shook as I felt the blood seep from my fingers. "No. That means..." *Have I been fucking my cousin?* That couldn't be true.

"Isaiah." Uncle Tate's hands came down on my shoulders, and I just stood there in unbelievable shock.

"Have I been fucking my cousin?!" I roared, whipping his hands off my body. *Jesus Christ.* The connection. Was it because we were fucking related? Why was this happening? Why did this feel like the walls were caving in? Why did I feel my heart had stopped beating but I was somehow still alive through it all? "There's no fucking way, Uncle Tate. Are you fucking telling me that I am in love with my cousin?"

"Isaiah." Cade's face came in front of mine as the room flipped on its side. "Calm down right fucking now! Open your ears, and listen to what he's saying!"

I reared back, ready to punch him so I could attack my uncle. How could he have kept this to himself? "My ears are fucking open! She's his daughter, Cade!"

I shook my head, taking a step back until I reached the far wall, and I pushed myself up against it. My uncle rushed over to me and pushed his forearm to my throat so I was forced to look at him. "Goddammnit, get a grip! She isn't your cousin, Isaiah!"

"What?" I yelled, gasping through uneven breaths. His forearm laid tightly on my throat as his green eyes drove into mine. *They even had the same color eyes!* Exact fucking shade of green.

"She isn't your cousin, Isaiah. You are not related."

"What the hell are you talking about? I just heard Beth!" My hand gestured toward the phone that was still laying on the floor. The room was quiet. So quiet you could hear a pin drop.

My uncle's arm slowly fell from my throat, and oxygen swarmed my lungs. He walked away, placing his hands on his hips. "I'm going to make this as short as possible, because she's missing, and every second that we stand here is another second that she is in trouble."

Good. We're on the same fucking page.

"I am not your uncle." My teeth came down on one another as I stood ramrod straight. "And I didn't leave the family business because I wanted to, Isaiah. I was kicked out of it."

I heard his words. I watched as his mouth moved. But I couldn't comprehend it.

"What?"

He nodded. "I am not your father's biological brother. Your grandmother took me in when I was left orphaned because of something your grandfather did to my parents." He swallowed. "Your dad and I didn't know we weren't real brothers until we were around your age. That's when your grandpa kicked me out of the family because I had the wrong blood running through my veins. He had always hated me, and I didn't know why until then." Uncle Tate kept his face even, but I detected the dip in his voice. The low tone of despair and guilt. "Long story short, he and I made a deal, with the convincing of your grandmother and father. He would spare me and do the one thing I asked, and then I would never ever speak of the family business, and I would change my name so I was no longer affiliated." His lips formed a straight line, the light-pale color appearing white as he tensed. "If he helped my friend, *Emily*, get out of some trouble, then I would leave and burn all the incriminating shit I had on him. He wanted to kill me, but believe it or not, your father convinced him not to. Then, of course, once he died, your father and I connected again. Your father didn't trust me. He'd changed over the years, but there was still a slight brotherly bond between us. Bain being here was a coincidence that ended in his favor, thus sending you here to do his dirty work."

"Emily," I whispered. "She was the friend you told me

about. The girl that was sent to the group home by the hands of Judge Stallard instead of going to prison."

He nodded solemnly. "I sent her to the fucking hands of a monster so she wouldn't have to go to prison."

Fuck.

"Emily is Gemma's mother. I didn't know she was pregnant. She didn't tell me, and every time I tried to contact her in the group home, I was shut down. As soon as the five years was up and I contacted Judge Stallard, they had said she finished out her sentence early and had left without even a goodbye. I had private investigators. Everything. She had just disappeared."

My fingers dug into my scalp as I pulled on the ends of my hair, remembering what Gemma had told me that night in the library when another memory stole her from me. "That's because he threw her into the Covens." I shook my head, pacing back and forth inside Gemma's tiny fucking room with too many sets of eyes tracking me. "She watched that sick fuck throw her mother into a padded room all because she didn't want to marry him. He raped her, and he all but told Gemma the same thing would happen to her if she didn't follow his rules." The pictures of her were surfacing in my mind, and I looked at Cade.

"Tell him, Isaiah. Tell him everything."

"He's doing the same to her." I pulled back at the sound of Mrs. Fitz's voice, stunned that she had stolen the words out of my mouth.

"How do you know that?" I asked.

Mrs. Fitz stepped forward with tears gathering. The papers in her hands were thrust outward, and I rushed over and stood beside my uncle...my *not uncle?*...whose entire body tensed like a concrete pillar.

Sketch after sketch of the most horrific drawings shook within Mrs. Fitz's fingers. "These are Gemma's drawings. I saw them while moving some things around in the supply closet. They were hidden, Tate, as if she didn't want anyone to see them."

Cade stepped forward. "That's what she's been drawing in the mornings, Isaiah. I saw her dip into the closet a few days ago when you were in the pool. I assumed she was just putting supplies away."

"What..." Uncle Tate's words slowly evaporated into thin air as his face hardened with each sketch placed in front of him.

These were so much worse than the pictures of her chained in the basement. These were gut-churning, soul-destroying sketches that were drawn so eloquently that only someone who lived them could create. There wasn't a detail out of place. There were scars on one of the figure's bodies—the figure I assumed to be Gemma. The chains hung with her wrists in them. I finally turned my back on the drawing that was half of Gemma's face, as if she had looked into a mirror and traced every last perfect detail of herself, while the other half were the words, *good girls don't break rules,* over and over again.

"Isaiah. Did you know about this?" My uncle sounded just as off as I felt.

I slowly turned back around and faced both him and Mrs. Fitz. "Yes." I found Cade, who was still standing by Sloane on her bed, and at the moment, I felt completely drained. Hopeless. Everything ached. "We snuck into Judge Stallard's house a few nights ago because I knew there was something else going on with Gemma. I also know he is connected to Dad, and the Covens, and Bain. I wanted more info."

"She wanted to run away?"

I nodded and shut my eyes to hold back the emotion. "I was helping her get away from him, and then after I dealt with Dad, I was going to deal with Judge Stallard to somehow fix it all for her. But there's more." *My plans were fucking shredded. What was I going to do?*

"There's more?" Cade questioned, just as confused as my uncle.

"I need to know everything, Isaiah." My uncle and I were feeling the same thing. I could hear it in his voice. Pure fear and desperation were coming down on us. I hardly even registered the words coming out of my mouth.

"Richard was planning on taking her when she turned eighteen. He wants to marry her, and..." I choked the next words out, dropping my head. "Turn her into Emily. Plastic surgery, everything. She found the files on his computer before she ran away the first time." I turned my back, looking directly at her bed. "So, did Richard show up early because of you? Does he know who you are to her? Or did he show up because of me?"

There was a slight shift in air, and the next voice to hit my ears had me stilling.

"He took her because of me."

My hand dug into the back of my shorts, and I spun around quickly, pointing the gun directly at Bain's head.

"Start fucking talking."

CHAPTER TWENTY-ONE

GEMMA

I WAS SO COLD. My body wouldn't stop shaking. The room was pitch black. My hands were tied behind my back, and although the skin around my wrists was tough from past scarring, I could still feel the slight burn of some type of rope binding me. I wanted to reach up and feel my eyes to see if they were actually closed instead of open. Maybe my body wasn't allowing me to open my eyes because of fear.

The fear settled deep in my belly. My stomach was twisting in unfathomable ways, and my heart had been pounding since I had regained consciousness. I wasn't sure how long I'd been out. My head throbbed with each breath I took, and if I even moved a little bit, the throbbing would be so intense that I would whimper.

He took me.

I sniffed the air softly, trying to calm my senses with the realization that I wasn't in the basement. There was no smell of mildew or dirt. The floor beneath my knees was cushiony instead of lined with the grittiness that laid over the concrete in that godforsaken area underneath Richard's house.

Isaiah.

My heart cracked in between the thundering beats. It had always been the plan to slip right through Isaiah's fingers, but it wasn't the plan to land in Richard's. Isaiah was making sure of that. *He will never touch you again.* But we were too late. We were too careless.

It wasn't Isaiah's fault. I'd waited until the very last second to let my guard down with him, which only made the pain that much worse.

He knew what Richard had done to me. He knew what he had planned. And he would know that Richard was the one to take me. The worry of *his* worries ate away at my stomach like little insects burrowing themselves.

Survive.

I was done fighting for freedom. If Gemma Richardson disappearing was what Richard wanted in the end, then I'd do it for Isaiah, to keep him safe and untouched.

I wouldn't strive for freedom.

I would strive for Isaiah's safety.

I would gladly trade myself for him. I'd do anything Richard wanted if that meant keeping Isaiah safe.

The stronger voice in the back of my head whispered lies and flawed ideas of a future where I could keep Isaiah safe and still escape Richard's plans, and it had me pausing for a moment.

What if? What if I could do what I'd been doing for years? Playing into Richard's hand but still finding a way out? Would I ever really give up? Was it just my fear talking? Shifting plans didn't mean I was giving up. I just had to be smarter.

Fuck him. I wasn't giving up.

The door opened, and I realized right then that my eyes were, in fact, open. The bright glow from the hall was like a punch to the head, and I cried out, dipping my chin to my chest. "There's my good girl with her little sleepyhead eyes on."

It was like nails on a chalkboard.

My chin stayed dipped to my chest as I refused to look at him. I was too afraid of what I'd see if I met his gaze. Would my resolve fall? Would I become submissive and do as he said to survive? Or would I fight back and hope that Isaiah was as strong as he said he was.

Isaiah wouldn't back down from Richard, and Richard wouldn't back down from Isaiah.

My only concern was that Richard had powerful friends that Isaiah didn't.

What was I going to do?

The lights overhead kicked on, and although my eyes were hardly open, the blinding light still hurt like hell. I remembered that he'd hit me really hard before I fell to the ground in my room. *I hoped Sloane was okay.* She would have told Isaiah everything. Panic skated right through me. *What if Richard took her too?*

"Enjoying your new room?" Richard's shoes appeared in my line of vision, and I almost spit on them. "I know your mother sure didn't."

That had my head raising. The second I glowered into Richard's disturbing eyes, his hand grabbed onto my arm, and he pulled me to my feet. The room moved before me, and I fought back nausea with the pain that surfaced.

I scanned the room slowly, wanting nothing more than to whip his disgusting fingers off my arm. I was surrounded by white. The walls looked as if they were made of clouds. Hundreds of them. Puffy, white cushions surrounded every single inch, and my stomach rolled again. I bent forward and bit my tongue so I didn't throw up. *This was the same room.* The memory came at me like sprinkles of broken glass. *My mom gripping me. Richard throwing me out of the room and into the hallway. The two men in black medical attire taking her away.*

"So, you've taken me to the Covens. How sentimental of you."

My face stung the second his hand collided with it, and my vision danced for a moment before I stood up straight and glared. *That hurt.* "I remember, you know," I croaked. "I remember the day you brought her here and locked her away. Tell me..." I sniffed as I felt something running over my lip. Probably blood. "Did she really kill herself, or did you kill her in the end?"

His lip was that of a wolf. A disgusting snarl. "Both. She knew what would happen if she didn't comply."

I kept my face steady. I wouldn't give him the satisfaction of a reaction. I wouldn't give him anything. Richard pushed me with force until my back rested along the cushioned wall. The door was still open behind him, leading out into a hallway, and the second my eyes landed on it, his beefy hand squeezed my chin tightly, forcing me back. I stared at his strong nose and the way his nostrils flared with angry breaths. "I should have never let that fucking social worker live. Nosy little bitch. I should have blinded them all: the ones who didn't want a payoff, the ones who wouldn't take bribes from the officials. I should have done away with them to keep you where you belonged. I never should have trusted you."

A choked laugh came from me. "You think I belong with you?"

His whiskey breath hit the side of my face, and I suddenly wondered how long I'd been out. He hadn't smelled of whiskey when he'd come to my room at St. Mary's. *How much time had passed?* Enough time to be thrown into a room with my hands tied behind my back. "Did he fuck you?"

I stilled, panic rushing. A chill coated me, and Richard snarled, looking down at my chest. "Does the thought of him make your perky little nipples hard?" His hand on my chin grew tighter, and I squeezed my eyes shut at the pain. My chin was likely to have bruises from the pressure. Suddenly, Richard's other hand left my torso, and he gripped the front of my shirt. I heard the tears of cotton as he ripped it from my chest, and I cried out, knowing I was completely bare underneath. His hand cupped me gently at first, and a tear escaped my eye. I knew he would no longer hold back. I knew he would no longer be waiting until I was too unconscious to understand or fight him off. I knew he would no longer wait to creep inside my bed late at night and hover over me with his hard length pressed to my middle only to scramble off in the end when I'd meet his eye.

Richard didn't care anymore.

He was no longer trying to manipulate me and make me love him.

He was going to love me even if I hated him.

Pain bit my skin as his touch turned rough. My eyes flared open, and my fear turned to anger. "Get the fuck off me." I bucked my hips violently, and it surprised us both. Everything else seemed to shut down, and I was in survival mode. Fight or flight. I was doing both. I was fighting so I could take flight. *I needed to get away from him.* "You do not get to touch me anymore! I am not your little doll, Richard!"

His hand came back down on my hip, and his nails dug into my bare skin. He pulled back, and the look in his eye was something I'd seen multiple times, but for some reason, it sent a new batch of dread into me. I was hesitant to do or say anything. "So you do remember," he remarked, brows crowding his dark eyes. His laugh echoed around me as he held me in place. "You're just like her, you know. You and your brother. I thought for a little while that you were more like your father—whoever the fuck he was. You never fought like her. Or Tobias. You were always so compliant."

"That's because you had brainwashed me. Even more so after you sent Tobias away."

His lip curved, and my throat closed. "*Sent* Tobias away?" The tilt of his head was menacing. He found humor in my words, and I didn't like that. I didn't like that at all. "You mean...after I killed Tobias."

My world stopped spinning.

My heart broke off in my chest, cracked my ribs, and fell to the floor.

He's lying. He's lying. He's lying.

"Oh yes, my sweet girl." His hand left my torso. He probably felt the fight leave my body just as I did. "Your mother is dead. Your brother is dead. And if I ever find out who your father is, he'll be dead too. You'll have no one but me."

Tobias was dead? No. No, he wasn't. But I was looking evil right in the eye, and I knew that evil could kill. Evil could destroy and kill, and Richard was the epitome of evil.

"So, let me ask you again." Richard's hand left my chin at some point and now rested over my throat, squeezing it just enough to gain my attention. "Did you fuck that boy? Isaiah? The Huntsman's son?"

I said nothing.

Not even the mention of Isaiah could bring back the fight inside of me.

Fight, Gemma! Survive!

"Oh, boys? Come on in here." The tone Richard carried felt like a storm brewing overhead. Thunder boomed. Lightning struck. I was in the middle of a fucking hailstorm, and I just kept getting pelted. "Go ahead and proceed with the exam. I need to know the truth. I no longer trust her."

"What truth?" I asked as he handed me off to two men wearing black scrubs. Their eyes were as dead and as dark as Richard's. *What the hell was going on?* One of the men, who had a bald head, looked at me like he was hungry. His gaze traveled over my body intimately, pausing at my chest, and I took a step back only to be pushed forward toward the white mattress on the floor. It was the same color and fabric that the walls were. *A padded room and a padded bed.* Both things were made of comfort, but I was as uncomfortable as I was in that basement so long ago.

"If you fucked him, of course. I need to know. The pictures were never as revealing as I would have liked..." Richard walked over to the other man standing above me while the bald one kept his hands on my shoulders. I felt dizzy and faint, and my heart was racing so fast I couldn't breathe.

"Let me go," I gasped, looking up with blurry eyes. "What are you doing?"

"Go ahead with the pelvic exam, and if I find that you are taking pleasure in touching what's mine, I will chop your fucking fingers off. I need to know if she's as tight as she should be. Do an STD test, too."

"What?!" My mouth gaped, and air seemed to be stuck in my lungs. Richard raised an eyebrow at me, as if I should have known this was coming. *No. No. No.* "Let go of me!" My voice was hoarse as I continued screaming. I thrashed as two strong hands landed on my thighs to steady me. Richard bent down and unzipped my jeans all while glaring at me from above.

"What is wrong with you?" I asked through choppy sobs.

I looked back at the two men who had no sign of life in their eyes. This wasn't real. It couldn't have been real.

I fought even harder as they pulled my jeans from my body. My shirt was split open, my breasts half hanging out. My jeans crumpled into a mess at my ankles. "No!" I screamed again, trying to rip my wrists out from the binding. I'd kill every last one of them. "I will never do what you want!

I will never submit. You'll have to cut my tongue out if you think I will *ever* keep my mouth shut."

"Oh, Gemma. You've been such a bad girl. It's almost as if you enjoy the punishments."

Just then, something pricked the side of my neck, and my movements grew slower just as Richard's face started to fade.

"*Good*," I whispered, feeling like I was in a fog. I didn't want to see his face anymore.

Then, suddenly, everything went quiet.

____

CHAPTER TWENTY-TWO

____

ISAIAH

THE GUN WAS heavy in my hand, and I knew it had nothing to do with the actual piece of metal. My fingers gripped the black handle as my pointer laid over the trigger. "I will blow your fucking head off, Bain. Do not tempt me. Where is she?"

Brantley was holding Bain by the back of his neck, but I knew that Bain could put up a good fight if he really wanted to. He was as large as Brantley and had been raised the same as we had. We all knew how to throw punches.

"I always thought your weakness was your loyalty to your family." Bain's smug grin filled my vision, and I swore to God the room dripped in blood. "I thought for sure that Jack would be your downfall. I mean, your father used him to do his bidding, yeah?" The room grew hot as Brantley pushed him further toward me. I didn't dare look at a single person. I stayed locked on his scheming face, and I felt my muscles tensing like they were preparing for something big. The room was one giant grenade, one exploding after the other. First, Gemma, then my uncle's revelation—or...Tate's, since apparently, we weren't related—and now Bain and his sick fucking game.

"What's the end game, Bain? Why? Why did you fucking have to drag her into this? What is the purpose? How does this benefit you?" I growled, taking a step closer to him. My uncle stepped over closer, too, but didn't get in my line of vision.

"I was wrong," Bain chuckled, glancing around the room at everyone. Even Mrs. Fitz, who I was certain looked as if she had swallowed a bat, stood there with bated breath. "Your weakness was never your family. It was just your inability to shut off those empowering feelings of loyalty and protection." He clicked his tongue. "Look where that got you."

I rushed at him, and his eyes sparked to life like the sick fuck he was. *He was more fucked up than I thought.* The gun was shoved into his chest, and Brantley pulled Bain's arms back with little to no effort.

"Isaiah." My uncle's warning didn't even come close to penetrating my rage.

"You won't shoot me, Rebel." Bain grew more serious. "You aren't like your father. You aren't like me."

"All you had to fucking do was wait one more goddamn day, and you would have had everything without taking down someone innocent like Gemma!" I screamed in his face, ready to blow him to pieces. My humanity was nonexistent when it came to Bain. The only thing that held me in place was the fact that *he* knew where Gemma had been taken. He was the one behind this. He was part of the reason that I suddenly came to the realization that, deep down, I wasn't as damaged as I thought. I used to think I didn't have a working heart, but I did. I did, because it beat for the girl that was taken so suddenly from my hands.

"Where and why?" I asked again, shoving the barrel even farther into his chest. Bain glanced down at it, and I wasn't sure if it was because he saw the coldness in my gaze or watched as my morals shifted, but he began speaking a second later.

"To secure the deal. That's why." Bain licked his lip as my uncle moved in closer. "Your father raised his prices on guns. Did you know that? The greedy fuck just couldn't help himself." Bain shrugged, and Brantley pulled his arms again, stretching the white uniformed shirt over his shoulders. "My dad saw it as a great opportunity and reached out to one of your biggest clients."

I snarled, interrupting him. "Your father is just as greedy as mine. He just can't fucking stand it that he's second best." It sounded as if I was sticking up for my father, but I wasn't. They were both pieces of shit, both too deep in a scheme of a business that did nothing but feed their egos and fulfilled their sick pleasures of becoming powerful and using killing to do so.

Bain nodded but quickly moved past. "Judge Stallard runs the Covens underneath that pesky little psych hospital. Judge Stallard's father was the one that started Operation KFS, did you know that? Never mind. That doesn't matter. Anyway, my father had worked with him in the past, hiring people here and there when need be."

My uncle tensed, and the room was covered in a blanket of ice. Operation KFS, the real story behind the rooms that laid beneath the psychiatric hospital. *The Covens.* Where men were created to kill and hired to do so. *Kill For Sale*—the biggest underground black market for gangsters that were nothing less than murderers and who were praised afterwards.

"So anyway, my father wanted to secure the deal and slowly move in and take all of your father's clients." He tipped his head to me, as if we were fucking friends. "You know all of this. That's why you followed me everywhere like a lost puppy."

"This has nothing to do with Gemma. I don't give a fuck about the business. Or the fucking Covens. Or that Richard runs it!" Gemma quickly moved to the top of the plan. The timeline had shifted dramatically. *At least Jack was safe.*

"Oh." Bain's eyebrows raised, and I wanted to punch him right between the fucking eyes. "But it does. She was my meal ticket. She was what secured the deal, Isaiah. Don't you get that? I knew that Judge Stallard had a niece. I had seen her before. A long, long time ago during a party that my father was invited to. I hardly recognized her, actually. I wouldn't have even known it was her until my father got to talking with Judge Stallard, and he let it slip that his niece was sent to the same boarding school that I was at. Close to the Covens. Not a coincidence there, ya know?"

My heart began thumping faster and faster, and my other hand almost came up to wrap around Bain's neck to drown out his smug tone of voice. *I could fucking kill him.* My bones were nearly shaking to attack.

"He had told my father that if I watched out for Gemma and reported back to him, he may consider switching dealers." Bain's lip twitched, and my stomach fell to the floor. "Imagine his concern when I told him that his precious little niece was *fucking* the Huntsman's son. Say goodbye to your business relationship with him." Bain blew out a heavy breath that hit me square in the jaw. I was too fucking shocked to even blink. *What the fuck.* "Man, he was fucking pissed when I showed him the photos. You better hope he never gets a hold of you."

I crowded Bain, the gun the only thing separating us as I got in his face. "So that's it? You have no humanity left, then? You wanted my father's clients so fucking bad that you gave up an innocent girl that is destined for a life of physical and sexual abuse?"

The pain rocked me so hard that it almost took the anger away. *Almost.*

Bain's brows dropped only a fraction, seeming to halt at the despair in my voice.

"Cade," I barked, knowing that I had to pull the plug now before things moved even further into this. "Go to Bain's room and cover every fucking inch of it. Grab anything that could lead us to Gemma."

The door opened and shut quickly, and I pulled back, lowering the gun from Bain's chest and taking a step back. "It seems my plan is coming a day early, Bain. Sit down and shut the fuck up."

CHAPTER TWENTY-THREE

ISAIAH

I PACED the small room a few times as Brantley shoved Bain down into Gemma's desk chair. Mrs. Fitz ran into the bathroom and gathered up some wet towels for Sloane and began cleaning her head up as everyone stayed silent. Part of me wanted to bark at everyone and throw them out so I could be alone with Bain, but I wasn't sure I could trust Mrs. Fitz not to call the authorities. I mean, I did just whip out a Glock with easy movements, and words like rape and abuse were being thrown around like fucking confetti, so it was probably best everyone just stayed where they were.

Except for Cade.

I needed him to leave. It wasn't because I didn't trust him. In fact, I probably trusted him the most. I resonated with him the most. But because I resonated with him and knew the things he felt for Journey, I needed him gone for just a few minutes.

"What plan, Isaiah?" My uncle walked over to me, and we locked gazes. We were both wound tight, but we were way too deep in this to stop and talk about our feelings like a therapist would recommend. The clock was ticking, and my gut churned at the thought of what Richard was doing to Gemma.

Turning my back on Uncle Tate, I walked over to Bain and stood above him. His long legs were straight in front of him, and his hands were tucked behind his head as he relaxed on the chair, looking pompous. He thought he had everything figured out. But he was wrong.

"If you would have waited one more day, you could have had it all without dragging her into this." My lip curved as I bent down to his level, resting the backs of my legs on my heels. "Now, here's the thing. I know you have a heart and some morals, otherwise you wouldn't have done what you did to Journey."

There was the smallest tick on his cheeks as the words flowed effortlessly out of my mouth. His body was unmoving, but the light behind his eyes switched almost immediately. It was the answer to a long-time question of mine. *Did he have something to do with Journey leaving this school?* I was *pretty* certain he was the main proprietor of the entire thing, although he probably thought I actually knew his secret since I called him out on it. Truth was, I didn't know shit.

"You needed her gone from this school. From this life. From Cade. You couldn't stand that she would have been knee deep in this shit. It's bad. You know it. I know it. This life that we both, along with Cade and Brantley"—I didn't even look at Shiner to see the uneasiness on his face from being the odd one out—"are destined to live. It's not safe for girls like her." My teeth ground along one another, and I felt the way my lips pulled back into a snarl. "Or Gemma."

Bain didn't say a word. He sat in the same position, taking in my accusation for what it was. I slowly rose to my feet, putting some space between us so I wouldn't be tempted to take his head and collide it with my knee. I may have appeared calm and in control on the outside, but I was panicky on the inside. I was frantically trying to pull things together with a string that felt knotted on both ends.

"After I got Gemma settled and got her out of this school, *just* like you did for Journey, I was going to make you a deal."

"A deal?"

I nodded solemnly. "You want my father's business so bad? Well, I was going to hand it right over."

Bain's eyes shifted to my uncle and then back to me. "That easy, eh? Just tell your ol' man that you're just going to give us your side of the state? All those clients? The dirty cops? The drug lords? All that money?" He threw his head back, and the room filled with manic laughter. "And you think I would have fallen for that?"

"Of course not." I walked closer to him, causing him to raise his head to look at me. "I was going to tell everyone what you did to Journey that balmy night just before summer hit." I didn't give him a chance to deny it, because I wouldn't have known what to say if he did. I was lying out of my ass, but I was solid with my instincts. I knew he had something to do with her, and if he had, he wouldn't test the waters in fear that I truly did have evidence. "Why do you think I sent Cade away? If he knew what you'd done...he'd break your fucking neck."

"I'm not afraid of Cade."

Brantley hissed out a breath. "You should be."

"So..." Bain crossed his arms over his chest, ignoring Brantley. "Your plan was to blackmail me so I would work with you? How, exactly? Stealing the clients out from your father? That would never work. He hardly trusts you." He laughed, but I sensed his curiosity.

"He trusts me enough. I thought we could work together, take him down, and then you could have it all, Bain. No more bloodshed. No more threats on your family from mine." I glanced up at Brantley, and his jaw was tight, but he shot me a curt nod, telling me that he was still on my side. "I know how to disappear. I'd hand it all over, and I'd be fucking gone. You wouldn't have to worry about the Huntsman any longer."

"And if I would have said no to your grand plan?"

My brow raised. "Would you have really risked it in the end? You have cops on your payroll, and so do we." I threw my hands up cautiously. "The better question is, would you risk Journey in the end? You sent her away; you made it seem like she was unstable." I dipped my head down and lowered my voice. "And I know why."

I didn't.

I had nothing solid that I could have truly shown for proof, but I knew that dangling Journey in front of him was the one thing that caused Bain to flinch and backtrack.

I breathed out an easy breath. "It would be a shame if the truth came out. Your father doesn't know about her, right?" I spun around, putting my back to him for a second. "So, let me ask you again...where the fuck is Gemma, Bain? We are done playing games."

"Isaiah." I felt Uncle Tate take a step forward, but I stayed lasered on Bain, who was undoubtedly thinking and processing everything I'd said. "I need to tell you something, and the only reason I'm willing to do this in front of him"— he nodded over to Bain—"is because we need him to find Gemma. Richard could have taken her anywhere."

The shuffling of papers behind me caught my attention. Over my shoulder, I could see Sloane and Mrs. Fitz both looking through the sketches that Gemma had drawn. I quickly swiped her leather-bound journal off the desk and threw it toward them. "Look in there, too. See if she left anything that could be valuable."

Turning back to Bain, I saw him and my uncle having a

stare off. I moved in a little closer, clenching my fists by my sides, feeling something bubble up in my stomach, threatening to climb out of my throat. "You were right, Bain. I am unable to shut off my loyalty and protection, but do you know what that means?" Hot, seedy breath left me, and my fingers began to tingle. "That means I have no limits when it comes to her. You will tell me, and you will work with me in getting her back." My finger pointed so close to his face that my uncle stepped in and pushed me away. "Or the fact that she's being raped and forced down to her fucking knees with chains around her wrists is on your fucking conscience."

And mine. It was on mine, too. My knees nearly buckled right then, but Uncle Tate's hand dug into the back of my neck, and he looked me dead in the eye. "We will get her back. But you can't kill him."

"I will if anything happens to her." My voice was gritty as I tried to pull back my emotions. I wanted to shut down. I wanted to lock it all down and take my fist and beat Bain until I didn't feel the panic twisting in my body. "She's... You didn't see the fucking photos of her. You didn't see where she was kept in that fucking house!" My voice reached levels that I didn't even know possible. The strain was against my throat, and I knew that if my uncle wasn't holding me upright, I would have fallen. I was terrified. I was fucking terrified and determined to kill every last person on this earth that even dared to touch her. I was spinning out of control and felt untamed, but I didn't even care.

"I'll tell you where she is." The entire room seemed to gravitate toward Bain and his compliance. We locked stares, and his jaw flexed. "If the deal is still on the table, I'll lead you right to her." He sighed. "And we'll take out Richard Stallard in the process."

That was too easy.

"There's a way around this." My uncle took a few steps

back, ripping his tie off with force. "I said I needed to tell you something, and this something can solve our problems right here, and right now."

"What?" I threw my hands out impatiently.

My uncle, the headmaster of this school, placed his hands on his hips and silenced the entire room with five little words. "I'm working with the feds."

Bain's eyes widened. Brantley took a step forward, and I took a step back. *What?*

"I'm working with Jacobi."

My head spun. "What does Jacobi have to do with this?"

"Who is Jacobi?"

We ignored Bain.

"Isaiah." My uncle's eyes softened, and I was stuck on the pleading within them. "Jacobi is in the FBI. He has been since he left." He swallowed, and I stalled. Complete shock and confusion wracked me. Cade chose to walk into the room right then, holding nothing useful, but I was too frozen by the way my uncle was walking toward me and the way his mouth was moving. "We don't have time for an explanation, but your father is about to meet his demise, Isaiah. Jacobi—and I—have been working to take him down for a while. All we needed was to put him somewhere that we could get him. A trap. The feds have so much intel, but…it's all speculation unless we get eyes on him, and someone calls him out on his identity. Your father is very careful. He's extremely smart and elusive. And the feds want more than just him. The feds want his customers too. This isn't just a small sting they're working on."

My uncle looked over at Bain. "You and your father remain unknown to them. They know the idea of you, but not who you are. If you work with us, take us to Gemma, we can make sure it stays that way. They don't want the small fish. They want the shark."

"My father won't step anywhere near this."

"And you?" I asked, once again eating up borrowed time. Jack's face hit the back of my mind, and I had to hope like hell that Jacobi knew what he was doing when he took him in for protection by my request. It was the first time I'd talked to my older brother in years, and he mentioned nothing of this to me. *What the fuck.*

"Is it true?" Bain asked.

"Is what true?"

"What you're saying about Richard and Gemma?"

I stomped over to Mrs. Fitz and Sloane, who were looking through Gemma's journal, and whipped some of the sketches off the bottom of the bed. I shoved them into Bain's lap, annoyed that he was touching something of hers. "What the fuck do you think?" I felt the pain hit the back of my eyes as I looked at her pieces of art. I blinked away the worry and sliced back at the hurt. "Where is she, Bain?"

He blew out a heavy breath. "I'm pretty sure she's at the Covens."

CHAPTER TWENTY-FOUR

GEMMA

I BLINKED SLOWLY, like my eyes were made of lead. The room was so bright that it gave me an instant headache, so I shut my eyes again.

I'll burn the world down for you, Gemma.

I hummed, smiling gently at the thought of Isaiah. It felt weird to smile. My lips cracked with the movement, and I tasted blood on my tongue. I tried to swallow, but my throat felt too dry. Like there was cotton shoved down it. I wanted to go back to sleep.

Just survive, Gemma. I'll come back for you.

"Tobias?" I whispered. My words sounded strange against my ears. Slow and mumbled. I ran my tongue over the roof of my mouth and teeth, searching for rocks. It sounded like rocks were inside my mouth, making my words grumbly.

"No. Not Tobias. I'm just here to give you some more meds. Richard said he wants to keep you sedated until he gets back so you'll stop screaming."

A girly voice hit my ears next. "Whatcha doing?"

My eyes stayed shut as I tried to figure out if I was sleeping or awake. I was too afraid to peek, but I took comfort in knowing that neither of the voices I heard were Richard's.

"What are you doing out of your room?"

The light, feminine voice floated in my ears as she answered whoever was hovering over me. I could feel the person's body heat, and part of me wanted to pull them in close. I was cold. So cold. My blood felt cold. My veins were like icicles. I was pretty sure I was shivering.

"Someone left my door open again, so I wandered."

Warm air wafted over my face as the person above me moved farther away. I slowly pulled one eye open, trying to adjust to the bright lights in the stark-white room. My head rested against the floor, and I remembered sliding off the mattress I was on last time I was awake because of what was done on it. *How long have I been like this?* I was in and out of consciousness and confused. It was like being back at Richard's all over again.

The floor felt so comfy against my skin, but with that comfort came a sickening, nauseated feeling, and I was afraid to dig further into my head to find out what had happened.

"Who'd you spread your legs for this time?"

The girly laugh snagged my attention, and when my eyes finally adjusted to the light, I zeroed in on her. She was pretty, even with the drab clothing she was wearing, and she was definitely my age. She had an innocence to her that felt too familiar to me.

Her blondish-brown hair was parted down the middle and split into easy waves over her shoulders. The slate-colored robe was tied tightly around her tiny middle, and she was barefoot, padding around the white cloud-like floor like she weighed no more than an ounce. The freckles on the bridge of her nose were faded, and her skin was pale, as if she hadn't seen sunlight in a really long time, but the thing that really caught my eye were the long, pink scars running up her forearms. I felt envy for a second because I'd always been so protective of the scars along my wrists, so much so that I wore long sleeves even when the temperature was warm. But this girl? Her cuffed robe sleeves were pushed all the way up to her elbows, and she wore her scars like trophies. The long, skinny, pink, raised marks were shining like diamonds in a desert against her pretty skin.

I wanted to be her.

Not just because she seemed proud of who she was and held an air of confidence to her, but because she was standing in the doorway and could walk the halls without anyone even stopping her.

The man wearing black scrubs crossed his arms over his chest as he gave her a look, waiting for her to answer his question. She shrugged. "Jealous I didn't spread my legs for you, big man?"

I squinted my eyes so it looked as if they were closed as I saw him standing over her. She didn't look fazed in the slightest. Who was she?

He tilted his head, still holding the syringe destined for my neck in his hand. "Maybe. Maybe I'll stick you with this and fuck you while you're unconscious, little one."

I bit my tongue. *Had he done that to me?* No. Richard wouldn't have allowed that. Would he? My heart started to skip in my chest, and I wished I had enough energy to spring to my feet and dart out of the open door, but it felt like my feet were numb. My whole body felt numb and tingly.

"You would never." The girl stood tall and wore an impenetrable expression. "You guys like my banter too much to do such a thing." I caught the flirty tip of her lip, and the man seemed to fall for it.

He rolled his eyes. "Go back to your room so I don't get my ass chewed for letting you roam."

"Who's that?" My eyes quickly shut, and I tried to appear like I was sleeping again, but I was pretty certain the girl had seen me. My movements were too slow. It felt like actual minutes before my eyelashes collided again.

"Newbie. None of your concern. Actually, this bottom floor is none of your concern. How many times have you been caught down here? For fuck's sake, the psych employees are so blinded by your charm."

"And you're not?" I peeled my eyes open once more when I heard the shuffling of fabric. I almost choked when I watched the girl take a step closer, running her hand down the side of his face. The sound of his beard against her skin made a scratchy sound, and her lips were a millisecond from touching his. "Remember the last time we got too close?"

The man's eyes darted down to her mouth, but I quickly moved my gaze to her hand that was moving in between them.

Was she…?

"Mmm, I remember," she whispered. "I wonder what would have happened if we hadn't gotten interrupted?"

I pulled back slowly, wincing at the fogginess in my brain as I watched his hands shoot down to her slender hips. He threw his head back, the veins along his neck prominent as her hand dove down into his pants. "Goddamnit. Stop. You shouldn't be acting like this."

"Maybe you should stop me." Her hand moved inside his pants faster. *What was going on?* I was confused but too stunned to look away or close my eyes. This girl was…different. Bold. Determined. She looked sweet at first. Her calm voice sounded like a child's, with an innocence that I'd held once upon a time. But now she appeared tough and seasoned.

My mouth gaped as the man's hips started thrusting, and the girl's eyes darted away, looking more disturbed than aroused like she'd seemed a few seconds ago. But that was when she caught my eye. She blinked once and froze for a moment before shaking her head, silently shushing me.

Her other hand pulled back slowly, and my eyes widened as I saw her slip something from the man's pocket into her own. He was too blinded by her hand in his pants to realize. His eyes were shut tightly, and his hips were rocking. Loud breaths were coming out of his mouth, and I shut my eyes quickly when his sultry voice rang out.

"You're a little minx."

"What do you expect when I'm stuck inside a prison cell all day being fed little white pills to make me *happy*?" She let out a little moan. "Plus, I like seeing you at your mercy for me. It feels good to be in control once in a while."

"Jesus Christ." His words were a mix of desperation and awe. "You're not in control."

Oh, but she was. She was distracting him so she could take something. *Was this real?*

"Fuck," the word was strained.

"Better hurry, someone's coming."

His breathing picked up, and after one grunt later, everything went silent. His breathing resumed to normal, and I heard a faint giggle before he muttered under his breath, "Go back to your room, now."

"I don't get a thank you?" I heard the amusement in her tone. "That was for not telling on me for being out of my room. Bye, big man."

A loud breath clamored through the room right before the door shut, and after a few seconds, I opened my eyes only to pull back with a scream lodged in my throat because the guy was standing over me with a beet-red face.

"Keep your fucking mouth shut." He hovered over me.

"It's the only way you'll survive here." Then, he pricked me again, and for a fleeting second, I was thankful.

————

THE ROOM SPUN AGAIN like I was on a merry-go-round.

He was here.

A tiny voice in the back of my head made the hair on my arms stand erect. There was a shadow in the depths of my mind that was threatening to come to light with the warning. Like some broken part of me that had been shoved down way too far was emerging so I could be prepared. But instead of being prepared, I shoved her down again.

No.

I want to go home.

But where was home? Not with Richard. Home wasn't the place that I had grown up in.

Was it St. Mary's? It was the first place I'd ever felt safe, even if it was proven that I wasn't.

Isaiah.

I felt safe with him. I felt good when I was with him.

A whimper left me, and the warmth of a single tear ran along my cool cheek. "*Isaiah.*"

"Say his name again, and you'll regret it."

I squeezed my eyes shut at the sound of Richard's voice. *Was it real?* It wasn't real. My head shook back and forth as my brain played ping-pong against the walls of my skull.

"How many times did he fuck you? You know better than to lie to me. Think of all the times you'd lied over the years. What happened after I found out the truth?"

The basement was so cold. It always was. I knew Richard was behind me. I felt his heavy presence, and I was pretty sure his hand had trailed down my naked spine. Was that what woke me up? Probably.

"Tell me, Gemma. Did you eat the last cookie? Because Tobias is saying it was him." Richard's laugh cut through my fear like a sharp sword. "A cookie. So insignificant, but I can't have you lying to me. I'm doing this for a reason. You will not break rules while in my home."

"I'm cold, Uncle Richard."

"What did I tell you to call me when you are down here?"

My eyes peeled open, and fear like no other hit me again. I hated it down here. The cookie wasn't worth it. Why did I take it?

"Daddy," I whispered, and then I screamed when something sliced at my back. The sound of leather against skin ricocheted through the dark room.

"I'm sorry!" I yelled out, pulling at the chains imprisoning my wrists.

"You're too old to be doing this, Gemma. Lying to me. You're supposed to be my good girl. I hate punishing you."

"You don't hate punishing me," my voice cracked, and I pulled my eyes open, looking back at Richard's dark eyes that were now aged with fine wrinkles around the edges. I wasn't in the basement. I was in the white room. I was at the Covens.

The sickest smile slithered onto his face. "You're tough this go-around. It was always so easy to break you in the past."

A growl started to curl deep in my throat. Anger lit me up inside, and not even Richard's darkness could put out the flame.

"What?" Richard's head tilted, and I saw that his white button-down shirt was undone at the top, showing off his dark curly chest hair. He looked slimmer, and the dark circles under his eyes did nothing but make him look that much more dangerous. I focused on the bright-pink scratches along his cheek. Where did he get those? "Did having some cock in your pussy give you some sort of confidence? Imagine what mine could do."

I was disgusted, and the remnants of fear surfaced. *No.* He didn't get to have me. "I am not yours, Richard. I won't let you touch me."

He laughed, throwing his head back. I tried raising my hands to lash out, but I couldn't. *What was wrong with my arms?* I looked down, taking my eyes off Richard, which was a mistake. His hand clamped onto my throat, and a scream got lodged. It hurt. It hurt really bad. My neck was sore, and his fingers felt as if they were digging into open wounds. "If you keep screaming and hitting me when I come in here, it'll only be worse for you. No one is coming for you, Gemma. You might as well give up now."

My head thrashed beneath his grip, and I pushed away the pain radiating to my temples. His hand came off my neck, and a look of excitement hit his muddy eyes. He liked when I fought him, and he probably didn't even realize it until now, because in the past, I didn't fight. I had let him have me because I thought it was the only way to survive.

And maybe it was.

"I will never give up."

What if he never let me go? What if I never made it out alive? Panic started to prickle at my vision, and I was seconds from letting it take me under, but I was too afraid of what was going to surface when it did.

A knock sounded, hardly audible through the lush, white, soft walls. I tried to move, wiggling to get away and toward the door. Maybe it was someone sane. Maybe it was someone who could hear me yelling.

Richard's large hand grabbed onto my leg, and that was when I realized I was wearing a gray medical gown, the same color that the pretty girl had been wearing the last time I was conscious. *Was that real? Was she real?*

"No!" I yelled, suddenly snatched from my confusion. "Stop!"

Richard's legs came down as he straddled me, his middle pressing against me so hard that I bit my tongue to direct the pain somewhere else. His hand came over my mouth as he glared like the devil down into my face. "Just be the good fucking girl you're supposed to be, Gemma. I've spent nearly eighteen years taking care of you and waiting for you to grow up. I am no longer going to be patient. You will do as I say. You'll be begging for me after they're through with you. I don't want to let them break you, but I think it's the only way. Why are you women so unaware of what a man like me could give to someone like you?"

My mouth opened wide against his skin, and I clamped down as hard as I could, tasting his blood in my mouth.

"You just have to be fucking difficult!" he yelled, anger taking a hold of his brown depths. His fist came up quickly as his face contorted, and I was suddenly silenced by the pain.

The room was wobbly as my head fell to the side. Dizziness swallowed me, and suddenly, I was back on the merry-go-round. My body was tired, and I was questioning reality again.

"Why is this happening?" I whispered, shutting my eyes because it felt so good to see nothing but the abyss.

Something sounded in my ears, and I opened my eyes again, sour vomit hitting the back of my tongue. The door was open, and I saw Richard standing there with blood dripping from his hand. *Did I do that?* I licked my lips. Yes, I did. I bit him.

"Good." My voice was louder than I thought, and he looked back at me for a brief second before looking at someone else. The room was like a tunnel, and hope sparked in my chest when I caught a blur of a maroon tie.

"Isaiah?" My eyes opened wider, and a ragged breath left

me. *Could I breathe?* I moaned. It felt hard to breathe. My chest hurt from the thumping inside.

Wait. I blinked a few more times, trying to right the room. "Can someone make the room stop moving?" I yelled out, but my voice didn't sound right. It was rough. My throat ached.

"It's none of your business, boy. I switched vendors for a few reasons, one of them being because the Huntsman raised his prices. Don't you think for a second that I owe you now. I don't owe anyone. It's the other way around."

The Huntsman.

"Help!" I yelled, fighting through the fogginess of my head.

"I understand what you're saying, but I have a proposition for you."

I recognized that voice.

Was that...? "*Bain?*"

Richard's glare snapped to me as Bain stepped farther into the room. He was half inside now, and when our eyes connected, his grew wide for a split second before he turned to look back at Richard. "You want Isaiah, right?"

Richard turned his back to me as I squeezed my eyes shut for a second. Everything was fuzzy, like a radio that had too much static. "I can lead him here. He'll want to come after Gemma. He will bring his father, too. He knows I'm the one that gave you the proof of their relationship. Not to mention, the Huntsman is aware that he is no longer in business with you. He knows that you've switched sellers. They'll want blood."

"No." My eyes were open again. *Did I say that?*

Richard and Bain were both looking at me. I could feel their stares without even truly seeing them. "Bain, no," I repeated, trying to focus on him. When we finally seemed to lock gazes, his mouth moved silently. "*It's okay*," he mouthed. "*Shh.*"

What? It was like seeing that girl again. Was this real?

I closed the room out because I was too confused, and the longer I kept my eyes open, the more nauseated I felt. I didn't want to see him anymore. Or Richard. I didn't want to believe what I was hearing.

Was Bain going to bring Isaiah here?

Richard would kill him. Richard killed my mom...and Tobias.

He would kill Isaiah too.

I cried.

I knew I was crying, because I could hear myself, even if I did feel like I was floating.

Something felt wrong.

It was like I could feel my body, but I couldn't feel my body.

"Survive, Gemma."

"Huh?"

"It won't be long."

I knew I was imagining things. The first voice sounded like Tobias, but the second sounded like Bain.

And neither of them would be telling me anything encouraging. One was dead, and the other had sold me to the devil.

CHAPTER TWENTY-FIVE

ISAIAH

"I'M NOT WAITING." The chair I was forced into toppled backward as I jumped to my feet.

My uncle was pacing back and forth in front of me, chewing on his nail. He sliced his attention over to me as he stopped dead in his tracks, and seeing his green eyes made my stomach roll. They were the same fucking shade as Gemma's, and now that I knew she was his daughter, it was hard to look at them.

"You will fucking wait, Isaiah. This is much bigger than your ego, so sit down."

My blood rushed. "This has nothing to do with my ego, *Tate.* He's probably fucking her right now! She's probably screaming for help, and no one is there to scoop her up and take her away from danger!

"You don't think I've thought that already?" The vein on my uncle's forehead was throbbing as we met chest to chest. It was only the two of us in his office. Brantley and Cade were getting things gathered and making sure Sloane and Mrs. Fitz were calm enough to leave alone with the nurse without ruining our plans before we even got a chance to step foot near the Covens. "She's my goddamn daughter, and I'm the whole reason this poor girl is stuck with a man like Richard Stallard!" He turned around and slammed his fists onto his wooden desk, and a few things fell off the side as his head dropped. "This is so fucked up. All of it is. From the moment Emily got caught... I wouldn't be surprised if your grandfather had known she was pregnant with my twins. He probably sent her there on purpose, allowing me to think I was doing a good thing by her, but really, he was sitting back, laughing his ass off over the fact that I was losing everything in my life."

"I don't trust Bain," I said, ignoring my uncle's revelation that my grandfather was a real piece of shit. My father was just like him. Later on, maybe he and I could bond over our paralleled fucked-up childhoods, but right now we needed to go get our girl.

Our girl.

My chest caved in one single swoop. This truly was fucked-up. All of it. Gemma and I were destined to burn from the second we connected. The messy web had grown wider, and it was tangled with a disturbing past and wicked lies. She and I were innocently thrown into a life neither of us wanted or deserved.

And after it was all said and done, I wouldn't be deserving of her at all. I would kill Richard and burn the Covens to the fucking ground and hope my father was inside, too. I didn't care. Bad people deserved bad things. And they were both monstrosities.

My uncle turned back around. "Was it true? What you said about Journey and Bain?"

"Does it matter? The blackmail seemed to work." I paused. "Unless he's playing us. I don't trust him. He could have been lying. We need to go to the Covens."

"We have to wait for Jacobi!"

As soon as my uncle had let the cat out of the bag that my older brother was in the FBI, we immediately went to his office and called him. He was on speaker, and the first thing out of my mouth was, "*Where is Jack?*" Apparently, he was safe, and although I'd hated my brother for years, and the first time I'd spoken to him in a long time was the other day when I told him he *owed* me and I demanded he take in Jack—*his little brother just as much as he was mine*—there was still a part of me that trusted him. I trusted Jack to be in Jacobi's care versus anywhere near my father when he realized that I'd betrayed him.

"No fucking offense, but I don't give a fuck about the FBI's plans to take down my father or Richard. Or the Covens. My only concern is Gemma, and that should be your only concern too!"

We were chest to chest again, and his face was as red as mine. Maddening heat covered every inch of my skin, and every time her name would fly off my tongue, it felt like another part of my soul cracked a little more.

Uncle Tate's hands wrapped around my face, his fingers pushing into my scalp. "Do you really think you'll be able to just walk into the Covens and get her? If she's really there, no one is going to give you the key, Isaiah. You'll probably be shot on the spot, especially if the Covens has switched allegiances. If they are no longer being supplied by your father, they will not think twice about shooting you right between the eyes! You should know this. Why do you think they've been hidden all these years? They're smart and ruthless, and they take any threat they see, whether it's true or not, and demolish it."

"I'll find another way in, then!" My entire body shook with...shock? Fear? Adrenaline? I was ready to break a neck or two if it meant getting his hands off her.

I'm coming, Gem.

"You will not be able to just walk in there, Isaiah! We need to wait for the phone call from Jacobi and figure out the best way to handle this! He's been working with the ATF, and they are constructing a plan right this second. We don't even know if Gemma is actually at the Covens. Can we trust Bain? Probably not. I should have never let him stay at this school. If it had been up to me, he would have been gone. But, Isaiah, you're going to cause more harm to her by harming yourself. Think about her! She will never forgive herself if you die trying to find her! She is just like her mother. She puts everyone before herself."

"Did someone just say Gemma?"

My uncle and I both spun around quickly, and my hands were already in fists. I locked onto two shadowed eyes, one of them black and blue, with dark hair hanging over his sliced eyebrow. He was my height but skinnier than me, standing right there in the threshold of my uncle's office. "Who the fuck are you?"

"He's with me." My stomach was like a catapult to the floor when the person speaking in a shy tone stepped to the left and farther into the room.

My uncle's hands fell to his side as his jaw unhinged. "Journey?"

———

"Did you just say Gemma?"

My throat constricted as I stared at Journey. It was like seeing a ghost. My eyes immediately flew to her bare arms with the wounds now turned into scars. *What was she wearing?* She had on a...dress? A gray, smock-like dress hid her skinny frame and cut off just above her bony knees. She had on thick gray socks that went up to mid-calf, but they were covered in dirt and mud. The guy she stood next to completely enveloped her short height with his. He took a step forward and placed his body half in front of hers protectively, and my thoughts immediately went to Cade. *He was going to go ballistic.*

"Journey," my uncle whispered, shock rooting him right to the floor.

I quickly moved past the surprise, ignoring the way everything in the room seemed to shrink even further, and saw two blue eyes that looked as cold as mine, staring directly at me. "How do you kno—"

Holy shit.

I was instantly coated in ice. A chill came over me as I took a step forward. "What the fuck," I mumbled, looking at my uncle and then to him. I did that a few more times, and I felt the blood drain from my face. It was obvious. So fucking obvious. "Tobias."

His chin hitched, and the sharp cut of his jaw had fading bruises. "Did you say the name Gemma?"

My uncle instantly crouched to the ground, both fisted hands coming together and up to his mouth. His head shook back and forth as he realized who had just walked in his door. It had to have been like looking into a mirror twenty years ago. The only difference between the two were their eyes. Gemma got her eyes from her father. Tobias must have gotten his from Emily.

"Oh my God," my uncle mumbled, slowly rising to his feet with his eyes shinier than I'd ever seen before. "How did you find me?"

Tobias' cut eyebrow bundled, looking at my uncle in confusion. Journey stepped forward, crossing her arms over her chest. "He didn't find you. I brought us here."

"Where have you been?" I asked. Journey had disappeared after that night, and Cade had let her. He had let her because he knew that if he was aware of where she was, he would have followed her and likely done more harm. We'd assumed that she was sent to a different school after receiving the medical treatment she needed. The farther away from us, the better.

Journey's little jaw wiggled as her eyes darted to my uncle. "Do you know where I was?"

My uncle's head shook as he graced her with a brief glance. "Sister Mary at the orphanage had said you were in the hospital, and afterwards, they would be placing you at a different school and with a foster family, if they could, uh... " My uncle cleared his throat. "Find one that would be willing to address the issues."

A high-pitched sarcastic laugh left Journey, and it was full of sarcasm. I'd know. It sounded a lot like mine most of the time. "That's funny."

"Journey, where were you?" I looked at Tobias as a heavy feeling fell upon my shoulders. "And how did you find him?"

Journey and Tobias turned toward each other before she addressed me. "I've been at the Covenant Psychiatric Hospital since the night I was taken from here."

The room was instantly clouded with something dark and disturbing. The walls changed to black, the lights grew dim, and my heart thundered within my chest. *Fuck*. My nostrils flared, and I hoped like hell that she was a patient on the top floor and had no idea what was on the bottom floor, but with the fact that Tobias was standing by her side, I didn't even want to know. I didn't want to ask.

All I wanted was to move past this, walk out the fucking door, and go get Gemma.

It was like mountain after mountain just kept popping up and getting in my way. The path was winding, and I was sick of not knowing which direction I was being pushed and pulled.

"What?" My uncle's fist was seconds from colliding with the desk again. "This whole goddamn town is corrupted by people like your father and Richard!" He pointed his finger at me, and I didn't disagree.

"Richard? You know Richard?" Tobias crept farther into the office, the door shutting behind him, which was good because we had a whole lot of shit to discuss and not a lot of time.

CHAPTER TWENTY-SIX

ISAIAH

"You mean to tell me that you *think* my sister is at the Covens right now? There's no way. I would have known. The workers talk there. They talk to me."

The tick in Tobias' jaw was moving back and forth, back and forth, much like mine. His voice creaked like a door that was seconds from flying off its hinges, and I was honestly pretty sure he, too, was seconds from flying off the hinges. His face was nearly purple after he got over the hump of shock that my not-so-real uncle, Tate Ellison, was actually his father.

"I need to see a picture of Gemma." Journey finally spoke for the first time since telling us that she had been at the psych hospital.

I stared at her with my leg hopping up and down from across the room. "Why? Did you see her there? She hasn't been there for long." I glanced at the clock and swallowed back panic. *Any amount of time would have been too long.*

"Give me a picture."

"Don't have any."

"She has brown hair. Green eyes. The same color as his." Tobias nodded over to my uncle, *his* father. "I haven't seen her in years, so I can't say much else."

"Scars around her wrists," I said, my voice no more than a whisper. I shut my eyes before opening them again to see Tobias' entire demeanor change.

"From the chains?"

My entire body shook. I gave him a quick nod before taking a deep breath to steady myself.

"Journey, did you see a girl before we left?"

Her hesitant gaze met Tobias' as she crossed her arms over her chest again. Her voice softened when she spoke to him, and my uncle and I shared a fleeting glance.

"Remember when you asked me how I was able to steal the keycard?" Tobias nodded slowly, eyeing her suspiciously. "And I told you to forget about it because we didn't have time for explanations?"

"And I knew you were stalling, and I reminded you that we told each other everything."

Her bottom lip trembled, and it was like going back in the past. Instead of seeing this new, raw version of her, I saw the girl that I'd found with her wrists slit, lying in the middle of the courtyard. So innocent-looking and vulnerable. "Well, I cornered Hank, did something to...distract him, and stole his card. He was the easiest target. So easily swayed. But right before I left the room he was in, I saw a girl. He was about to give her an injection. I'd never seen a girl down there before. I thought it was weird, and I asked who she was, but he blew me off, and my goal was getting us out, and I knew we didn't have much time."

"Journey, what did she look like?"

My uncle asked that question as Tobias and I shared the

same blank expression. There was a goddamn war happening in the thick of my brain, and I couldn't form sentences as it fabricated images of Gemma inside that place.

"Not good. She...she looked bad. There were marks around her neck like she'd been choked, some cuts on her face. It looked like her head had bled at some point, too." I climbed to my feet. "I didn't get a good look at her. It was a quick glance, but...her hands were tied behind her back. There was blood on her gown."

"Where at? Where was the blood?"

Journey bit her lip, glancing away from Tobias. "Where do you think?"

"I'm not waiting. I'm going to get her." I stormed to the door with Tobias hot on my heels.

"I can get us in. I'll be enough of a distraction for them. Let's go."

"And what's the plan?" My uncle rushed after us, and I didn't know Tobias at all, but we were instantly on the same side, working together. We were going to get Gemma, and no one was getting in the way.

A blur of dark-blonde hair whizzed in front of us. Journey reached up to her tiptoes and grabbed onto Tobias' shirt. "Do not go back there, Tobias! You promised me that once you were out, you were never going back! No matter what! Not even for revenge!"

His hands landed on her arms gently as he pushed her out of the way. "That was before I knew my sister was there. I've spent four years trying to get back to her. I've spent four fucking years in that place, allowing them to break me over and over again just so I could finally fool them and get the fuck out. Nothing will stop me. Not even you."

"Tobias!" she shouted, tears rolling down her cheeks. "Don't go back in there."

My uncle entered the hallway from his office, his phone

pressed to his ear. "I can't stop them." He paused, glancing at the three of us. "Isaiah and...Gemma's brother. He just showed up. He's...he's been at the Covens this whole time."

"Tobias!" Journey stepped in front of him again as he began to shift forward. His jaw flexed, and he heaved a heavy sigh, not even bothering to hide his agitation.

"Journey. I said I would come here with you and make sure you were safe. After that, I was going to find my sister. For once, fate was on my side. I'm being led right to her! Now please get out of my way."

"Remember what they did to you! You can't go back there. They'll kill you if they know you aren't what they thought you were."

He scoffed. "I'm already fucking dead, Journey."

And with that, her hands fell as hurt covered her features. Tobias glanced at me, and I nodded, and we both stepped around her.

"Isaiah." My steps faltered as I heard Cade bellow down the hall. "Is everything set in motion? My dad just called and said your father is on his way to meet with Ric—"

There wasn't a single sound to be heard. I couldn't even hear Jacobi on the other line with Uncle Tate. The doors to St. Mary's were open, and not even the cool night air could lessen the tension inside this entryway.

I glanced over my shoulder and saw Cade standing there, hands down by his sides with his face free of emotion. It was as if he'd seen a ghost, too, and to be honest, Journey was a ghost to us.

"Journ."

Tobias flung his dark hair over his cut eyebrow. He slowly angled his head to Cade, and I saw murder in his eyes.

Cade sliced his attention over to Tobias, and I could feel the tension rise. "Who are you?"

"Are you Cade?"

Journey stayed completely silent as my uncle began talking to Jacobi on the phone again. "We're on our way. Yeah, yeah. Okay. I got it. I'll call you when we're at the spot. Do you have eyes on Carlisle? Cade just said that Carlisle is on his way. I'm assuming to meet Richard regarding his shift in business partners."

Cade stepped closer. "Yeah, I'm Cade. Who are you?"

Right there. That sick grin that covered Tobias' face proved to me at that exact moment that he knew more about Journey than we wanted. His feet took him over gracefully, like he was on the hunt for prey.

"Tobias," Journey warned, taking a step forward. But it was too late. Tobias' arm came back, and he sucker punched Cade without even a flinch of emotion. Blood instantly rushed, and Cade's entire gaze turned dark. He turned toward Journey, but she quickly glanced away, looking afraid instead of ashamed. *Huh.*

I quickly spun all the way around and rushed over to Tobias. "We don't have fucking time for this!" I got in between them. "Let's go. You two can have your WWE match later. It doesn't matter right now."

And with that, we all left St. Mary's behind, knowing we were walking right into a gunfight.

———

THE AIR in my uncle's car was suffocating. The windows felt like the walls inside a prison. No one spoke. Not a single word. Journey stayed behind, and although she had put up a fight, I could see the relief settle when Tobias pulled her aside and spoke quietly into her ear, getting her to agree in the end.

I wasn't sure what would be waiting at the Covens when we showed up. Jacobi and his team were already there, setting up invisible parameters along with ATF. They'd been working together to take down my father and his crew for quite a while now, which made me wonder if they'd been following me, too, at some point. Although I wasn't the one who carried out the sales, I'd still been involved and had been to the Covens multiple times in the near and distant past. None of that really mattered, though. The only thing on my mind was Gemma. Once I got her out of there and safe, then we could worry about Richard and my father, along with their gun-running business scheme.

That was, if I made it out alive.

If something went sideways and my father slipped out undetected—because he was notorious for being invisible—he would come after me. He would do nothing but hunt me down and kill me. After all, his other persona went by *The Huntsman*.

"So, you know my sister."

I kept my face straight, looking out the windshield. My uncle drove, Cade sat up front for obvious reasons, Brantley sat to my right, and Tobias to my left. We were crammed, and it did nothing but heighten my already rising blood pressure.

"Yeah."

"What is she like now?"

The car turned in jerky movements as my uncle followed the GPS. Jacobi gave him a different location to head to so we were inconspicuous when we arrived, and if we didn't show up at the Covens in the next few minutes, I would open the door and walk there myself. This wasn't the route we usually took.

"At first, she was kind of snappy with me." My lips wanted to curve upward despite the hole in my chest.

Tobias' head whizzed over to me. "She was?"

I nodded solemnly. "Yeah. She seemed annoyed with me, and she was determined to stay on track without anyone poking into her business. She was guarded." My fist clenched over my lacrosse shorts. I still hadn't changed from earlier when we were about to get on the bus for the away game. "For good reason. She was independent. Determined. Strong."

My uncle caught my eye in the rearview mirror, but I looked away.

"But she eventually trusted you? And told you things?"

I tasted blood in my mouth and truly felt sorry for Tobias. He seemed broken, and the curiosity that had piqued in his voice seemed to turn to guilt at the last second—a hopeful guilt, but still guilt.

I nodded. "Yes, she did."

"Does that mean she found out Richard's plans? That he was going to make her his wife? Force her to play make-believe in that fucked-up house he was so proud of. He told me he was going to—"

"Why aren't we there yet?" I interrupted Tobias because everything he was saying was making my anger spike. I was becoming antsier as the road became narrower. I could sense my uncle's anxiety, too, like he was thinking the same thing I was.

Tobias glanced out the window, and Brantley did the same.

"*Tate*." I didn't call him Uncle, and his mouth formed a straight line.

"I don't know, Isaiah." The car suddenly came to a stop, and he pulled his phone closer and started to zoom in on the map.

"He doesn't want me there," I interjected, realizing that we were going in the wrong fucking direction. "Jacobi is controlling and..." I pushed back on the small amount of despair I felt. "Protective. He was always so protective, which was why it was so hard to believe that he'd actually left me. He doesn't want me there. Turn the fucking car around."

My uncle muttered a string of curse words under his breath as he whipped the car around and flew down the same road that we were already on. The center console was opened next as his left hand stayed glue to the wheel. I caught the glint of a small black pistol and nodded in approval.

CHAPTER TWENTY-SEVEN

GEMMA

"THE HUNTSMAN IS on his way, along with his two right-hand men." Richard's laugh made my ears ring. "They'll feel right at home here, yeah?"

I stared at him, feeling so much hate and dread swimming around my head. I was no longer dizzy. The second time I'd woken up, my head wasn't spinning. It hurt, but the room was actually standing upright for the first time since I'd arrived—I thought.

Time was confusing, just like it had been when I was in the basement with Richard all those times.

"Isaiah will be here sooner than him, I bet." Bain's smug smile burned a hole through my stomach. I'd always had a small fraction of hope that he wasn't as terrible as he acted. But I was wrong. I was so wrong about so many things.

"Good. I can't wait to get my hands on him. And you'll take care of his father? Is your father coming, too? I really couldn't care less about The Huntsman and his little minions now that I have a new seller, but a deal is a deal."

Bain nodded. "My father is leaving it up to me."

Richard's eyebrows raised in approval. The conversation suddenly switched from murder and illegal firearm deals to talking about a father being proud of his son. "I have to say, I was nervous about switching vendors, but the local police have been whispering to me that ATF is on The Huntsman's tail." He elbowed Bain, and he smiled, although it didn't reach his eyes. "I have local and county on my payroll, so they give me all the details. Switching to you and your father has been a bit of a blessing."

Richard's stare pinned me to my spot against the wall, and I did everything I could not to flinch under his scrutiny. "I wouldn't have known about Gemma's little escapades, either, if it weren't for you."

There was something stirring inside my belly. Hate was crowding my head, and there wasn't really any point in playing his games any longer. "Oh, you mean spreading my legs for Isaiah Underwood? How do you know I didn't just do it to spite you?" Because at first, a part of me did. A tainted part of me wanted to do everything I could to take back the control that my *uncle* had taken from my grasp. I wanted to prove to myself that he didn't rule me.

"Keep talkin'. It'll make later that much sweeter for me. It's obvious you like it when I punish you, so I won't even feel bad when I bend you over and spank you."

A flush crept up my neck like a fire-burning trail. I tingled all over and *almost* climbed to my feet. For what? I wasn't sure. Richard was bigger than me and stronger, and not to mention, my arms were tied.

My teeth ground along one another, and my mouth was so dry I was surprised I could even form words, but with the adrenaline flowing through my blood, I felt like I could do pretty much anything—like take Richard down and warn Isaiah before he got too close.

I didn't have a plan. I was flying blindly, and I hated that. I'd acted without a plan in the past, and it only ended terribly, but even when I had a plan set in place, it didn't mean that things would go smoothly.

I mean, look at me now. Tied up, beaten, violated, and broken.

That wouldn't stop me, though. Broken pieces were that much sharper.

A head peeked in the white padded room, and Bain and Richard both pushed off from the wall, pausing their totally mundane conversation as if a girl wasn't tied up in the corner.

"Sir, your guests have arrived." My head tilted when I recognized the man. *That was the guy who gave me the injection.* His eyes flew to mine momentarily, and I realized that what I saw earlier was real. There was a girl in here. A girl who stole his keycard. Hope sprung to my very being. *Maybe she would come back for me.* "I would also like to inform you that a patient is missing."

Richard's hands went to his waist. "A patient? From our floor?"

The man's head fell in defeat, and I casually looked over to Bain. My breath halted when I saw him staring directly at me. My brows crowded as something passed behind his eyes. *Was he trying to tell me something?*

"Both, sir. Two patients are missing. One from the psych floor, and one from this one."

"Bain." Bain quickly took his gaze from mine. "Stay in here until I yell for you. I'm going to step out with Hank here and bring The Huntsman in. I guess he arrived before his son. I may be the one to take care of him, depending on how quickly our conversation moves."

"He'll tell me everything you say, so if you want to keep the punishment to a minimum later, I suggest you keep quiet," Richard threatened me.

Then, he walked out into the hall, keeping the door slightly ajar.

Bain's back was to me, and my heart raced. My wrists ached, and my head suddenly pounded as if it were only blocking out the pain while Richard was nearby. My body refused to show any kind of vulnerability while near him.

"How could you do this?" I whispered, shutting my eyes for a moment to ease the throbbing. "Was it all worth it? Did you know who I was from the beginning? Did you plan to use me just to take a customer from Isaiah's father?"

"Gemma, shut up," Bain seethed, still standing near the door. His head turned slightly to meet my stare, and the face he was making didn't match the evil notch in his tone. His amber eyes were pleading. There was a small indent in between his brows, and suddenly, I was back to wondering if this was real. "Shh," he mouthed, and I felt my resolve fall.

Don't trust.

The small voice inside my head was back, and she was pounding against my skull. That leery feeling of trusting someone boomed like thunder, and I listened to it.

"How long have you known who I was? When did it finally click?"

Bain's shoulders tensed. I could see the hardened curves even through his uniform shirt. Did he come here in a hurry? Did he come with Richard after I was taken? I bet Isaiah trashed every last room, trying to find him.

"Did he take Sloane, too? Did you know that you were not only sending Isaiah to his death, but me, too? Do you know what it's like to live with someone like that? Do you know how hard it is to please someone you want dead?"

I swore I saw his head nod, but our attention went back to the door. There were voices outside now. They were muffled, but I could hear the low murmurs. One of them was as familiar to me as Richard's. *Isaiah's father.* His voice had lived inside the deepest parts of my memories. He was the one who had nearly raped me when he caught me just outside the back door to this psychotic place. If Richard knew that Isaiah's father had touched me the way that he did, he would kill him on the spot. Or maybe he wouldn't. Maybe he would play with him like he liked to play with me. Richard liked to taunt and tease. It was always a cat-and-mouse game with him, except he would keep one mouse alive forever.

And that was me.

Their laughter carried into the room through the slight opening of the door. I almost screamed out, but I wasn't sure I could. My voice was hardly above a whisper no matter how hard I tried to speak up. I wasn't even sure how Bain could hear me from across the room. My throat was like sandpaper. Too hoarse to make much of a sound.

I felt a tear escape from the corner of my eye at the thought, and I pursed my lips. *Why was I crying?* Negative thoughts started to peg me, and fear began to dance in the distance. My resolve was falling. The helplessness that surfaced made me double over. *Isaiah.* He was about to get caught in the crossfire, and I would have to live with that guilt for the rest of my life. This was my fault. There wouldn't have been this big of a target on his back if I'd never allowed him to kiss me or touch me...or love me. I should have stayed away like my fear had warned me to do.

Richard's voice grew closer, and my head flew up, my body locking down all emotion I allowed myself to feel. "Yes, I assume you think I called you here to discuss our business arrangement, but that's not exactly the case. We share a mutual problem, Carlisle."

Richard's voice faded, as if he were walking past my room, and I jumped when Bain quickly spun around. He was over to me in seconds, and I pressed my tender back up against the wall when he dipped down in front of me.

"We don't have much time."

"What?" I asked, frustrated that I hardly had a voice. "What are you doing?"

My wrists were jerked, and I let out a whimper. *Oh my God.* They had to have been torn to shreds. The rope felt worse than the chains.

Bain's steely gaze collided with mine, and I hated to admit it, but his voice was soothing. I had no idea why, but he felt safer to me than anyone else so far in this place. "You've always been good at games, Gemma. Play along so we both make it out of here alive. Keep your arms behind your back so he doesn't know I loosened them, and don't run until—"

I squinted with confusion, but Bain quickly stood up when the door swung open. He turned around, and I bit my lip to keep myself from looking startled. My body trembled from the shock and skepticism, but as soon as I saw Richard, I straightened my shoulders and played along like Bain had said.

"What are you doing?" Richard asked as he made his way over to us.

Bain stepped aside. "She was about to scream because she heard people walk past the door. I was telling her to be quiet."

Richard eyed him curiously. He glanced at me, and I glared back when I felt the contact from his hand on my arm. "Well, it's show time. There's movement outside, and I have a good feeling that it's your little boyfriend." He directed the last part of his sentence to me, and not only did dread hit me, but so did hope.

"Where are you taking her?" Bain asked, stepping beside Richard. "Things might get hairy. Isaiah will not come unprepared now that he knows she is here."

Richard threw his head back and laughed. "I'm going to have her watch as I kill him. The ultimate punishment. Maybe now she'll learn that she is mine, and no one else is allowed to touch her." His eyes were like black holes on his face, and I pulled back in horror.

"You want to kill The Huntsman before or after?" he asked Bain, bypassing my horrific expression. *It was now or never.*

I didn't wait for Bain's answer. I saw the open door and the opportunity that I would never be given again. I easily ripped free from Richard's hold because he wasn't expecting it. I fought through the throbs and aches in my body and took off through the opening, dragging my heavy feet with me. *Isaiah.* I had to warn him. I wasn't sure what Bain was up to, but I knew, without a doubt, that Isaiah was about to die by the hands of Richard because of me, and I would fight with everything I had to change his fate.

The hallway was long and bare of anything. The memories of when I was younger tried to break through my resolve, but I was good at throwing walls up, and that was exactly what I did. Each time my hand hit the hard surface as I half-ran/half-stumbled down the hall, another wall would build in my head. I took a left when I got to the end and didn't look back to see if Richard was coming after me, because I knew he would be. In the deepest pits of my brain, I knew my way around this hall, and just as I tried to put walls up to block out the past, there was an instinctual part of me that was trying to tear them down, too.

I'd drawn this before. My memories had been a map of this building—it was the last place that I'd seen my mother—and I was finally going to use it.

"Where is it?" I whispered, heart racing and mind spinning. "Where is the fucking door?"

"Gemma! You cannot escape. You might as well stop

running." Richard's voice was distant, and it gave me the motivation to keep going farther. If he thought I would stop running just by his command, he was even more dense than I thought.

There were loud sounds coming from somewhere close by, grunting and yelling, but it was too muffled to hear with the pounding in my ears. I spun around in a circle, coming to a standstill as Richard popped up at the end of the hall. It was like something out of a horror film. The hallway was bright, and he crept down the length of it like the Grim Reaper. There was an obvious glint in his eye, showing that he enjoyed the chase. *Shit!*

Loud bangs echoed, and I covered my ears to drown out the sound. My back hit the far wall, and there was nowhere to go. I was cornered. *Where was the fucking door? The door was supposed to be here!* In fact, there weren't any doors at all. None. Just one long, skinny hallway with stark-white walls that seemed to go on forever. Did I remember it wrong? Did my five-year-old memory make up a map inside my head to allow me to think there was ever a way out? Did I create some alternate version of this place to drown out the real one? Was I truly trapped? And where was Bain?

"Did you hear that?" Richard shouted as he continued to walk toward me. I almost fell to my knees. "Three gunshots means three men are currently dead. Your boyfriend's father just met his maker." Richard laughed, and it was like being back in his house, sitting across from him at the dinner table as his mother would place hot food in front of us before rushing back to the group home. He was easygoing, like he had the world in his hands. And to him, he probably did. He'd corrupted so many people and had been changing fates by slamming his gavel on the judge's bench for as long as I'd known him. He thought he was the almighty. Untouchable.

"Go to hell!" I roared, which came out like a screeching

whisper. I tasted the salt on my lips from my tears, and I quickly pushed them away, pausing at the sight of my wrists. *Oh my God.* They were torn, and I couldn't tell which was fresh blood and which was dried.

"You think I'm destined for hell? After all that I've given you over the years? Stability, love, steady direction, protection. I've nurtured you, Gemma." My body flattened against the wall as he grew closer, and I didn't know what to do. Fear was wracking my insides, and I knew that if I tried to run around him, he'd catch me. I was looking death right in the eye.

I would die by his hands one day. Maybe not physically, but emotionally, I would be dead.

"Gemma!" My chest rocked as I stifled a sob. That sounded like Isaiah's voice inside my head, urging me to fight a little longer. But this was it. There was no other choice now. The hope I'd felt a little while ago was diminished as I stood alone in the hallway, staring at Richard with a clearer head than before.

"Don't kill him," I whispered, breaking down and meeting my resolve. "I'll do what you want, if you spare him." I swallowed roughly, wincing at the pain it caused. "If you let Isaiah live, I'll do everything you ask. But if you don't, I will scream every second of every day. I'll fight you every step of the way. I will never ever be your wife and play family with you, if you kill him." The thought made me want to vomit. In fact, I felt the burn against my raw throat, but I still kept my chin up and my gaze level.

I knew I was trying to leverage and that it likely wouldn't work.

Richard's hand came up around my throat, and I gasped, beginning to claw at his hands. "You think you can bargain with me? For him?"

I saw the blow before I felt it. My head cocked back and

hit the hard wall behind me, my vision completely vanishing. My legs didn't work, and I couldn't feel the floor beneath me. "You think you have any control here, Emily?"

Emily. He called me Emily. My fingers scratched at his skin, and I felt his flesh beneath my nails. My breath was seizing, and my head was a bomb, exploding with pain. My vision came back in quick jabs, like flashes from a lightning storm. His grip on my neck lessened for a quick second before he squeezed again and shoved me back farther. "Open your fucking eyes when I talk to you. You will watch me kill your little crush, and you'll be sorry you ever let him touch you. I told you the rules, and you broke them. What did I always tell you, Gemma? Good girls don't break rules, and you *are* my good girl."

He shoved me back once more, and I swore every one of my organs jostled on the inside. I wanted to fight back and cry and scream, but my body wasn't acting the way that I needed it to. I could feel the blood dripping over my face and the oxygen leaving my body. *He's going to kill me.*

My heart beat quickly, thumping harder and harder as I tried to stay present. It was the only thing I felt before there was a popping sound, and I suddenly collapsed to the ground.

I fell flat as soon as my knees hit the floor. My head slammed down like a ton of bricks.

My vision was foggy, but I could see Richard lying beside me, writhing around. "You fucking piece of shit! Who are you? You just shot me!"

"If I didn't think sending you to prison was a better idea, that bullet would have gone right in between your eyes. You'll go away for life, Richard. You can't pay off the FBI and ATF."

I groaned, reaching up with a shaky hand and touching my head. It was sticky. *Was my hand sticky? Or my head? Both?* I blinked again, suddenly feeling very cold. Someone in a black mask was standing over Richard with a gun pointed at his head. "If I find out that you've touched Journey like you have Gemma, I will fucking kill you with my own bare hands."

Then, his boot raised, and he dropped it down onto Richard's face, silencing every word on the tip of his tongue.

"Bain?" I groaned. *Was that Bain?* It sounded like him.

I felt a light slap to my face, and my eyes opened again. The black mask was moving all over the place, and it was hard to focus. "Keep your eyes open."

Just then, I heard the crash of something, and the person in the mask suddenly stood up. He was there one second, but then he was gone. I turned my head to the left, my head flopped hard, and I cried out. Richard was lying beside me with his eyes shut, and although I felt like I was unable to move, I still tried to get away from him.

"No," I whispered, shoving myself backward, except there was something hard behind me. A wall?

"Gemma!" There was a blur of something dark up ahead. I knew something was coming for me because the dark color stood out in the white hallway.

Wait. Isaiah! I had to make him leave.

"No!" I shouted. "Isaiah...ru...run."

But then, my face hit the floor again, and it was dark.

CHAPTER TWENTY-EIGHT

ISAIAH

IT WAS CHAOS. A heavy bout of turmoil seemed to blast me from behind, but I kept moving forward. My feet slapped against the glossy tiled floor, and although I'd been in this place before, it all felt so foreign to me because my mind was centered on one thing: the small body lying at the end of the hall that I'd just watched crash to the ground in a heap of blood with my name on the end of her lips.

There was a lot of blood. I zeroed in on it, and the panic hammered through my skin like the bullets I could hear at my back.

I wasn't sure who was shooting: the enemy or the rescuer. I didn't care as long as I got to her. It was selfish, but I was man enough to admit that.

Jesus Christ. My knees hit the ground as I bypassed an unconscious Richard Stallard. If we were in any other situation and Gemma wasn't lying in a pool of red blood, I would have pulled my gun out and killed him right then, but she outweighed any amount of anger that I felt. My heart was in my hands, beating for her and only her, and it canceled out every single thing going on around me.

"Gemma," I gasped. My face was wet, and my hands were shaking. I was always in control until it came to her. Even when I had found Journey bleeding in the courtyard last spring, I'd had my head straight on my shoulders as I picked her up and called an ambulance. I was worried but controlled. With Gemma, I was fucking lost.

Her limp body felt like a feather in my arms as I rushed down the hall, going past the FBI and ATF like they were completely invisible. They ran past me with their guns pointed, and I ran past them with my eyes set on the door.

"Get me a fucking ambulance!" my voice rang through the raging chaos, and Tobias and my uncle, who were two steps behind me when we'd entered the Covens, stopped dead in their tracks at the sound of my demand. Tobias' mouth fell, and the hard shell that he'd formed around himself from the second he stepped in my uncle's office an hour and half ago was shattered like glass.

They rushed over to me as everyone went in the opposite direction. Tobias' hand came up to wipe at his face, but he didn't dare touch her. "*Gemma*, what did he do to you?"

There were marks all over her body. Bruises and blood and her fucking wrists. I *almost* turned on my heel and went back down the hall to grab Richard by his throat, but I didn't. Gemma needed help—right fucking now.

We were back outside a second later, and both Gemma's brother and my uncle were beside me. "Jacobi! Where the fuck is Jacobi? I need an ambulance."

Everything had been a blur from the moment we had gotten here. I went into the side door of the Covens before the FBI and ATF. I didn't know it until I heard my brother's voice from behind, telling me to stand down, but I didn't listen. Neither did my uncle, Tobias, Brantley, or Cade. We stormed the place. Brantley, Cade, and Tobias went in one direction, looking for the guards that should have been there, and then it seemed, seconds later, we had SWAT at our backs.

For all I knew, shit could have still been going down inside the Covens. I wouldn't know, though, because as soon as I grabbed Gemma, I did what I intended to do.

The mist in the air did nothing but add to the sweat glistening on my skin as I ran with Gemma in my arms toward the sight of my older brother wearing his FBI jacket.

"Jacobi, I need a fucking ambulance!" I didn't even recognize the sound of my voice. I felt a heavy hand on my shoulder as Jacobi looked down at Gemma and pushed us toward flashing lights. He pulled his radio up and mumbled something about needing medical attention right away, and then Gemma was ripped from my arms, and Jacobi was in my face, forcing me backward.

"Let them take care of her, brother!" His eyes were the same color as my mom's, and it split me right down the middle. I glanced behind his shoulder and watched as two paramedics started working on Gemma, feeling for a pulse, opening her eyes with a small flashlight and then slamming the doors and turning their sirens on.

"No!" I pushed at Jacobi as his fingers dug into my chest. Tobias and my uncle were holding my arms back as I thrashed. "Let me go with her! I have to go with her. She can't be alone!"

"She is safe, Isaiah. I promise you. She is safe with them." Jacobi's pleads flew into my ears, but it did nothing to settle me. Nothing was getting through the adrenaline and panic.

"How do you know?" That came from Tobias, and I could tell he was just as irritated as I was. "Do you know how many fucking dirty cops there are in the world? Do you know how many men knew about this place and did nothing to stop it?

Do you know how many men were fucking *created* here? How can we trust anyone?"

Jacobi's hands left my chest, and my fists clenched by my sides as I stared down the darkened road. The flashing lights were only at my back now instead of at my front. *I'm going after her.*

"I would never send her with someone I didn't trust. I will send some of my trusted men to the hospital. You can go there now. I don't want you near your father."

Our father. He meant our father. "He's still alive?"

He nodded. "Three shots went off right before you flew through the side door. My men were already on their way down the stairs. They went through the psych unit to secure it first. Your father, along with Cade's and Brantley's all had flesh wounds. They were trying to flee, along with some guards, but we got them." Jacobi looked at my uncle. "Take them and go."

"I want to stay."

That came from Tobias, and my back stiffened. "What?"

There was a cloud behind his blue eyes, something dark and troubled. "I trust you to keep my sister safe. She'll want to see you when she wakes."

If. If she wakes.

The thought did not escape me once, and the pain that came with it radiated all the way down to my heels and back.

"That's good. We need you to stay. We have questions, and I think you'll be able to answer them."

"I'll answer anything you want as long as you let me see Richard. Dead or alive."

Murder was in his tone, but nonetheless, Jacobi nodded and inched his head to everything unfolding behind us. Tobias turned without saying a word, and I could tell that my uncle wanted to go after him, but the second he stepped a foot forward, Tobias glanced back. "She needs to know you are her father. She needs to know there is one sane person left in our family."

My uncle stopped mid-step as Jacobi interjected. "I'll have an officer escort you to the hospital, along with Cade and Brantley. They're already with Special Agent Gibbons. *A bunch of fucking teenagers swarming the Covens,*" he mumbled the last part under his breath and then pulled his radio and began spouting things off as we watched Tobias head toward a group of men and women all wearing the same FBI gear my older brother was wearing.

Jacobi looked at me for a painfully long second, something passing between us that I was unable to sort through with my mind somewhere else. He nodded. I nodded back. And then my uncle and I were both in the back of a squad car, on our way to see Gemma.

To see if she was alive.

———

THE DOCTOR WAS SPEAKING to my uncle about Gemma, although it took a lot of coaxing and explaining.

"Gemma is my student—no, sorry. She is my daughter. But I just found out that she is my daughter."

"The man she lived with abused her."

"He said he was her uncle, but they were not related. He has had her in his custody for her entire life, but it was not formally legal."

"Yes. Judge Stallard."

"He did this to her!"

Finally, Special Agent Gibbons stepped forward and flashed a badge and corroborated on everything, and the doctor finally gave us an update.

"Medically induced coma."

"Possible brain injury."

"Rape kit."

"Severe trauma."

"We need to let her heal and watch her closely. Her body has been through a lot."

I stood there with my arms down by my sides, feeling as if my entire world had been put on hold. The adrenaline was slowly leaving my bloodstream, and the shock was setting in. My legs weren't the least bit steady, and my arms quaked. My face was wet, and my chest felt cracked wide open. If I could take her place, I would. In a heartbeat. She'd been cleaned up for the most part and placed in a clean gown. The blankets were pulled up, so I walked a little closer and began pulling the cotton sheet down so I could hold her hand. I wanted her to know that someone was here. That I was here. She looked so fragile, but I knew she was the furthest thing from it.

"Sir, you can't do that! You really shouldn't even be in here."

Fuck off.

"Let him." I paused at the sound of my older brother's voice and rolled my eyes as he began pulling out his badge, guiding the nurse away for a moment to discuss the situation. It amazed me how pulling a badge out could sway people in different directions. Some people had more power than others, and if that landed in the wrong hands, things like *this* happened—where people got fucking hurt, when they didn't deserve it all, because someone else held the power.

My finger rubbed softly on the white gauze wrapped around Gemma's wrist, and my throat grew tight. I shut my eyes as her beautiful face floated into my head. The sassy look she'd given me on the day I met her. The way her features were pulled in tight as she yelled at me for making the school think something had happened between us in the art supply closet during that first week. How excitement shined bright in her green eyes when we darted through the forest with something much more than attraction pulling us together. It all seemed so trivial now, so innocent and insignificant given everything we'd been through, but there wasn't a moment spent with Gemma that was insignificant. We had no idea the shit we were up against that first time I kissed her. I hadn't known how deep it all truly went.

And I had no idea that she would be able to crawl under my skin and bring to life my deepest, darkest fears. She proved to me that I had true insecurities lying underneath my guarded exterior, and one of the biggest threats was that I would bring harm to someone that I loved because of my choices. I thought I was doing right by her, and in the end, she still ended up here.

There were victories, and there were defeats.

And if she didn't wake up, there would be no victory in this. Nothing would matter anymore. Not my father or his entire empire as it came crashing to the ground. Not Richard or the punishment he would be given and the justice that came with it. Nothing mattered but this moment right here.

Gemma and I were destined to burn from the start, but it felt like I was the only one burning alive.

CHAPTER TWENTY-NINE

GEMMA

I COULDN'T REMEMBER ANYTHING, and that was so infuriating. Most of my life, I'd been pushing away the dark thoughts and memories that tried to sneak up on me, but now, I was trying like hell to actually remember something, and nothing was coming to mind.

What was the last thing I remembered?

Isaiah? Coming to my room to say goodbye before the game?

I felt my eyes moving behind my closed eyelids as I strained to hear the sounds. Fear was holding me back and blocking things out. I was familiar with the feeling that was nestled deep in my belly. The twisting and bundling of nerves that begged me to keep my eyes closed as I fought to make sense of what was going on.

Richard.

There were beeping sounds that were gaining traction in my ears. They became more persistent as my thoughts jumped in several different directions. *The Covens.* I was at the

Covens. Oh my God. Have they hooked me up to a machine? Was that the beeping? Maybe to keep me sedated and to feed me more drugs?

My eyes flung open. "Isaiah." Did he ever show up? Where did Bain go? Did Richard get to Isaiah?

Things were happening too fast, and I knew I needed to breathe, but I couldn't. I glanced down quickly and saw I was wearing a medical gown. I pulled the covers off my legs next, and I winced at the bruises for a quick second before flipping on my side and clamoring to the floor with a loud thud. Something fell off my finger that held a wire, but the only thing I could focus on was being on the ground.

"Ugh," I groaned, feeling stiff in places that I didn't know existed. My fingers hit the cool tile, and I saw more wires and tubes coming from my arm that trailed to a shiny pole that held something in a clear bag. *Drugs?* I had to get out of here. I pushed myself up on two shaky arms and ignored the bandages around my wrists. I felt weak, too weak to fight Richard if he came here, but maybe, just maybe, I could get to that door and...what? What was I going to do?

My knees wobbled on the hard surface as I began crawling. I heard voices. I pushed past everything that was scheming in the back of my head, telling me to be afraid, but instead, I got to my feet. I hung tightly onto the pole that was following me around like a little shadow.

"Help," I whispered through clenched teeth. My voice was still gritty sounding. My hand landed on the doorknob, and I realized that the room I was in looked nothing like the room from before. I remembered it being white, but this room wasn't white. It was a light blue.

I shook my head, surprised that it didn't hurt that much. The color of the room didn't matter. I needed to get the hell out of here.

The door flung open on its own with my hand on the

knob. I instantly fell forward, crashing to the ground with the metal pole clunking over the tiles. "No!" I jerked back, and my eyes widened at the face standing over me. "Just let me go! Pretend you didn't see me! At least let me warn him!"

"Whoa, whoa." The guy standing over me had beautiful, soft-blue eyes. His face was free of any markings, and he didn't look like any of the men that I'd seen after Richard had taken me. There was something alive in his gaze. Not the dead-to-the-world look that I couldn't forget if I tried. The longer I stared into this person's gaze, the more memories started to surface.

I still wasn't sure where I was, but I didn't think I was at the Covens anymore.

"Is Isaiah okay?" As soon as the words were out, I wanted to suck them back in. What if he wasn't? What if he did show up like Richard had said and...and... My hand flew up to my mouth. "Did he kill him?" And what about Sloane? Then the thought came of my brother and how Richard had told me that he'd killed him long ago.

I shuddered, my shoulders caving. My mind was everywhere. Too many emotions were pulling at me like puppet strings, and I didn't know what to say or do.

The blue-eyed man dropped down to my level. "You're going to be okay, Gemma." He touched my arm, and I pulled back instantly, and then my attention was drawn to the left as I heard something fall to the ground. A Styrofoam cup had crashed, and a black liquid spilled everywhere like tiny droplets from a rain puddle. I traveled up a set of long legs, and it was as if my eyes had truly opened for the first time since waking up.

His gasp landed on my ears as he rushed down the hall, sliding to his knees and picking me up in his arms. I was shaking. My teeth were clattering.

"*You're okay. You're okay. You're okay.*" My head was pressed to Isaiah's chest, and my senses sprung wide open. "It's okay. Just breathe. Take a breath, baby."

His head turned up at the sound of the man who had found me. "I'll get a nurse and her fath—" There was a hesitation. "I'll be back."

The footsteps faded, and I pulled back slightly, taking Isaiah's scent with me. "Isaiah. Where am I?" Our eyes met, and relief fell over me, but I was too afraid to let myself feel it. I shut my eyes and buried my head into his chest again. *Everything was fine. I was fine. I was alive, and he was alive.* "Please tell me that we are far away from that place. *Please.*"

"We're in the hospital, and I promise you that you are safe now. Damn, you're shaking. I need you to calm down, okay? They'll sedate you again, and fuck, just stay with me this time." Isaiah's hands ran down my arms, and I shuddered as things started to come back faster. *Richard had me by the throat.* My fingers uncurled from Isaiah's shirt once again. "Isaiah, where is Richard? He's going to kill you. He knows everything! He told me he had pictures of us...from—" I gasped, feeling panicky. I rubbed at my neck. "From Bain. *Bain!* He was luring you to the Covens! They're going to kill your dad, too! I heard him. Bain was there, and he...untied me?...and then..." I stopped as Isaiah stole my hand from my neck, replacing mine with his. His fingers brushed over the skin as he finished my sentence.

"I know. I know everything." His head dropped as if he were too guilty to look at me. "There are some things you don't know, but all that matters is that you're alive and in my arms for the first time in weeks."

"Weeks?" I swallowed with a dry throat. "I think I need water."

"Come on, I've got you." I peered up at Isaiah, and there were so many things hidden behind his blue eyes. The blue eyes that I pictured when I was taken from St. Mary's and shoved into a white padded room. The blue eyes that I pictured every single time I came to from being hit, or drugged, or worse. His thumb gently swiped at my bottom lip as it trembled, and I smashed them together to keep myself from breaking.

"Don't do that," he whispered. "If you cry, I'll wipe your tears. If you have nightmares, I'll wake you up. If you break down right here in front of me, I will piece you back together. I'm not leaving your side, and you aren't leaving mine, either."

A shaky breath left me as he nodded once, making sure I understood, and then he scooped me up and took me back into the room, scolding a nurse for not coming sooner.

"She finally wakes up, and no one is here to check her vitals. Un-fucking-believable," he grumbled angrily before sitting us both down onto the bed, keeping a hold of me the entire time.

CHAPTER THIRTY

ISAIAH

SHE NEVER BROKE her resolve once, even when there were several people in the room, all waiting for her to cry or at least question everything being thrown at her. Anyone else in her situation would have covered their ears and winced at the things coming from Jacobi's mouth, but Gemma was strong.

Stronger than me.

Stronger than anyone I'd ever met before.

The IV was finally taken out of her arm, and there was a slight pinkish hue covering her cheeks that made my stomach dip at the sight. She was beginning to look more like the Gemma I knew, and all I wanted to do was keep her to myself.

She pushed a piece of brown hair behind her ear, showing off how delicate her high cheekbone was. The bruises on her neck were mostly gone now, but they had taken a long time to heal. Every time I caught a glimpse of the fingerprint marks, my vision would turn crimson. I was sure Richard thought he was in a shitty place at the moment and probably couldn't even fathom how a man with his power could end up behind bars, but if he were breathing outside of that metal box, I would take my hands and choke him like he'd choked her.

"So..." Gemma shifted uncomfortably, pushing herself up farther on the bed. It had been quite a few hours since she'd woken, and per the doctor's orders, we were to give her some time before we overwhelmed her with information, but Gemma insisted, and me being me, I advocated for her. She deserved to know everything when she was ready, and if she was ready now, then she was fucking ready.

She had started off at St. Mary's on wobbly feet, but she left on sturdier ones. She didn't shy away from the past any longer. She welcomed it with open arms.

"So...my mom was sent to the group home because she had gotten in trouble with the law? And that was how she met Richard?" Gemma was repeating what Jacobi had told her because it was a clusterfuck.

My uncle—well, not technically my *uncle,* but it was hard not to think of him like that—shifted on the window ledge of the sterile-smelling room, glancing away from Gemma's curious look. "Well, technically, she met Richard when she went for sentencing. He—"

Gemma nodded. "He sent girls to the group home instead of jail. I knew that...I just didn't fully know my mom was one of them. I had suspected a time or two, but from what I remembered when I was little, my mom never really went over to the group home. We lived in the big house. Richard's house."

Uncle Tate's vein was back again, throbbing right there in the middle of his forehead. I knew that, deep down, he felt that it was his fault that Emily had been there. It was a favor from Judge Stallard and the last tie between him and my grandfather. A deal. My grandfather would keep Emily from prison with the help of his ol' pal Judge Stallard, and Uncle

Tate would destroy the incriminating files he had regarding the family business and leave without a word.

It wasn't his fault, though. Although, I knew why he felt that way. It was insignificant at this point. There was so much more that Gemma didn't know.

"Right," Jacobi answered. "From what we've gathered, your mother and Richard had some sort of an affair during her time there, and that would have gone against every ethic and moral that Judge Stallard stood for. So, he kept it a secret, along with you and your brother."

"My mother didn't want to be with him anymore. I remember her telling him no, and he got angry. He said she was mentally unstable and left her at the psych hospital, later saying she had killed herself."

Jacobi nodded again, and I could sense that Gemma was feeling uncomfortable.

I whispered into her ear, "Do you want to take a break?"

Her head shook instantly, so I pulled back and kept a hold of her hand.

"From a psychological viewpoint, Richard seemed to have been obsessed with your mother and with the idea of creating a family with her. When she told him no, his obsession moved to you, and crossing that with an obvious personality disorder along with the different facets of his life..."

"What are you saying?" she asked.

I spoke for my brother. "Richard is fucking crazy."

Gemma laughed. She actually laughed, and her cheeks looked pinker, too. "Um, yeah. I know. But what now?" She looked at Jacobi and suddenly grew serious. "You say you're in the FBI."

He nodded slowly. "We, speaking for the FBI, were working closely with ATF, the Bureau of Alcohol, Tobacco, Firearms, and Explosives, and you seemed to come up on the radar." Jacobi hummed, smiling slightly. "You kind of wrapped everything up for us in a nice and tidy bow, Gemma. We owe you. Not only did we take down one of the biggest illegal gun suppliers in the western hemisphere, we took down their biggest client: Judge Stallard and the Covens, which is wildly popular on the dark web. You were at the center of it all, as complicated as it was."

My brother's half-assed compliment didn't seem to register with Gemma. Her fingers started de-threading the blanket covering our legs, and her nerves were evident. "How many people are on Richard's payroll, though? On the FBI? He has power... I've seen him use it."

I placed my hand on Gemma's, and she stilled, looking up at me, appearing so fucking vulnerable, and I wanted to somehow force it into her head that no one was coming close to her now. "He will not be cut loose, Gemma."

"How do you know that, though? What?" She panicked, looking back at my brother and my uncle—*her father*, which she had no idea about...*yet*. "Is it his word against mine? All the abuse? Who's to say he won't just lie and say I'm crazy like my mother? He's threatened that before! Who's to say I can trust you?"

"Not only do we have him on the abuse, but we have charges relating to the Covens, too. And it isn't just his word against yours..."

Gemma was leery. "What do you mean? Do you have witnesses? Do you have proof of everything he did to me? And I don't even know what *really* went on at the psych hospital...but I can tell you that it wasn't good. The men that came into my room were... What did Richard even have to do with that place? I remember some things that were said and done from when I was younger, but..." She pulled into herself. "The men that I saw in that place were bad people. They..."

My heart thudded to the ground. My uncle visibly tensed, and Jacobi winced. "We know what went on at the psych hospital. Judge Stallard deemed men mentally ill and sent them to the hospital, but instead of treating them for mental illness in the true psych hospital, he..."

Jacobi slowly shifted his attention to me, and I nodded, allowing him to continue. Gemma would tell us when she wanted to stop, but I had a hunch she wouldn't want to.

"He gave those men an option of lessening their sentences for something else in life."

"Like what?"

I answered, staring at the wall. "Gun-runners. Drug-sellers. Hitmen."

Her head snapped to mine. "Hitmen? Like..."

"Professional killers hired on the black market. Yes. That's where Isaiah's father—"

I pointed my finger at Jacobi, correcting him. "Our."

Gemma was already aware that Jacobi was my brother, so she wasn't shocked by this.

"That's where *our* father came into play. He supplied the guns to the Covens for the hitmen. He'd been selling them to Richard for years, thus bringing us all together here today."

"That is not the reason we're here today." Uncle Tate lowered his legs to the ground from the window seat and placed his hands on his knees. I felt the shift in the room and bit my tongue.

"What...what do you mean?" I could hear the exhaustion within Gemma, so I pulled her back, and she rested along my chest, taking a deep breath. *I know, baby. I know.*

My hands rubbed at her bare arms and placed a kiss on her hair.

"You and Isaiah were in the middle of something neither one of you should have had to deal with. You being in Richard's care from birth made you a casualty in a sick game of illegal activities. Not only the abuse that you have suffered but so much more." My uncle turned to me. "And you, being your father's son, had to figure out a way to save the one girl that you loved from not only your future but hers too. You two have been at the center of this the entire time. Like a bridge between two evils."

"I don't know if this..." I started to interject when I felt Gemma shift uncomfortably. She was looking up at me, and I clamped my mouth shut. *She needed to know.*

"I'm not Isaiah's uncle, Gemma."

I grabbed her hand tightly, and she squeezed it right back. "Then who are you?"

His eyes shut briefly. "I'm your father."

CHAPTER THIRTY-ONE

GEMMA

MY MOUTH OPENED. Then closed. Then opened again. All while the room fell silent. There were four of us in here, but it felt like just me and...Headmaster Ellison...my father.

"Gem." Isaiah's thumb rubbed slow circles over my hand. Headmaster Ellison looked equal parts relieved and horrified.

"I..." My voice was a whisper again, and I cleared my throat, forcing my mouth to move through the emotion straining my vocals. "I don't... I'm confused."

Headmaster Ellison's hands rested over his thighs evenly. His chest rose and stayed for a second before it deflated, and he spilled.

"Your mother and I were a lot like you and Isaiah. We came from completely different backgrounds but were drawn together nonetheless. We were in a sort of secret relationship due to a number of things, but she...helped me through some messed up stuff, and when she got caught in a bad spot—felony theft—I helped her out. Or I thought I was helping. I bargained with my father—or who I *thought* to be my father —Isaiah's grandfather, to help her. Our family had been doing business with the Stallards for a very long time. So, Isaiah's grandfather asked Judge Stallard, *Richard*, for a favor in keeping your mother out of prison, all in exchange for me to leave the family because it turned out I was an orphan, just like your mother was. I'm not an Underwood. I'm not related to Isaiah. And his grandfather knew that from the beginning and wanted me out of the family." Headmaster Ellison's eyes were glossy, and the agony was there, evident on his face, and I felt it just as much. The guilt. He had to have had so much guilt. "I thought I was helping her. I thought I was helping her stay out of prison."

"Did you..." I unclogged my tight throat, looking away. "Did you know she was pregnant with me and Tobias? Did you know who I was the second I showed up at St. Mary's?"

"No!" Headmaster Ellison popped to his feet and walked over to the bed, so I was forced to look up at him. "I tried to talk to your mother after her sentencing, but every time I would try to have contact with her in the group home, I would get shut down. My letters would go unanswered, and eventually, I believed that she just didn't want to talk to me anymore. But I think now I know why. Richard didn't want her to have contact with me or anyone from her past life. He must have seen something in her... Maybe he saw a future with a beautiful young girl who was stuck in a bad spot with two little babies. Maybe he knew I was your father all along. Although, if he had known that, I doubt he would have sent you to me.

"After her sentence ended, I tried to find her again. Ann, Richard's mother, had said that she'd disappeared. I hired private investigators, everything. There was no trail of her. Anywhere."

My head fell in defeat. "That makes sense. There would be no paper trail when you are no longer alive, and not to mention, Richard is well versed in covering things up. He told Tobias and me that she committed suicide because she was so sick. That's why she left us in the first place. To go to the hospital to get better and...that she killed herself." I slowly raised my head and looked at Jacobi, all while squeezing Isaiah's hand. "That's not true. Richard killed her. Or someone in that place did."

His jaw tensed as he nodded and began scribbling it down in his notebook.

"I'm so sorry, Gemma." I came back and met Headmaster Ellison again. The familiarity of his presence and calmness he always gave me was still there and even more palpable.

"You remind me of Tobias." I bit my lip, squeezing my eyes for a second before opening them back up and taking a deep breath. I pushed up off Isaiah's hard and sturdy chest, suddenly missing the way his heart beat along my back. "From the second I met you, I...you felt so familiar to me. Like I knew you somehow." The realization hit me like a ton of bricks, and I wanted to cry. I really did. There was so much hurt jabbing at me, but one thing was for certain: Headmaster Ellison, my *father,* was not the one at fault. The true evil here was Richard Stallard. All his lies, his cover-ups, his payouts. He was the one who needed to take the blame. All of it.

"It wasn't your fault," I whispered, placing my hand on his. The headmaster's head flew up in surprise. "I know you think you have their blood on your hands, but you don't. It's Richard's fault. Not yours. There were plenty of young girls at the group home that he could have chosen from. Who knows? Maybe this isn't the first time he's become obsessed."

We stayed locked on each other for far too long. My heart hurt, but at the same time, it felt stitched back together. It was banged up, and parts of it would likely never heal. The wounds of losing someone forever would stay, but there were parts of me that were still hanging on. There were parts of me that could care for someone and learn to trust them. I learned that from what I felt for Isaiah.

"Gemma," Jacobi interrupted Headmaster Ellison's and my tense moment. "There is something else that you need to know." He stood up, shifting his attention to Isaiah and then to Headmaster Ellison, which only spiked my blood with more dread.

"Now what?" I asked, feeling as if I were teetering over the edge.

"Like I said, it isn't just your word against his. There are photos that we have collected from the house you grew up in, along with many corroborators who have come forward after the press release on the accusations of Richard, along with those who he tried to bribe and/or pay off. Like a..." Jacobi shuffled through some papers before nodding. "Miss Ann Scova. She was the social worker who had taken on your case after some girls from the group home began speaking up about the *girl in the big house*. That social worker is a tough cookie. Anyway, Richard had tried to pay her to turn a blind eye, but she didn't."

I nodded. "She was the reason I was sent to Wellington Prep. Richard said he had no choice but to send me to an actual school because of a social worker poking around. And then that led to sending me to St. Mary's."

"Yes, and..." Jacobi looked at Isaiah again, and he tensed behind me. I spun around and looked at the wariness pulling along his dark features.

"Gemma, what did Richard say to you about Tobias?" His brows slanted, and his tongue darted out to lick his lips. He pulled himself up higher on my hospital bed and bent a knee, resting his arm on it as I sat in between his legs. "Didn't you tell me that you knew Tobias was still alive? That's why you went to the Covens that one night, yeah?"

My head dropped again, but I thought better of hiding the hurt. Instead, I peeked back up and let Isaiah read my face for what it was. "Richard told me he killed him when I had made a remark. And I know what you're thinking. Why would I believe anything he says? But you didn't see the look in his eye, Isaiah. And it makes sense..." I shrugged, not wanting to believe the truth that had been in the back of my mind for the last several years. "I couldn't find *anything* in that house that was connected to my brother. There were no leads, no clues, nothing. And you even said it yourself: he wasn't at the Covens. Where else would he be?" My heart thrashed, and if the nurse came in here right now and took my blood pressure, I was certain it would be much higher than it was an hour ago. "He killed him."

"Gem," Headmaster Ellison's voice was soft, and like before, I felt calm near him. Almost just as calm as I did with Isaiah. "Your brother is alive."

Chills coated my arms, except this time it wasn't from fear. It was from shock. My heart whacked inside. "He's alive?"

"He's our other witness. There is no way anyone in their right mind could let Richard Stallard walk freely on this earth after the evidence and statements from the pair of you. Even given his judicial stance. There is too much against him now for a cover-up. I won't let it happen."

"Just like you won't let Dad walk either?" That came from Isaiah, but I'd forgotten that his father even had a role in this. Jacobi gave him a look and said something, but I couldn't focus on what he'd said.

Tobias was alive.

My twin brother was alive.

"Do you have him? My brother?" I sat up taller, ignoring

the stiffness in my body. "Is he okay? Where was he? Is he here right now?"

The words were spilling out so fast, and my body was moving quickly as I tried to hop off the bed. Isaiah grabbed onto my waist and pulled me back. "Gemma, take it easy. You're still recovering."

My head turned to him, and I knew that he could see the hope blossoming. "Tobias is alive, Isaiah! My brother is alive."

His lips curved slightly, but there was something sad lingering there too. I knew Isaiah, and I could tell when something wasn't right. "I know, baby. But..."

"But what?"

He sighed, bringing me closer to him as if there wasn't anyone else in the room. I peered up into his blue eyes, and I could see him stalling. "Isaiah, I can handle it. What?"

He chuckled. "Oh, I know you can. I just don't know if I can handle the hurt I'm going to see." My mouth tugged down as he continued. "He's been at the Covens this entire time." He swallowed, licking his lips again. "And...he's working on some things. On himself."

"So..."

"So, he doesn't want to see you...not yet."

My shoulders dropped as hurt crashed and burned around me. *He didn't want to see me?* "Oh."

"Hey, he'll get back on track, okay? He's just..."

"He just wants to be alone right now."

I turned to the headmaster... My father... *Our* father. "Does...he know that you're our father?"

He nodded. "He knows everything."

I nodded in unison with him as I tried to wrap my head around everything. The rollercoaster of emotions and revelations. The ups and down of devastation and hope and then more devastation was making my head hurt again. I didn't know what to say or feel. I should have been grateful that I was alive and sitting beside Isaiah, but now I just felt empty, like my body was locking down emotion because it was just too much.

"Alright. Out." Isaiah pointed to the door as if he read my mind.

I slinked back onto his chest without even realizing I'd done so.

Jacobi stood up, glancing over at me once more. He and Isaiah looked a lot alike, except Isaiah was bad-boy handsome with his coy grin and dark features, and Jacobi was a serene type of handsome. Smooth and put together. Chivalrous. "You are safe now, Gemma. You and Tobias both. Okay? Get some rest." Then, he looked at Isaiah once more and turned around and walked out the door.

Headmaster Ellison patted my leg and slowly began to back away, looking more confused than ever. I felt the same.

"Headma—" I paused. "Ta—" I paused again. *What should I call him?* I shook my head, looking down. "If you talk to my brother, can you just tell him...that..." The vulnerability was so heavy I could hardly speak. "Can you just tell him that I love him? And whatever he's feeling, it's okay?"

His lips gently curved, and the uneasiness that I saw just seconds ago was gone. "I will. Get some rest. I'll be back in a bit."

Once the door shut, Isaiah's hand was on my chin, and he angled my head on his chest to look up at him. His eyes bounced back and forth between mine as his thumb rubbed over my bottom lip again. I was pretty sure it was wobbling. "You are unbelievable. The strongest person I know."

The tears were there, making his face blurry for a second before I blinked them away. I was swimming in everything I'd just been told, and there was shock and fear and a whole bunch of other stuff that was threatening to come out of my mouth, but instead of talking about the fact that my brother was alive, or that I now had a father, I said something that surprised us both. "I love you." Those three little words were the one thing I was sure of in the moment, and it felt good to get them out.

A flicker of shock reached Isaiah, and it was as if everything else just paused for a few seconds. My eyes watered again, and I buried my face back in his chest. "I just wanted you to know that. I didn't say it before, but I felt it. I felt it a long time ago."

"I know. I felt it, too." Then, his arms came around me as his leg popped back down. Mine hooked over his, and we lay like that for so long I thought he might be asleep.

"So now what," I whispered, talking to myself more than anything.

He answered quickly. "Things are going to get messier. We're still stuck in a fucking web. There will be trials. Statements to be made. All of it. My father's entire empire just came crashing down. Some of his people went into hiding, and others are currently being arrested. Richard's name is plastered everywhere, and it's an uproar. The entire state is in shambles."

"What about Jack? And Sloane?"

"They're both okay. I sent Jack to Jacobi before I even knew he was in the FBI, working toward the same goal I was."

I nodded, squeezing him tighter. The future looked even scarier than before, but at least the people I cared about were okay.

"I'll be here no matter what. Okay? We just have to find a new normal."

A small grin covered my face as I tried to lighten the mood. "So, no more hiding underneath the dining hall tables in the middle of the night to reach under my skirt so no one sees us?"

Isaiah's chuckle was abrupt, and my face shook against his chest as he laughed. Somehow, I still managed to let out a light laugh, too.

"Fuck that. I'll have you on top of the table this time. In front of the whole school. Ask me if I care."

I smiled, my cheeks feeling hot, but then a thought occurred to me. "What happened to Bain?" I popped up, and we locked eyes. "He untied me, Isaiah. I think. In that room. He..."

"Don't try to make sense of it."

"Where did he go, though? He was there, and then..."

"He helped us get to you. He had put you there, but he helped get you back after he realized..." He shook his head. "I need you to understand something. Bain won't hurt you. When and if you come back to school, he will be there, but he will not fucking touch you. Okay? Do you trust me? We do not have to worry about Bain."

"Yes, I trust you," I answered swiftly, still stuck on Bain. There was something off about him at the Covens. He wasn't his usual, put-a-knife-in-your-back self. What had happened while I was out the last couple of weeks? *Was Bain the one in the mask after I ran? Did he say those things to Richard? That he would kill him?* What was real and what wasn't?

Isaiah must have sensed that my mind was pulling me again, because the next thing I knew, he was pushing my face closer to his and silencing me with his mouth. His lips covered mine softly, and the things I felt when he kissed me, that had been dormant since I was taken, were suddenly turned back on, canceling out the questions and confusion.

A tiny noise left me as I pushed closer to him. Isaiah's teeth sunk into my bottom lip as he clenched his eyes. He pulled back, and looking into his eyes was like the ocean was pulling me. He drank me in, every inch of my face, especially my lips. "Knock it off, Good Girl."

I smiled.

The twitch of his lips had mine rising higher. He shrugged and said, "Never mind. Don't knock it off." And then he pulled me in again and chased my tongue with his.

CHAPTER THIRTY-TWO

ISAIAH

"Go away, Isaiah. She's mine. You've had her to yourself for weeks." Sloane's eyebrow hitched, and there was an evil glint lingering, which was her usual look when it came to me.

My arms were crossed over my uniform as I rested lazily against the far wall of the girls' hallway. It was wild in here at the crack of dawn. Like a fucking zoo. There were girls rushing down the hall with wet hair, and some had green shit on their skin, covering every inch of their face except their eyes. It was frightening, and the excess in estrogen did nothing but make me antsy.

One chick ran past with only a towel on, and when she saw me standing there in a mist of hairspray and perfume, she screamed, and her towel fell. I quickly shut my eyes and pushed forward, running right into Sloane. "She's my girl-friend, Sloane. And yes, I had her for weeks to myself, but she was in a fucking coma. Doesn't really count."

"Does too."

"Oh my goodness, you two! Just let him in, or he'll never

go away. You know how persistent he is." The humor in Gemma's voice made the entire five minutes that I stood in the girls' hallway worth it. In the past, I'd only ever come down here during the late night, even before Gemma. It was a whole new era in the mornings.

"Ugh, fine." Sloane huffed and shut the door behind me, silencing all the catty chatter happening on the outside.

"It's crazy out there," I said, stepping farther into the room. I glanced around their girly dorm and searched for the only person I really wanted to see.

"Says the guy who carried me out of a literal gun fight." Gemma popped out of her bathroom, and it was jarring to see her like this. Her cheeks were painted with a tint of pink, her green eyes brighter than ever. The bags underneath had faded, and it looked as if she had actually gotten some sleep.

I, however, had not. I worried all night long that she would have a nightmare and I wouldn't be there to help her, but she reminded me that she'd been having nightmares and remembering things that she'd forced away for years, and this was no different. Except now, she truly felt safe. Even with Bain here, she said she felt safe. He was still a rat in my eyes, and the Rebels and I would never stop watching him, but he had saved her, and he'd stayed true to his word. So, I would stay true to mine.

Gemma insisted that she get back to classes as soon as the doctor cleared her, despite everything that was unfolding outside of this palatial school. Her name, along with Tobias', had been withheld from the news, and they remained anonymous, so Tate couldn't think of any other reason to keep her from normalcy. If she wanted to come back to school, then she could come back to school.

He'd reminded me that Gemma felt at home here above anywhere else, and it was the perfect place to put her, given that her newfound father also resided here.

Tate—who I now refrained from calling Uncle—had been busy since returning back. There were messes to clean up and explanations to the SMC on his whereabouts—along with mine and Gemma's. And let's not forget the fact that he now had to place two new students at St. Mary's: one being Journey, which was surely going to be the new talk of the gossip blog, Mary's Murmurs, and the other being Tobias—when he was ready.

For now, he stayed away. There was a lot Gemma and I weren't aware of, but I knew that Tate was keeping a watchful eye on him and helping him as much as he could. Tobias was Tate's son, but according to what he'd said to me one night at the hospital when Gemma was still recovering, there may never be a bond between them. There may never be hope for a relationship. Tobias wasn't the same boy he was when Gemma knew him, and Tobias was smart enough to realize that, which was why he was still staying away. I respected that.

And Gemma understood. She knew how damaging trauma could be. But it still hurt her that she hadn't seen him yet. She was quiet about it. Reserved.

But I knew her. I felt her feelings as if they were my own.

Just like I knew that she was nervous for today.

Not because of what had happened over the last few weeks—because, again, no one knew but a few of us. She was nervous because I told her that I was going to pick her up around her waist, place her hot little ass on the dining hall table during breakfast and kiss her senseless in front of everyone because we now had the freedom to do so.

Considering that we were never truly exclusive, I wanted to make a point to show everyone that we were. I explained very calmly that now that she was mine and the dangers that we were faced with no longer hid in the shadows, neither would we.

Gemma was my girlfriend, and the whole fucking lot of St. Mary's would know it. Maybe I was a little possessive, but there was a difference between possessive and controlling. *She was mine for as long as she wanted me.*

"Ready?" I finally asked as Sloane and Gemma packed their bags.

Gemma looked at me out of the corner of her eye, and I winked. "Isaiah, you better not."

"Oh, I am."

She tried to fight a smile, but I saw the cute little way her lips tugged.

"He better not what?" Sloane asked, spraying some perfume on her uniform.

My eyebrows waggled. "I'm markin' my claim."

"You're what?"

Gemma sighed, walking closer to me, but not before shooting me a look. "He said he's going to kiss me in front of everyone to indicate that we are boyfriend and girlfriend."

I shook my finger. "That is not what I said. I said I was going to plop your hot little ass on the dining table and kiss you in front of everyone because I can and I will."

Sloane's lips smashed together as she held back a laugh. "Gemma, your face is so red right now."

"Shut up! Both of you!" She turned back to me. "You know I hate attention."

"But you love me." I winked and grabbed her hand, pulling her toward the chaos. Sloane was right at our backs.

"Everyone knows you two are a thing anyway. It won't be much of a surprise to the students. But maybe to the teachers." Sloane turned to me as we walked down the hall, which was much less wild now. *How did they disappear that fast?* "Are you off probation now? Or was that a lie too?"

I held back an eye roll. Sloane was still a little bitter that we hadn't filled her in on everything when Gemma was taken.

Eventually Cade and Brantley pulled her aside, along with Shiner, while I was at the hospital, and laid it all out for her. Well, Brantley was the one who'd straightened everything out. Cade was still in his feels about Journey showing up out of nowhere. I hadn't talked with him much, but from the times that I did, I could tell he was completely fucked up—especially because she was still at the orphanage until Tate got things settled. It was slowly killing Cade.

"I'm off probation now. That wasn't a lie. The SMC really was going to expel me if I didn't stop fucking around and get my grades up." I pulled Gemma into my chest for a second, pecking her on the nose before we descended the steps toward the dining hall. "Thank God for my tutor."

Gemma laughed, but before we knew it, we were walking into the dining hall. The girl whose towel fell in front of me no more than twenty minutes ago darted past us with her head glued to her chest.

"What was that all about?" Gemma asked, looking back at the girl scurrying away.

I brushed it off, but Sloane answered as we made our way toward Cade, Brantley, Mercedes, and Shiner. "Her towel fell as your boyfriend was waiting in the hall to come into our room. Pretty sure she's horrified."

"Oh my God. That's...embarrassing."

Sloane shrugged. "She could have willingly opened her towel for him, and in that case, we would have had to set her straight. Isaiah Underwood is taken!"

Gemma's face blushed as she elbowed her friend. "Oh my gosh. You're as bad as him!"

Sloane pulled away from Gem and walked over to sit beside Mercedes as if Gemma hadn't just elbowed her.

She and I were left in the middle of the dining hall, and *fuck*, I just got a little nervous. *Did I seriously just get fucking butterflies?*

Gemma's green gaze tilted toward mine, and I dipped down, my tie hanging between us. I whispered into her ear, "I won't do it if you don't want me to."

She paused, looking torn. *Did she want me to?* My lips curled, and she was pinned to them. The thought of her perfect ass on that table did all sorts of things to me. The memory of the last time I'd placed her on the table was not long forgotten. I dipped down to her ear again, seeing a flush creep up her cleavage that had been playing peek-a-boo with me all morning. "But I know damn well, deep down, you want me to. You know you like breaking rules with me, Gem. And I have to say, sitting on the table in the middle of breakfast, tongue-fucking your new boyfriend...is kind of against the rules."

It took half a second for her lips to split in two and one more for my hands to dip underneath her skirt, gripping her firm ass that was hardly covered by her panties and plopping her down in front of everyone.

"You're the baddest good girl I've ever met, Gemma Richardson."

Her brow flicked. "Well, maybe I'm not a good girl, Isaiah Underwood."

And then my mouth was on hers, and the entire dining hall fell silent.

EPILOGUE

GEMMA

THE NEWSPAPER CAUGHT my eye the second I walked toward the dining room with Isaiah at my back. He pulled out my chair for me, and I shot him a playful smile all while Cade, Brantley, and Shiner made no attempt at hiding their snickering. They didn't think their best friend, head Rebel of the school, was a gentleman, but they were wrong. Isaiah was different with me. He was different from what he'd always portrayed himself as on the outside.

I thought, deep down, his best friends knew that too.

They just liked to screw with him.

As soon as I sat down, the guys started talking again about lacrosse and how they wished it weren't an all-year sport for our school. There was a giant elephant in the room, but they pretended there wasn't.

Things were weird.

There...I said it. Sitting here, at my newly found father's home, a very large house behind St. Mary's, having family dinner at his table, was just awkward.

After things had calmed down and I returned to school, Tate had pulled me into his office, looking more disheveled than I'd ever seen him. His tie was loose, his sleeves were pushed up to his elbows, and three half-empty cups of cold coffee sat on the edge of his desk. He very hesitantly told me that he was moving from the servant's cottage just below the school to the actual house that was just a mile or two down the road. He said he'd never wanted to live there because, *"What would a single man like me need a house that big for?"* But now, things were changing. Jacobi, along with Ann Scova, the social worker that had never once forgotten about me *or* Richard, had come together and were allowing Jack, Isaiah's little brother, to move in with Tate. Isaiah's father was behind bars and would be for a very long time given the severity of charges against him, and paired with the fact that their mother was being moved to a medical facility for further care, he had nowhere else to go. Jacobi's job in the FBI wasn't the most accommodating for young children, so this was their best option. Plus, Jack wanted to be with Isaiah, and this was as close as they could get. Jack would attend the primary school down the road and come back home in the evenings. Isaiah would still stay at the boarding school, but he could come and go as he pleased, even if Tate wasn't actually blood related to either of them.

Instead, he was blood related to me.

He offered for me to stay here, too, but I declined politely. It wasn't because I didn't want to have a relationship with him; it was just that things were moving too quickly, and the rest of the school wasn't aware that he was my father.

I was sure it would come out eventually, but for now, no one really knew except our closest friends, and that was how I wanted to keep it.

Now, if my brother came back, then my mind might change.

He was still staying away, and each day that passed that I didn't hear from him made the knife dig in a little further.

But I tried not to focus on it. He was alive and safe, and that was all that mattered.

Grabbing the napkin off the side of the plate, I pulled it to my lap and looked back at the newspaper laying at the end of the table once more.

The headline caused my heart to slip.

"The Girl *in the* Basement Story Unfolds with New Witness Statements"

It was no surprise that the news article was about me, and the future of having to talk with more lawyers and law enforcement did not dampen my foresight at all. Things were going to get harder, but I pushed the anxiety away, reminding myself that I wasn't alone in this.

I had Isaiah, and our friends, and Tate. I also had Tobias, even if he wasn't presently here with me.

As soon as Tate walked into the dining room, holding a box of pizza, Jack—who I'd yet to formally meet—came rushing in behind him with cute little glasses on the edge of his nose, beaming at his older brother and his three friends.

"Isaiahhhhhh!" He ran up to the side of his seat and clenched his arms around Isaiah's middle.

"Hey, little man! Cool bedroom, am I right? I helped paint it."

"No, you didn't. You sat back and watched Gemma. Uncle Tate told me so." Jack released his older brother and turned and looked at me before pushing his glasses up from the edge of his nose. "Are you Gemma?"

I smiled. "I am. Do you like your room?"

He nodded vigorously, his glasses falling down again. "I *love* it. Did you seriously draw Hogwarts on my wall? All by yourself?"

The awe in his blue eyes warmed my heart. I nodded slowly. "I did. Does it look okay? I've never seen *Harry Potter,* so I just looked at a picture on the Internet and tried my best."

His little mouth flew open, and he snapped his head to Isaiah. "She's never seen *Harry Potter*, Isaiah!"

Everyone in the room laughed, even Tate.

"I know, dude. What are we gonna do about that?"

Jack shook his head, taking the seat beside Isaiah. "Well, we have to watch *Harry Potter* after dinner. We have to!" He looked up at Tate, who was still holding the pizza in his hands. "Can we, Uncle Tate? Just the first movie?"

Tate gave him a warm grin. "Sure, if Gemma wants to. They all have to get back to the school here in a bit, though."

"Pizza?" Isaiah asked, leaning back in his seat. His hand made its way to my leg, and small prickles of heat coated my skin. "I thought you said you were cooking."

The pizza was placed down on the table, and his shoulders sagged. "I burned it."

Shiner let out a laugh. "I wasn't gonna say anything, but I could smell that you burned something before I even sat down."

Tate ran a hand through his hair. "I'm... I've never really cooked before. I always ate at the school."

"Aw, look at Tate trying to be a family man." Isaiah's voice was on the brink of laughter, and I knew he was just giving him a hard time, but I thought it was sweet that he was actually trying. He was so unsure when he'd asked me to come to dinner, allowing me to invite Isaiah, too, which then turned into Cade, Brantley, and Shiner inviting themselves along. I was certain once Sloane and Mercedes caught wind that all the guys came, they'd want to come too. Tate was putting in an effort to be there for me, all while not pressuring me to act a certain way or to take control of my life.

"I can cook next week," I said, biting my lip nervously when everyone stared at me. I desperately wanted to pull my hands to my lap to hide my wrists, but I promised myself I wasn't going to hide my scars any longer. It was one more thing I could take back from Richard. He didn't have control over me anymore, nor did I have to hide the scars that he'd put there.

"Oh, good idea. May I put in a request, Queen Rebel?"

I laughed, looking over at Shiner. The nickname started as soon as I had come back to school and everyone realized that Isaiah and I were a thing. It was so stupid, but I secretly loved it, too.

"No, you can't." Brantley sat back in his seat and shook his head. "No one wants to eat fucking liver and onions, Shiner. It's gross, okay?"

"You haven't had it prepared right, then." Shiner clapped his hands as Isaiah sat forward and pulled a slice of pizza from the box. "I have a great idea. We should all take turns. Sunday dinner every week, *but...*" He held up his finger, silencing the room. To be honest, I think we all wanted to know what would come out of his mouth next, because he was so entertaining. "We switch. One week Gemma will cook. Next, I will cook. Then Brantley, Cade, Isaiah, and so on. We should have a competition. Jack can determine who is the best cook, although we all know it's me." He pulled a piece of pizza up to his mouth. "We all know that I'm a winner."

Everyone laughed—even Cade, who had been very withdrawn since everything had happened. I knew it had to do with Journey, who I also hadn't formally met yet. I desperately wanted to meet her, though. I didn't even know her, and

I wanted to wrap my arms around her to thank her for helping my brother get out of the Covens. Maybe it was a mutual thing. Or maybe Tobias helped her. Either way, I felt like she was a piece of Tobias, and I would take what I could get.

After we all got our pizza, I saw Tate casually push the newspaper underneath his plate so no one would see it. We caught eyes, and he paused, knowing that I saw it, but I gave him a little smile and shook my head. Isaiah squeezed my leg, and I began eating until Tate cleared his throat.

"So, about Sunday dinners, then. Is that...a thing?" He was looking directly at me. "Would you like to make this a reoccurring thing?"

There it was again, that small amount of unease that etched over his tired features. He was trying so hard, and it felt so good to have someone not force me into anything. He had no idea how much I respected that.

I nodded. "Sure, I think I would like that." The relief came over him quickly, and his eyes lit up. I turned to Shiner. "But I'm not eating liver and onions."

He threw his hands up as Isaiah laughed from beside me. "Oh, come on! What?"

The table was full of laughter and easy conversation. I couldn't help but feel lighter sitting here, even though this moment and these relationships came from the most messed-up situation ever. It still felt good, though. I felt like I was surrounded by family, and it was then that I realized that feeling at *home* had nothing to do with where you grew up, how you grew up, or who raised you, and it had everything to do with where you felt the safest and the most loved.

And from where I was sitting, I felt loved and safe.

There was still a piece of me missing, but as for the pieces that were there, they were happy. I was happy and at ease. It felt so comforting that I didn't have to watch my back and have fear creeping up behind me.

Shiner was still going on about liver and onions when there was a knock on the door. The table grew silent, and we all turned to Tate. There was a tiny crease present in between his eyebrows as he slowly stood up, placing his slice of pizza back on the table. As soon as he left the room, we all stood up, even Jack, and followed after him.

He turned around right before opening the door and rolled his eyes. "Go back to the dining room."

None of us moved, and he sighed before reaching for the doorknob. The door swung open a second later, and Isaiah, being taller than me, must have seen who it was. His hand grabbed onto mine, and he clenched it.

"What's wrong?" My body instantly went into fear mode. My heart began to thump, and I felt hot.

I slowly peeked around Tate and sucked in every bit of air in the room. A gasp got stuck in my throat, and my legs almost gave out on me.

A voice I recognized, even in this next life, hit my ears. "I think I'm ready to take you up on your offer now. I think I'm ready to see my sister."

Tate took a step back, and there, in the doorway, with the sun setting in the distance, was my twin brother holding a duffel bag over his shoulder.

"Tobias." My whisper was the only thing floating in between us. It seemed everyone was holding their breath.

My eyes watered as Tobias took a step forward, and my heart leapt into the air. He looked different. So different. He was no longer a boy, and he was no longer the light that I grasped onto in some of the darkest times of our lives.

As soon as he was in front of me, he said, "Hey, sis."

My hand slowly fell from Isaiah's, and I shakily reached up and touched the side of Tobias' face. There was a tiny thin scar that cut through his eyebrow that I zeroed in on as my palm collided with his skin. My chest caved, and I wanted to sob. *He was so different.*

"What did he do to you?" I whispered, dropping my hand to wrap my arms around him. At first, he was tense, so tense that I could feel every hardened muscle along his stomach, but eventually, his arms wrapped around me.

His whisper was hardly present. I doubted anyone could hear it but me. "I could ask you the same."

I pulled back slowly, ignoring the tears on my face. Tobias was free of any emotion, but I wasn't expecting much. "We can only go up from here, right?"

He showed me a tired smile. "Yeah."

A few more moments passed before Tate closed the door, grabbing Tobias' bag. "Well...do you want some pizza?"

Tobias let go of me and took a hefty step back. "Sure."

And one by one, we all shuffled back into the dining room. Isaiah's hand was back in mine, and a soft kiss pelted the side of my head. I peered up at him, and he gave me a reassuring smile.

Things were far from being perfect, but that was okay.

Perfect was overrated, and this right here was better than anything I'd ever had before.

The End

AUTHOR'S NOTE

FINALLY! Isaiah and Gemma got their happily ever after! You will see more of them in upcoming books (although their story is finished) so don't worry about missing them too much! I hope you enjoyed all the ups and downs that these two had to endure. When I first started writing their story, I had no idea it would turn into *this*. St. Mary's is a world that I will be living in for a while. There are more stories to come, and your questions will eventually be answered (because I know, I know — you have questions!). Journey and Cade for starters, and Tobias? Bain? SO MANY QUESTIONS AND POSSIBILITIES! Rest assured that there is more to come and some things were not explained because it would spoil future books! Until next time, friends.

Please note: Journey and Cade's book, Dead Girls Never Talk, will be available May of 2022!

XO

Ps. If you enjoyed the St. Mary's Duet and haven't read my English Prep Series, continue reading for the blurb of book one, All the Little Lies: A High School Bully Romance.

All the Little Lies Blurb:

English Prep stands tall with its ivy-covered exterior and old, wrought-iron doors. The stone gargoyles sit at the school's entrance, knowing just as much as anyone: I don't belong.

Once upon a time, I did. I belonged in the "it" crowd with all the other well-endowed kids, but now, I am no longer welcome.

Not after five years away from this place.

Not after the scandal that landed me on the wrong side of the tracks.

I'd be lying if I said I'm not looking forward to seeing the one person who was always by my side. My old best friend. My safe place.

Only, Christian isn't the same boy I left behind. His cold, brooding, devastatingly attractive glare sends chills down my spine. My old best friend doesn't welcome me with open arms, and I have no idea why. Lies continue to fall from our lips.

Christian wants me gone. But I'm determined to stay.

All the Little Lies is stand-alone, High School Bully Romance intended for readers 18+. This book deals with subjects that some may find triggering.

You can find this book on Amazon or at sjsylvis.com

ALSO BY SJ SYLVIS

English Prep Series

All the Little Lies

All the Little Secrets

All the Little Truths

St. Mary's Series

Good Girls Never Rise

Bad Boys Never Fall

Dead Girls Never Talk

Standalones

Three Summers

Yours Truly, Cammie

Chasing Ivy

Falling for Fallon

Truth

All of SJ Sylvis' books are FREE in Kindle Unlimited!

ABOUT THE AUTHOR

S.J. Sylvis is a romance author who is best known for her angsty new adult romances and romantic comedies. She currently resides in Arizona with her husband, two small kiddos, and dog. She is obsessed with coffee, becomes easily attached to fictional characters, and spends most of her evenings buried in a book!

sjsylvis.com

ACKNOWLEDGMENTS

As always, I would like to mention my *amazing* family for making me smile daily and for always supporting me. I love you forever and ever. <3

To my author friends (I can't list you all. I would feel too bad if I accidentally left someone out, so you know who you are!!)--where would I be without you? To our daily voice messages, shares, likes, encouraging words, and writing sprints—I love you all SO much and I am so grateful for your friendship. Here's to many more books!

To my Betas (Andrea, Danah, Emma, & Megan)—Thank you SO much for helping me with plot holes, confusing scenes, and for reminding me that I need to flip imposter syndrome the bird. You four helped me in ways you don't even realize. xo.

To my Editor, Jenn, Thank you for always making my work shine. I would not be where I am without you! xo.

To my Proofer/PA, I honestly have no idea where I would be without you, Mary! Thank you for reminding me to do the things that I forget about, for picking up my slack, and for everything else. xo.

To my Cover Designer/person who keeps me sane—
Danah, thank you for everything and for making the St.
Mary's covers AMAZING. (Shout out to Lukeographyau and
Beau Privato too!) xo.

Laura, you are so much more than just an author friend. I
love you and your friendship! Thank you for helping me with
anything I throw your way! xo.

To my readers, bloggers, ARC readers, Tiktokers, anyone
who helps spread the word about my books—WOW. You are
the reason I can make this writing gig an actual career.
Without your support, reviews, & shares, I wouldn't be where
I am today. Thank you so incredibly much for everything you
do. It does not go unnoticed.

Xo,

SJ